Witch's Brew

A Phila Street Novel

Ella M. Hayes

Valenza Publishing

Valenza Publishing
Schroon Lake, NY 12835

First published in 2025

Edited by Dr. Stephen Hull

ISBN: 979-8-9919345-2-7

More by Valenza Publishing

Praise for Ella M. Hayes

"A tribute to the romance genre and a candid exploration of the trials of upholding one's essence in an ever-changing society. Crafted with charm and depth by Ella M. Hayes, the novel is a compelling invitation to anyone at the crossroads of following their heart or conforming to societal expectations."

-Chris Jones, Overly Honest Reviews, on "Bookends"

"...an exceptionally cute and fun read... This book had a good bit of a twist in it and overall, I highly recommend. Especially if you are looking for a refreshing and fun read. This book pairs well with a cup of tea, a comfy chair, and a free afternoon."

-Jade Nimoa, author of "Fate's Tether," on "Bookends"

"A rich blend of cozy, steamy, paranormal romance with intrigue and characters that keep you guessing."

-Morgan Christensen, author of The Matriarch Chronicles

"The perfect fall witchy read..."

-Madison Lovely, author of "Devious"

"...a charming read with paranormal components and a dash of spice..."

-J.M. Gokey, author of "The Chosen"

Dedication:

To all of those who have been staying strong and pushing
through, looking for salvation.

Epigraph

"So sweet with a mean streak, nearly brought me to my knees."
-Cigarette Daydreams

"Dfbnbzhxdujzsjuzsdxjdszdjdxxdjmhnsxzmnbgfdsanm8bv65 c4x3" - my Sam walking across my keyboard which my wife told me to keep in.

The Playlist

Season of the Witch - Lana Del Rey
Willow - Taylor Swift
Lighthouse - Bleach Lab
Whiskey - Maria Hill
Blue Romance - Black Honey
Die for Me! - VANA
Antidote - Greywind
Cigarette Daydream - Cage the Elephant

1. The Haunted Girl

What is it your heart desires? What is it you're willing to pay a small fortune for? Maybe you want a more arousing love life, or maybe for your boss to see you in a better light? Are you in need of something certain, or open to exploring the mysterious depths of your soul you're scared to let see the light? Witch's Brew can help with that. As I said, for a small fortune, but I'll make it worth your while.

Ask around, I have plenty of satisfied customers. Take for instance the girl next door. Poor thing had a messy history with the boys. The first one neglected her, the next one lied to her. When he broke her heart, everything else fell apart around her. That's what happens when you let someone control your heart too much. She never paid me much mind, but once she opened up… oh how I changed her life. From what I can tell, she hasn't had a bad day since.

Just know I have some conditions to my services. I love a good curse as much as the next girl. Some people just have it coming. But a good curse has to come from a good place. And if you ask me to do something purely out of spite… let's just say it might find its way back to you.

So what will it be? How about we put a little bit of spice in your life?

"I think I have a ghost problem…"

I feel like an asshole now. I blocked off my night, got my room all set up for this appointment, and all it is is a ghost problem I can't even deal with from here.

"Have you cleansed the area?" I ask.

"Yes! I burned sage in my apartment until I couldn't breathe!" Maria is a girl I've seen in my store a million times. I have hope for her and try to educate when I can, but up until now she has been an aesthetic buyer. She lacks the proper respect for the craft and it's obvious why her attempts have failed.

"What kind of sage?"

"White. I think. I don't know, I just went with whatever the internet said. But it's not working and I still feel this presence in my apartment."

At least she burns the right kind. Perhaps my assumption was wrong about her. The problem must be deeper than that.

She goes on. "It's not like, evil, I don't think. Oh god, I hope not. It's just there, you know? But no one else ever feels it. Like when my boyfriend comes over he thinks I'm just crazy. And that really bothers me, but it also bothers me that it bothers me 'cause like, then I feel defensive over this ghost like, come on, he's right there! Don't treat him like he's not! But that's weird isn't it? That I feel bad for him? The ghost I mean. I don't know, maybe I'm just like… such an empath or something. Like I think I'm a really caring person."

Everybody's an empath now.

"If it makes you feel better, I don't think you're crazy. How long have you been living there?" For as much as she rambles, I don't believe she's exaggerating anything. I lean in closer over the candle-lit table and rest my head in my hands. My sleeves fall down a few inches and I see her eyes drop down.

Maria loses focus and reaches out for my hands. "Ooo these are so pretty. Where do you get yours done?" She asks about the tattoos on the backside of my right hand; a bead chain around my wrist and over the back of my hand, and runes on my fingers.

I smile politely but don't want to get off track. "Not around here. Please, Maria, your apartment."

"I've been wanting to get sleeves like this. I only have a small one on my side right now. But like, it seems like all witches like you have really cool body art so maybe I'm just not like, embracing it all enough you know? Oh! Do you think that's why I'm not good with the sage?"

Like I said, they like the aesthetic. Next year it will be something new.

I take my hands back from her and cross them on the table. "I think it's a lack of focus and understanding." I see her begin to fall back in either offense or shock. "So let's fix the understanding part. How long have you been living there?"

Maria immediately drops the attitude. I assume this isn't the first time someone has called her out for this. "I've always lived here.

My parent's own the building, but this apartment was always rented out to other people. I started renting it from them, I think… April. Yeah, I moved in back in April, I think. Late April."

"And is that when you felt this presence? Or has it always been a part of this house?"

"Well, no, never. Wait! No, that's not true, I lied." She's leaned in and talking fast again. "I felt it first a month earlier when I checked out the place to like, get a feel for living here. My parents *never* let me in when there was someone renting it. But like when, no, *before* I moved in officially, when I was just checking it out, I think I did feel something but I didn't think a whole lot of it. I mean it's an old apartment and everything. And for a while, I thought I felt something in the time between then and moving in, but that didn't make sense."

Now my interest is really piqued. "Why do you think not?"

Her cheeks go red. "I don't know, doesn't that like, break the rules of a haunted house? I mean, no one died there recently as far as I know. No one ever complained about ghosts, so why would it show up just now?"

I can't help but smirk. "Darling, I don't think it's the house that's haunted."

"What do you mean?"

"Don't get scared, but, I think it's you."

Maria gasps and holds her hand over her mouth. With anyone else, I'd think she was trying to play me for a fool. Not Maria though. She's too innocent and earnest. I can't wait to tell her what all of this means for her.

"I wouldn't call this a bad thing just yet. Sometimes it's the aura of a person that can attract spirits. It's not a matter of time or place; those are irrelevant for things such as this." To help her remain calm I hold out my hands again and she gently rests hers on mine. "Tell me about the energy you feel when they're around."

She takes a deep breath like the news was equivalent to being told a family member has a terrible disease. "I mean... it's not... like, bad. You know? Honestly, I'm kinda used to it now." She giggles and says, "Sometimes when I come home I say 'hello' to it. Just like, at first as a joke, but now it's a habit."

"So would you say it's a positive energy?"

She blushes again. "Sometimes..." Her tone shifts after a short pause. "But that's weird, isn't it? I mean, it's like I'm living with someone. My boyfriend doesn't even get to stay the night!" She giggles again.

What a shame, Maria. There's some magic in that too.

"I think I'm getting the right picture," I say. "You have nothing to fear, Maria. Spirits like this are completely natural and aren't seeking to hurt you."

She lets out a deep sigh and laughs. "Phew! That's a relief."

"I can't know anything for sure though unless I feel it first hand."

"Oh! Yeah of course!" She's quick to push her chair back and stand. "If you need a ride I don't mind driving you."

"Darling, I really don't do house calls. Your home is your own-"

Before I can finish the sentence she's rummaging through

13

her purse. The small wad of twenty dollar bills is very convincing.

Three hundred dollars later we're at her apartment. It's a quaint place on the upper floor of an ancient house in northern Saratoga. This place must be over a hundred years old. From the moment I step onto the yard, I'm overcome with the energy of a thousand happy memories. Smells from holiday cooking and the warmth of children being hugged by their parents.

"This is a good home," I tell Maria.

We walk up the stairs to her apartment, up old steps that creak with the slightest pressure. Her apartment holds a similar energy and right away I identify the presence she called me for.

"I was right," I say to her. "You have nothing to be afraid of. Your smudging wasn't working because there are no negative energies here. Spirits like this one should be your friend."

Maria wanders around her living space, looking around the room as if expecting to see the spirit manifest. "But it's my home. As… comforting as they feel, it's like having someone always watching me. Even when I'm…" She's scared to say what we both know she's thinking. Must have had strict parents.

"This home was never yours." I expect another offended reaction, but hers is pure curiosity. I find a seat on one of her couches to drive home my point. "This space belongs to the spirits. All of nature does. We merely occupy it for our brief time here until we can join them. While we're here, we must be respectful."

Maria is still looking around like a child. "How can I be respectful if I don't understand it?"

"Imagine you have guests over at your place," I begin. "You

want them to feel comfortable and welcome. Maybe you make them a cup of tea." I bob my head towards her kitchen.

It takes her a second, but Maria takes the hint and jumps to heat up the kettle.

As she makes the tea, I continue, "And as the guest, you want to be courteous to your host. Respect their space. Don't overstep."

Maria lights her old-fashioned gas stove top. Three clicks and the flames burst out under the kettle. "So, are you saying I can't get rid of him? I mean... it?"

"That's not at all what I'm saying. Anyone can be evicted, darling. But do you really want to?"

She purses her lips and looks down at her feet. It's adorable how easy she is to read.

"If you want my advice-"

"Yes! Of course!" She shouts, unaware of her volume.

I pause, letting the room settle, then say, "Embrace your roommate. This is their home, too. Some people don't move on because they have unfinished business. But some don't move on because this is where they will be happiest, surrounded by the memories of their lifetime, and the ones they inherit when they join with nature."

Maria leans over the counter that divides the parlor and the kitchen. "You are so wise... and you got all this from just walking in the room?"

I look out the window and see the waxing moon. "It's a good moon tonight. Helps with understanding. But this is all only the start of the matter. As I said, in your case, this spirit is concerned with you, not the home anymore."

"I still don't understand what that means. Am I going to be possessed or something like that?"

I laugh at her ignorance. "No, no, don't worry, darling. When you began living in this place for the first time, the spirit connected with you. It's extremely rare for something like that to happen. Usually, our worlds are such as two rooms divided by a window. We can see the other world; sometimes hear and feel their presence, but rarely do we actively try to cross over. This spirit is different. You two connected, presumably emotionally, as if they saw a friend in you."

"So... he's latched onto me? Like, all the time?"

It's curious that she continues to refer to the spirit as a 'he.'

"Do you follow your friends everywhere they go? At all times?"

She shakes her head.

"This home is theirs as well as yours. But when you leave, they will not always be with you. There's that respect. So, what's your choice?"

Maria pours the tea. It's probably the first moment since I met her in my covenstead that she's let herself think before speaking. "Well... I mean... If he's not... bad?"

My work here is done. I rise from the couch and pull one of the hundred-dollar bills out of my pocket. "Here's your refund," I say, placing it on the counter. "Do you have a tumbler I can borrow for that?"

She looks at me, clearly taken aback.

I smirk and tell her, "You'll get it back next time you come into the store. And I'll want to hear about whatever happens here."

To be completely honest, I don't really want to leave this house. Every inch of this place is oversaturated with joyful spirits, their presence made more clear with the aroma of the tea. I want to wander the halls and knock on all of the apartment doors, asking the residents if I can come in and meditate with them. But it's almost midnight, and that'd be weird. Instead, I make a mental note to look into the history of this building.

For now, I have other business to attend to.

2. Night Swim

A few miles outside of town, deep in the woods is a pond I fancy as my own. Only in terms of people that visit it, though. I'm not too arrogant to believe I can truly own this place.

It's nestled quietly deep in the forest, behind a wall of brush, far away from any public paths. One of my sisters introduced it to me before she fell out of our coven. I come here now to meditate and prepare myself for spellcasting. It's the only place I've found where I can truly block out everything and find sanctuary in unadulterated nature.

The moon and stars reflect beautifully off the still water of the shallow pond. Not even a tadpole will want to disturb the peace here. But a tadpole isn't here to deepen its bond with nature.

The July water is warm, like dipping my toes into a bath. I step in further. As the water surrounds my calves I want to jump in like a child and swim laps, it feels so nice. But I restrain myself. I'm not here to indulge. The water only comes up to my breasts at its deepest spot, and once there in the center, I lay on my back and let the music the night makes enter me.

With my eyes closed, I feel like I'm floating in the void. I see the universe before me and I wade through its seas. I take what is given to me, and I return it in full. When the universe calls, I answer. And when I am in need, the stars and moon, and the goods of the earth provide.

I am alive.

I am refreshed.

I am ready to cast my spells.

As the sun rises, I wake from my trance and swim back to the shore.

3. Spellbinding

It's time to prepare for the wave of customers. Every summer, tourists flock to Saratoga Springs for the horse racing. I think it's cruel, but what does my opinion matter, I just live here. Regardless of why they're here, the influx of rich people is good for business.

Now, I could sit back and let whoever comes come. But here's the perk to being a witch. With the right respect given to the universe, the universe is happy to give back.

I've done my meditations, so now it's time to craft.

On days like this, I like to cast a spell for prosperity. The first step is lighting the candles. This part I do in the covenstead, the back room where I hold all after-hour appointments. I light seven green sticks and spread them out on the edges of the table. Green for wealth, as well as a symbol of nature and growth. After they're in place, I gather my herbs for smudging. Clover, chamomile, dill, and sage are my primaries. I also like to throw a bit of rosemary in to help with stress. This reasoning is twofold; on my end, if I do have a busy day, I need to keep myself at peace. For the customer, if they aren't overwhelmed by the abundance of wares in my store, they'll have an easier time finding what they're looking for and better enjoy the experience. A bite out of the pie for me, and a bite for them.

Before I begin the smudging, I proclaim my incantations. I adorn my necklace of the Fehu rune, and with two fingers on it I implore the stars;

"As I give to you, grant back to me. Bring me coin, and bring me green. Let this home see growth, and let this servant prosper."

It's a work of my own, I hope you like it.

I feel the rune necklace pulse between my breasts.

I am heard.

Now comes the time to smudge. I light the stick with the flame from one of the candles and walk around Witch's Brew with it, attentive to smudge the more commonly walked areas as well as the doorway. For the sake of peace of mind, I might as well smudge outside, too.

My cat Willow hisses at Damien as I open the door and she scurries out as if she's been waiting for me to drop my guard. The dumb cat spooks a familiar face walking by.

"Oh, fuck!" Damien jumps. "Can't you keep that thing on a leash?"

"I should put you on a leash," I scowl. "Where have you been? I haven't heard from you all week."

He flashes a cheesy smile. "Babe, I've been busy. I can't be on my phone *all* the time." He kisses my cheek as he walks through the door and goes towards the back.

"Why come back now?" I ask, following him into the covenstead. It's obvious from his stride he's going to my upstairs apartment.

"Just wanted to come by and see my girl." He opens the door at the top of the stairs as I catch up to him, and beelines it for the bedroom.

"Damien, I know what you're up to and I don't have the time right now."

"Oh come on…" He turns and pulls me in, then whispers, "I haven't seen you all week." Damien's lips are on my neck, a gesture that should feel romantic. It used to make my knees weak just feeling his breath on my neck but, truth be told, the gesture has now completely lost its hold on me.

"I know a way we can spend time together," I say, careful not to make it sound like a tease.

He doesn't take the hint and a hand moves up my leg under my dress. "Oh yeah?" He asks, trying to sound sexy. "Tell me it doesn't involve this dress." I let him caress my loins, except, the way he does it is less 'caressing' and more 'squishing.'

All I have to say to him is, "Hm," and his expression goes flat. Damien realizes the fool he's making of himself and pulls back.

He begins pacing around. "What the fuck is all this then?" He waves at my outfit. "I can basically see your tits through that!"

"It's hot today. You want me wearing a parka?"

Damien scoffs and drops onto my bed.

23

"Don't sit there. You're disturbing my room."

"Dis- disturbing your room?" He laughs. "Fuck, Nyx what the hell is going on with you? You show no interest in me anymore, you smell like a fucking swamp, and now I can't even sit down in the bed we're supposed to fuck on?"

The arrogance of this man both annoys and humors me. I hate to admit it, but I enjoy seeing him worked up like this. I give him a light lip bite just to tease.

"You and *I* aren't *supposed* to do anything in *my* bed." I walk over to him slowly with my hands on my hips. "*You* get to have me when *I* allow it." When I'm right in front of him I plant one foot on the bed, just next to his leg. The dress rides up teasing just enough thigh to get him to listen. I then reach out and trace my finger up his neck and to his chin. "Got it?"

He opens his mouth to speak and I just know it's going to be some stupid argument.

"Uh uh," I say with my finger over his mouth. "Yes… or no?"

Damien nods.

"Good boy. Now, if you want this…" I pull up my dress just a bit so he can see whats beneath. You can look, but don't touch. "…then you behave. And when I ask you where you've been all week, you tell me."

Damien looks like he's about to crumble and worship the ground I walk on. Works every time.

"I've been busy," he says. "Working with my Dad upstate."

It's an obvious lie, so I'll show him what liars get.

I fake a smile and straddle him. His hard cock is desperate to break out of his pants. With my arms wrapped around his neck, I grind on him. "You've been working hard?" I ask with a pout. "Just need to come by your girl Nyx's place to relax?"

Damien throws his head back and groans. "Keep talking like that baby…"

"How about you work a little harder for me?"

"Anything, anything, baby." He moans.

I whisper in his ear, "Help me down on the floor."

I try to contain my laughter as I watch his face go from thinking I want him to fuck me on the floor, to the disappointed realization that he was way off.

"What?"

"These legs are staying closed for now, but the store opens soon." I halt my grinding. "I could really use a hand, and you said 'anything'."

His head falls back against the wall so hard I'm surprised he doesn't punch a hole.

I climb off him and make my way to the stairs. "Put on a brave face, darling," I call to him. "It's gonna be a busy day."

4. First Day of the Season

With Damien manning the register, I'm free to take breaks when it suits me. There aren't many, but at lulls in the day I like to step outside and sit with Willow and smoke. Smoking the cabriole is an attraction for the aesthetic witches. They see me smoking it and think, 'Oh that's a witch who knows what's up,' but between you and me, that's all it is. A fun way to stylize my addictions. At the very least, they're homemade rolls, not the chemical-filled death sticks that ruined tobacco's reputation. Tobacco used to be respected as an herb for healing in Mayan culture. In all fairness, it's doing nothing to heal my body, but it does help my mind.

Willow, on the other hand, is one hundred percent authentic. It's funny that some people used to associate them with the presence of evil. A witch and her cat were inherently evil things. Now, if I were living back in the 1600s, just minding my own business, using magic to help my crops grow and some kid comes around, pointing fingers at me, shouting and screaming and ruining my meditations… well, I don't see how you expect me not to mix them into my cauldron.

I jest, don't worry. It's fun to play with the stereotypes sometimes.

Even though it's been months, it's weird not seeing Silvia Wright and Bookends next door. They officially went out of business last Christmas. I *did* offer to cast a spell for their success, but some people in their skepticism often ignore my help. At least she came around later and I don't think she'll doubt anymore. I think all of us on Phila Street are looking forward to see who moves into that spot next. If it's a good year for me, I might extend out and renovate that place. Witch's Brew is wonderful, but on summers like I expect this one to be, it gets rather crammed. Plus everyone on this street knows *I'm* the one that could do some good with the spot.

In fact, I think this street would be much better with more of my input. Let's take the bar across the street for example. Drab by every standard. First of all, this isn't the street for bars. Pack up and go to Caroline Street. If they don't get wise and do something new like a tea den soon they'll be sure to end up like Bookends. Come to think of it, maybe that's what I should do if I buy the place. Some soothing ambiance music, a candlelit vibe and sitting pillows. Doesn't that sound lovely, darling?

"Sure, yeah it's great. Can I get some help inside?" Damien asks.

Sometimes I really can't tell the difference between my daydreams and discussions. But why should I? What's the difference except the audience? And if the audience isn't interested, why should I care?

I take one final drag of the cigarette and pause before

answering him. "Miss me already? I didn't realize it'd been a week."

Without looking, I can feel his eyes roll. "Come on, Nyx. It's your place, just fuckin' help out."

Oh, so *now* it's mine. "You didn't say the magic word."

He grunts, "Ugh... please, babe?"

That's better. I hold out my hand and he helps me up. I give him a kiss on the cheek to show my appreciation and then it's time to attend to my customers.

It's hot enough today outside, but inside with everyone so close together it's almost boiling. I thank myself for smudging the room beforehand to help everyone's mindset.

Crystals are particularly popular today. I don't put the most faith in them but, like everything in my store, I wouldn't sell them if I didn't believe they had a bit of magic to them.

I display a blue-violet iolite crystal necklace with a short oval cut, for a pair of young girls. One of them used to come in all the time, usually after school based on the uniforms she wore. Knowing that, I try to cater to possible needs. "This may be what you're looking for"

One of the girls refuses to acknowledge me, but the other looks up. "What's this one good for?" she asks.

I smile my best saleswoman smile. "This is iolite. It's good for bringing wisdom. What are you this year, Jenna? Senior, right?" I place the necklace on her as if she's already made up her mind. "Wouldn't be bad to have some extra help with all these exams to get into a good college, huh?"

She holds the crystal in her palms and gazes at it. "Actually,

I'm in college now. How'd you know my name?" Her voice is timid, but her eyes are filled with wonder.

I've got her now.

"Hm. Lucky guess," I tease.

Jenna laughs, "So cool," then takes the necklace off. "But I'm looking for something else."

"Oh?" I'm intrigued. Someone who might actually know their stuff?

"Do you have anything pretty with rose quartz or moonstone?"

There are very few things girls this age would want those for, and I have to say, their priorities are in the wrong place. I try to smile again and pick up a different necklace. "Here," I hold it out for them. "Cathedral quartz. I think this is closer to what you're looking for"

Jenna holds the necklace but doesn't put it on. "And this is to help-"

"With exactly what you need," I close her hands around the necklace and give her a wink. A warm energy surrounds our hands and I see her eyes light up. Another happy customer.

As I turn to care for another customer who's been waving me down, Jenna taps me on the shoulder. "Excuse me. Do you read tarot? My friend said you take appointments."

"You don't need an appointment for a tarot reading, darling. Just give me a few minutes to help this woman." I turn away again, but Jenna is insistent.

"It's not just the tarot reading I'm asking about. My friend said you can also…cast spells. Is it like, real?"

I give her a challenging eye.

"I mean like, *real* witchcraft."

"Darling, all of this is real. But it's less likely to show itself to the skeptic."

Her voice drops low as if we're speaking taboos. Under the volume of the crowd though, it's totally unnecessary. Perhaps she's only embarrassed about what her friend thinks of her. Her friend shows zero interest in anything in the store. She picks something up to give it a once over and puts it back down. "So it's like real potions and magic wands right?"

Ah yes, another girl wondering if I can snap my finger and turn someone into a toad. But to be fair, who says I can't?

"Appointments like that are for adults only." On principle, I won't cast spells for teens, regardless of the sincerity of the request. They need to learn from their mistakes before trying to craft their way out of them. And often, it's for something silly like I'm reading from Jenna, like wanting a boy to love her back, or change something fundamental to who they are. Who are we without our mistakes? So appointments with me are eighteen and up.

"Jeez, didn't know you needed to show I.D. anywhere other than a bar," she laughs and pulls out her driver's license, then nudges her friend to do the same, though the friend seems reluctant at first. They both check out.

"I told you, I'm in college now." Jenna grabs her friend's arm. "We're roommates, soon-to-be, at the school up the road."

I consider it for a moment then decide if anything, I'll charge her extra.

"See that curtain over there?" I point to my covenstead.

Jenna looks, then turns back and nods enthusiastically.

"Give me a few minutes and I'll show you some real magic."

Her eyes go wide and I hear her beg her friend to stay a few more minutes as I walk across the room to attend to my next customer.

"Can you help me with the candles, please?" A simple request, but halfway through helping her find the best option for her spellcasting, another customer calls for my help.

Before I realize it, I'm bouncing from one request to the next. This woman's looking for new tarot cards in *this* theme. This woman's arguing with me about what crystals are good for what. One young man tries to tease me about the broom in the corner, asking if I can really fly on it.

"Yes, and if you're not careful, I'll fly right to your home in the middle of the night and snatch you away for my stew." I shoo him away but remember his face. If I have the time tonight I'll attempt to cast a spell over him, a shroud over his mind when he comes by the store. The closer he comes, the less he'll see, and distractions will pop up. It will be like this store doesn't exist to him. That's how I like to deal with annoying skeptics.

"Do you have any availability for appointments? My girlfriend cheated on me again, I need you to curse her." Interesting.

"Do you ever sell ready-made potions?" If only I had the time.

"Where are your spellbooks?"

"Do you have anything like history of witchcraft?"

The heat is getting to me.

"Are you part of a coven? What do I have to do to join?"

"Do you actually believe in this stuff?"

"But it's not like real magic, right?"

"This is all a scam."

"Do the potions come with alcohol in them?"

"This stuff is so cool!"

Holy shit, I can not get a second to breathe!

"Damien!" I call across the busy store. "You need to help me over here!"

He signals back something, maybe saying he can't hear me, so I gesture toward the last person that needed my assistance. Damien throws up his hands in protest then points at the register. In response I grab my tits, the only language this man understands, and mouth *do you want them or not?*

Damien rolls his eyes and abandons his post so I can attend to Jenna.

I glide through the curtain to my covenstead, doing my best to make a magical impression with my entrance. The lights are low. Jenna and her friend sit at the table, their backs toward me. Only Jenna turns to watch my entrance.

The light shifts and it's like the sun reverted back to its rise the way it comes in at an angle, illuminating my silhouette with a golden trim. Jenna sees what I want her to. The small things like this will help her to keep her mind open through this.

"Now, pick a card," a deck of playing cards appears from my sleeve and I hold it out to Jenna and her friend as I sit down across from them.

They both laugh. Jenna curiously, the friend skeptically.

"You wanted to see magic, didn't you?" I ask, playing into the friend's skepticism.

Jenna and her friend look at each other and Jenna reaches out.

"Uh uh. Not you, Jenna." I look over at her friend. "You. Please."

The friend's eyes are locked on mine. Something in them changes. Energy flashes between us, we can both feel it.

She reaches out slowly and pulls a card out of the deck. As her fingers draw near, I flick out one of mine to graze her. Zoe's her name. Beautiful.

Jenna and Zoe look at the card.

"I... I thought this was a tarot reading." Jenna says.

I light two light blue candles and place them on the table.

"This *is*." I correct Jenna. "Turn the card around."

Zoe does as directed. She flips it once and sees what was meant for her. I notice the confusion on her face. "The fool?" The confusion turns to annoyance. "What's up with this?"

"Be not so quick to assume anything, Zoe."

Both of the faces go pale. They know neither one let her name slip.

"The fool in your case is a good thing," I continue. "It's a symbol of a new beginning. Something big is about to change in your life."

Jenna interjects. "We're starting college this semester. *That's* a big change."

"No, I think it's something much greater. Some change inside of you. Whether you accept it now or not, I believe by the time you walk out today, you'll be on a new path."

Zoe's face goes red. It makes me giggle.

"Now it's your turn, darling." I spread the cards out across the table, and the girls realize the whole deck is now tarot.

"How are you doing that?" Zoe asks.

I don't answer but give her a wink. Yes, she's stepping onto the right path.

"Okay, Jenna. Let's see where your fate lies." I flip the first card over.

The Tower.

Jenna reaches out to rotate the card, but I stop her. "No! This is how you're meant to read it. I know why you're here, Jenna. This card only proves it."

Her eyes make it clear she's been just as skeptical as her friend from the beginning. Jenna's here today in a desperate attempt at love, I assume her final attempt. She'd do anything to save her relationship. But now the tower lies reversed before her.

"In love, the Reverse Tower means the end is coming. I know you see the cracks in your romance, and the tower of your love has weak foundations. You must get out while you can, or it will fall on top of you, and you'll never escape the rubble."

Jenna pauses, and it's Zoe who answers. "She's right, Jen. That's what I've been telling you!"

Tears swell in Jenna's eyes. Her shoulders start to shudder.

It's never fun revealing that card to someone so young.

"Come, darling. I think I have something for you." I take Jenna by the hand and lead her to the tea cabinet in the back of the room. At the moment our skin makes contact, her heartbreak flows into me. This relationship has probably lasted for years, likely the only one she's ever had and she's unsure if she'll survive a breakup. Young love is so tragic.

"Here," I give her a small jar of homemade tea pouches. "This is for healing. After all is done, drink this and meditate. It will help."

Jenna is hesitant to accept the tea.

"It's free, darling. But the reading isn't, unfortunately. You'll pay for that and the crystal up front." I put the tea into her hands. "Come now, you've got healing to do." I walk her to the curtain and hold it open for her to exit my covenstead.

Jenna looks back again as she approaches the register. Her cheeks are red. Damien doesn't notice the sadness on her face as he rings her up, and that's probably for the best. Instead, his eyes tell me he needs more help on the floor. How does this man not understand I'm busy?

"How did you do that?" Zoe asks, still sitting at the table, eyeing the tarot cards.

The curtain falls.

"Still skeptical, are we?" I ask.

The room is dark, illuminated only by the few candles on the table. I pace slowly around her, attempting to read her energy.

"It's just a trick," she tries to convince herself. "You switched out the card." Zoe shivers as I lay a hand on her shoulder.

36

"Maybe I did. From three feet away, though?"

Zoe's head turns, and her eyes look up into mine. "Show me how you did it. If it's really real."

She looks so innocent with those big hazel eyes. There's some magic in there waiting to show itself, a lust for this world she stumbled into. One of two things will happen after today. She'll walk out of here, curious about what she saw but eventually dismiss it as a cheap sleight-of-hand trick. If she doesn't dismiss it, she'll dip her toes in further to witchcraft. In that case, who will I be but a humble teacher?

"Jenna isn't the one for you. Come back tomorrow night, darling. I'll open your eyes."

Zoe nods slowly. Her lip quivers.

"Tomorrow night," I remind her.

5. No Magic Here

Witch's Brew closes at eight. The second after I turn the lock, Damien's hands are on my hips.

"Not now, Damien. I'm tired." I scold.

"Oh, come on, enough teasing." His hands slide across my naval and down to my crotch.

I look out the glass door. There's still some light out and I wish I'd escaped fast enough to avoid his advances. But to be fair, I did promise him.

"Fine, you've been a good worker today. I suppose you deserve a treat."

Willow stands guard at the door and makes sure no one tries to break in while Damien leads me upstairs.

He's so quick to take my dress off it almost tears.

"Careful!"

Damien doesn't listen. He only turns me around and bends me over the bed. I hear him spit and feel his saliva on my pussy. Damien thrusts, only half-hard.

"Yeah, take that," he says, almost to himself.

I stare at the blank yellow wall in front of me, finding it more interesting than the sad attempt at fucking Damien makes.

This is ridiculous. He's been gone for over a week while I've been slaving away here, yet I'm still relegated to being just something to fuck? No, I'm the one that deserves to be pleasured.

Damien throws a hand under my leg to turn me over, rotates me on the bed, and then climbs on top. Before he realizes it's happened, I wrap my legs around him and spin us around so I'm on top. His cock hardens. It feels the tiniest bit better inside me, but not enough to make me cum. That I'll have to do on my own.

I focus my thoughts inward, concentrating on the sensation in my loins. When Damien reaches for my breasts, I pin his wrists to the bed. I have to clear all distractions from my mind. When he speaks, I make myself deaf to his exaggerated moans and praises.

Ecstasy begins to swell inside me. An orgasm may actually come. I steady my breaths, letting it rise, letting the magic do its work, giving myself the love I deserve-

It all comes to ruin when I feel Damien cum inside me and throw me off.

"Oh, fuck... baby... FUCK! I needed that. Fuck!"

"Would you quit it with the 'fuck?' It's unnecessary." I finger myself and feel his cum leaking out of me. The idiot didn't even think to give me a warning to get off in time. Wonderful. I stand and head for the bathroom, not bothering to put a robe on. It's too hot in here, anyway.

Across the room, I hear him say, "I'm sorry, but can you

blame me when you look that good? When'd you get that back tat anyway? It's hot."

I squat down on the toilet and answer to myself, "I've had it three months." The tattoo is a broom and crescent moon on my spine. Damien was there when I got it, but it'd do no good reminding him. He won't remember in ten minutes anyway.

Instead of starting another argument I shout from the bathroom, "I'll need your help again tomorrow."

Damien groans in annoyance. "I can't tomorrow. I've got shit going on."

I'll need a glass of hot tea if I'm going to put up with his complaining. I flush and walk over to the tiny apartment kitchen.

"Figure something else out then, whatever it is. I need your help."

He pulls his pants back on, and I notice his eyes wander for his shoes.

"Maybe next week, Nyx."

"No more 'Babe'?" I reach for a tea bag in the cabinet above the counter next to the refrigerator.

"What?" he stops dressing.

"Nothing. Do you want something to eat?"

"No, I should get going. Gotta drive back upstate."

"Just stay the night, Damien. It's late already."

"Won't get mad I sleep in your bed?" he teases, thinking he's funnier than he really is.

I turn around to put the kettle on the stove. His eyes are focused on my breasts.

"Cut it out, Damien."

He pushes himself off the bed and grunts like his knees are about to give out. "I don't get you, Nyx. 'Get out of my bed,' 'stay the night,' 'look how thin my dress is,' 'don't look at my tits.' What do you want from me?"

I swear I could smash this mug right here on the goddamn counter. "I want someone I can rely on, Damien! I want someone who doesn't just drop by when he wants something to fuck!"

His eyes harden. "Okay, if you want to play that card, don't treat me like a goddamn employee and maybe like your boyfriend for once."

"A boyfriend shows up more than once a week when you live down the road!"

"I'd be here more often if you let me stay the night!"

"Then stay the night! The bed's already soaked in your sweat!"

"I can't tonight! I have to go, Nyx."

He heads for the door but I'm on his heels, following him. "Then what are you complaining about, not staying the night?"

"Forget it, Nyx." He's storming down the stairs.

"No! What's going on with you? Where the hell have you been all week? I know damn well you haven't been with your *dad* all week."

We cross through my covenstead into the store. Anybody could walk across the window and see me in all my naked glory, but screw them.

"Cut it out. I'll call you tomorrow." Damien grabs the

doorknob and twists, forgetting it's locked. He pulls it so hard the door almost breaks off the hinges.

"Just stay, Damien!"

"Why?" He turns around violently. "So you can put me to work or because you want me here as… as your man or whatever."

"I want you here because I want *YOU*!"

We both see through the lie. Damien flicks the lock on the door. "I'll call you tomorrow."

6. The Witch's Apprentice

It pains me having to sit behind the register. On the positive side, there's no need to cast any spells for prosperity today. Yesterday looked like a ghost town compared to this! Everyone is bumping into each other and knocking things over. But for all the shouting, no one is talking to each other.

When someone does come by the counter for help, it pains me to only be able to point them in the right direction. I can't fully explain the 'why' of what they need. The one thing that gives me hope is Zoe's appointment tonight. That is, as long as I can survive until then.

I want to step outside my body. I'd let Physical Nyx watch the register while my spirit roams, nudging the customers to find what they're looking for. I just know if I do that, I'll be a blank face at the register again and struggle to ring stuff up like last time.

I hate to be that girl, but judging from the parade of high end outfits walking through the store, the customers today are almost exclusively horse track elites. There is no real interest in the craft, only something cute to check out while they're in town.

Now, here's a decently pleasant surprise. Just before noon, a bright smiling face walks in. Maria pushes her way through the crowd and waves me down. "Hey! Nyx! Guess what!"

Her expression is unlike anything I've ever seen on her. She always has this ditzy smile, but now every pore on her face beams with excitement. This should be interesting.

Maria arrives at the counter, cutting through the line of shoppers and breathes hard like she just ran a marathon. "Do you have a few minutes? I need to tell you about the ghost!"

"Darling, I'd love to," I say, handing a woman in a conservative sundress her receipt. "But now isn't a great time. You know better, let's make an appointment and-"

"No no no no, Nyx, seriously! This is big! I think I made contact with him!"

A nearby woman turns her head, but quickly goes back to her business.

"Maria, I'd love to talk more about this when I have the time. I'm free Monday nigh-"

"You don't get it!" she says excitedly. "You were right! About him and me! He's talked to me!"

I don't want to tell her outright how ridiculous that is. It is, to be clear, and if I heard anyone else making claims like that I'd have no issue shooting them down. But this is Maria, and at the very least her heart is in the right place.

"I find it hard to believe any spirit has contacted you. It just doesn't work like that. But please," I gesture at the line of patiently waiting customers. "I'm busy. Come back on Monday and we'll talk."

A tall gentleman with messy dark hair begins to step up to the counter, but Maria acts like he isn't there.

"There I was in my room, and like, I felt his presence again. So I tried meditating, you know, embracing him like you said I should do. I kept calling out to him-"

"Maria, that isn't meditating. That's summoning. And frankly, darling, I really don't think that's a safe option."

She doesn't hear a word I say, only continues talking. "... Calling and calling until it's like I'm wrapped in a cold blanket of this ghost! And that's when I heard him! I did! I really did, Nyx! He said my name! I mean it!"

Messy Hair gives me a look and shakes his head. *Yes, sir, I'm sorry she cut you, and she doesn't know what she's talking about, but to be fair, this is important.*

"Maria, right over there are some books on the spirit world. See it?"

She looks where I point, and before I even tell her which one to find, she's off.

Messy Hair steps forward. His hands are empty. He doesn't look like a tourist, nor someone with any interest in the craft. My guess is he's looking for something for his girlfriend but feels totally lost in the store.

"Excuse me, you hiring by any chance?"

What a way to introduce yourself, sir.

I purse my lips and try to smile politely. "No, thank you, sorry. I don't have time to talk to applicants. Who's next?"

The next customer steps up, but Messy Hair stands his ground. "You really look like you can use an extra hand around here."

"Thank you, but I'm doing fine. Could you please step to the side?" I shoo him away, and the next customer steps up holding a few dozen incense sticks.

As I count them, I see from the corner of my eye that Messy Hair is still standing there with his hands in his pockets.

"I'm sure other shops on Broadway are hiring."

He shakes his head. "And you look like you're struggling the most to keep up."

I shoot him a glare. "We're doing just fine, thank you." Then to the woman with incense, "$2.89. Cash only please under $5."

"Didn't you just miss out on an 'important appointment?'"

Just as he taunts, Maria returns with a full stack of books, dropping them all on the counter before the woman with incense can take her receipt. She's picked one of every book I have dealing with spirits, summoning, and the afterlife.

"Maria! Quit cutting the line!" I feel sweat on my brow. The heat of the day is only worsened by all the people in the store turning this place into an oven.

People groan behind her but Maria acts like she can't hear them. "Sorry, I'm in a rush. My boyfriend is waiting for me in the car. So, you really think these will help me connect more with him? The ghost I mean? Tommy still thinks I'm crazy for all this, but I'm hoping I can open his eyes a bit."

"Maria, I don't care what rush you're in. You can't cut the line like that."

She's taken aback, clearly offended.

"Just wait in line. Come around Monday night and we can talk, okay?"

Maria gathers her books and scowls at me as she trudges to the back of the checkout line.

Ironically, the next person who steps up inquires about after-hours appointments. I check my calendar and find an opening for the following Wednesday. We go back and forth trying to find a time that works, and through it all, Messy Hair is still there. When his presence becomes too annoying to ignore, I throw my head back. "Fine! I'll give you a call if I need an extra hand? Okay?"

Messy Hair flashes a cheesy smile of relief. "Great! Here, let me give-" He pulls out his phone and I cut him off.

"I got your number already. Just go. You're ruining the energy in here."

His eyes question me. He clearly doesn't remember giving me his phone number. I'll say whatever it takes to get this guy out of my store. Maybe it's sinking in now that I would *not* ever hire him.

Messy Hair drops his phone back into his pocket. "All right, then. Thanks for your time. If you change your mind, my name's L-"

"Thank you. I'm all set."

Even the woman booking an appointment gives him an eye to tell him to fuck off. She's cool.

* * *

By the time I close up at eight, I still haven't gotten a call or text from Damien. I shouldn't truly have expected him to call back. I'll see him again in maybe another week, or longer if he's seriously angry that I asked him to help out here once in a while. Whatever, thinking about it is additional stress I don't need.

My feet feel like they're about to fall off from standing all day in those restricting slippers. As soon as the last person was out of the store I threw them off. All I need now is someone to rub them. I should have asked Damien to do it last night. As long as it involves touching my body, Damien will do anything for me. *Almost anything,* I remind myself, thinking of his inability to make me finish.

I'm tired and hungry, but only have a few minutes until Zoe comes by for her appointment.

I change out of my sweaty clothes into something more comfortable for a hot summer night, eat some leftovers, and rush to set up the covenstead.

We'll start with something simple tonight. I don't want to overwhelm her. More than anything, I want all skepticism out of her mind.

As the sun sets, Zoe finds her way back into Witch's Brew.

"Hello?" she calls gingerly. "Is anyone here?"

All the lights are off on the floor. The only light she can see is the glow of the candles bleeding through the curtains of my covenstead.

"This way, darling," she hears my voice beckon her.

I watch her as she navigates around the room, careful not to bump into anything.

Zoe pulls the curtain to the side and finds the candlelit table with a small black book sitting on it.

"Hello? I was told to be here tonight."

"I'm glad you could come. Please, have a seat."

As Zoe sits at the table the candles burn brighter. Now's the time to make my entrance.

I slowly step into the room from the stairwell. "Do you know why you're here tonight?"

It's easy to see Zoe is beauty-stricken by me and how I wear my scarlet robe.

"You said I should come back. So I could see how you do your magic."

I laugh, "Ha! That may be what you tell yourself, but it's only the doorway to the real answer." I take my place at her side. She has a pretty face. It's a shame Jenna doesn't see her in the same light. "You don't have to say it for me. Say it to yourself. Why are you here tonight?"

Zoe swallows, uncomfortable admitting it out loud. "I want her to love me back."

I smile sympathetically and touch her cheek. Her eyes are locked in mine and she doesn't react to my touch. There's a connection here we both feel.

"You are here because the universe wants you to be. Your wants don't match with the universe's plans for you."

Her eyes drop in disappointment and I take her hands.

"And that's why it's wonderful to be a witch," I continue. "If anyone has a semblance of control in this world, it's girls like us. So, what do you say?" I slide the black book closer to her and open it on a blank page.

"What is this?" She asks.

I rise and stand behind her with my hands on her shoulders. "You can read through all the books in my store, but if you want to truly learn magic like mine, all you have to do is sign your name."

When she looks from me back to the book, she notices the pen.

"I just…write in 'Zoe?'"

"No, darling," I laugh. "Your real name. What is your heart telling you?"

"I… I don't know what you mean."

I flip through to the first page of the book of the spellbook. "I didn't sign this book as 'Samantha,' the name my parents gave me." Zoe reads 'Nyx' written in big letters. "This is the name the universe gave to me. Now it's your turn to listen and discover yours."

"What am I getting into? Is this a coven?"

"I have sisters, but no. My magic is my own. I share it with those I feel deserve it. And I've read your heart, darling. When I first touched your hand yesterday I felt the magic in you. And as the tarot read…" I flip back to her blank page, but now the card of the Fool is wedged between the pages. "It's time for a new beginning."

Zoe's pupils grow as she sucks in a quiet breath. She reaches for the pen and holds it over the paper.

I whisper in her ear, "Don't deny yourself any longer."

The pen scratches the paper. Her heart takes over. It's like watching someone read a Ouiji board the way her hand moves and spells out "Jade."

At the instant the "E" is finished, Jade drops the pen and

jumps up, turning to face me. Her hands plant on the table to keep herself up. We're only inches apart. Her breasts rise and fall with every deep breath she takes.

"What happens now?" Jade asks.

"Now the magic happens, darling."

We spend the night discovering which type of witch she's meant to be. Many today lean towards green witchcraft. We discuss that, hearth, cottage & kitchen witchcraft, hedge, elemental, cosmic, and eclectic witchcraft. She eats it all up like it's her last meal. Of all the varieties of witchcraft though, she leans most towards crystal witchcraft.

We go back and forth for hours with her questions. I'm overjoyed to be able to help her on this journey. There's no denying her yearning for more but, throughout the conversations, I feel hold-ups in her. Let's be clear, not skepticism anymore, but distractions. She wants more snap-of-the finger type magic.

"It all takes patience and practice, Jade," I tell her. "Some things can be done with a snap of the finger, or however your spell calls for it. But you have to push the worldly notions of magic out of your mind. Learn to appreciate the magic in a cup of tea or meditation. Let me show you." I light a stick of incense and invite her to sit with me on the floor pillows in the back corner of the room.

"Take my hands," I offer.

Jade closes her eyes and takes my hands. I instruct her how to calm her mind and focus inward on herself. She's still anxious around me. There's a mix of emotion in her heart when we touch.

I tell her, "Your mind lingers too much on others."

"I'm sorry," She jumbles out. "I'm trying."

"It's okay," I tell her patiently. "It's okay to want. But you need control of your heart before you give it away. As we practice, do your best to drive distractions out of your mind. Bad focus makes bad magic. Do you understand?"

"Yes, Nyx."

Our meditation lasts an hour. By the time we're done, I feel a stillness inside of her. I send her off into the night with some literature on witchcraft and a special tea. We plan to meet again in another week, and I'm excited to see how she develops.

7. A Day Off

Witch's Brew is closed on Sundays. It's a much-needed and well-deserved break. I let myself enjoy the peace and quiet. After breakfast, I sit down to read. It's some smutty book called "Binds" I picked up just to bother my brother because his ex started dating the author or something like that. I was never the biggest fan of the girl when they were together, but I'll give her credit; she's got good taste in smut.

In the back of my mind, I catch myself dwelling on Damien not calling back. What starts as a small voice grows slowly into an unavoidable anger if I don't do anything.

I should just call him.

No, I shouldn't, I don't need to bother myself with him. He'll crawl back when he's ready but I'm not going to let it get me on my day off.

But how long is it going to take him to call back this time?

It doesn't matter.

It does matter.

This conflict over Damien is infuriating. There is no need to devote so much of my energy to a man like him. Just focus on the book, Nyx.

Michael tightened the collar around Gabrielle's neck. "Now get on your knees," he demanded, and she did as she was ordered.

Gabrielle walked on all fours toward the bed. Michael sat down and spread his legs.

"Be a good girl," he said.

She inched closer to him, his hard cock demanding her attention. Gabriella opened her mouth and traced her tongue from the base of his cock to the tip, then filled her mouth.

Are you serious? No, I'm sorry but this should be the other way around. For all this girl is built up to be, she's just going to cave to this guy's needs when he whips his dick out? That's how you know it was written by a man.

Whatever, at least it's sexy.

I read on and just as my eyes find the word I left off on, my phone rings. It's Harry, my brother.

"What do you want?" I ask, annoyed to be taken away from this fun, if cringy, book.

"You home today?"

"Let me guess, Aria booted you out again?"

"She's that predictable?"

"*You're* that predictable. I'll be down in a sec." Oh well, no smutty reading today for this girl, and now I have to put clothes on.

Harry is quick to make himself comfortable in my apartment. Every time he comes over, he acts like he's in a museum the way he stares at the decor. Sometimes I get the notion he's not totally oblivious to the depths of my beliefs, but he still manages to make a fool of himself every time he comes by.

"Jesus, Nyx. Not gonna put anything on?" He asks as he enters my domain.

What is it with guys not understanding it is *hot* in the summer?

"I'm covered, you'll be fine." I tighten the cord around my robe to emphasize myself. "What'd you do this time?"

Harry kicks his feet up on the sofa. "*I* didn't do anything. Aria's just a fucking nut."

"This is why you don't date your friends." I push his feet off the sofa and sit back down on the love seat.

"Binds" is on the table. I catch Harry spot it then roll his eyes. He's still a little sour about the whole "Daniel Cassidy" thing with his ex.

He does his best to ignore the book and says, "No, it's not like that. One minute she's all about 'the next step' in our relationship and the next she wants to break up. Like, what's the next step, Nyx? Moving in together isn't good enough?"

The Aria/Harry drama makes my head hurt. I rub my temples and try to think of something that sounds sympathetic. "Okayyy… maybe… shit, I don't know. How long have you two been together?"

"Five months I think?" He gets up and walks over to the

kitchen. "You got anything to drink?" Before I can answer, he's already scrounging around the fridge and pulls out a bottle. "What's this? One of your potions?" He teases.

It's not even worth getting up from my seat. "It's kombucha, dumbass."

"Homemade?" He asks and smells it.

"Trader Joes. If you came here to complain, can you just complain and get it over with?"

"Actually, I'm not here *just* to complain. I need to crash. *And* complain." Harry takes a sip of the kombucha and his face contorts in disgust. "Shit, you actually drink this?"

"I can't keep letting you crash here, Harry."

"Why?" He makes his way back to the couch. "Damien isn't here, is he?"

"No."

"Good, I hate that guy."

"You hate every guy."

"I have good reason to hate Damien. He's even got the name of the fucking devil kid from 'The Omen,' as if that wasn't bad enough reason to bail."

"Maybe that's what I like about him," I joke.

"Don't even- don't... don't joke with that shit. The witchcraft and whatever, go for it. But fuck off with that Satanic shit. Everyone knows it's all for show and bein' a contrarian. Besides, I thought you had a rule against that kinda stuff."

I sit up straighter. He's right, but I enjoy making him uncomfortable. "Who knows I didn't already sign his little black book?"

He waves away the remark.

"You're right. I didn't sign his. I've got my own, cause I don't belong to no one."

His right eyebrow raises. "You remember those kids in high-school that thought they were just 'misunderstood' and 'edgy,' and 'cool' because of that, but really they were just cringy? Yeah, that's you."

I fall back in the chair. That's nothing new from Harry, and he still comes by when he needs my help, so what do I care?

"Yeah well, I'm the one that runs her own business, and *you* got kicked out of your apartment again. Which one's more 'cringy?'"

"The Satanic shit," he shoots back without hesitation, and falls back down on the couch. "Where is the Antichrist, anyway?"

"He's with his Dad this week." I don't even realize it until the words are out, but my tone has fallen flat and avoidant.

He takes a swig of the kombucha and scrunches his face again in disgust, but holds it down. I expect a response, something sarcastic like, 'who'da thought?', but nothing. Just prolonged eye contact through sour fermented tea.

We hold that look for a minute, testing to see who will shit talk Damien first. If it's Harry, then we both know I'll get defensive. If it's me, it's just what he expects to hear, and he wins.

"Aria," I finally say.

Harry sinks in his chair just a bit.

"Five months and she wants more?"

He shrugs. "I don't know what she expects. Even the move in I thought was too fast. Like, Silvia? We only lived together 'cause of COVID. Look how that turned out."

"And she hasn't told you *what* the next step is that she's looking for?"

Harry rolls his eyes. "For as much as she talks, it's never anything productive." He laughs to himself then asks, "Anything you can do to read her mind?"

Oh how easy he makes it to loathe all men. And it's clear that he's not going to accept any blame for his predicament during this conversation, so arguing is all for naught. "Today's my day off. You can come back over tonight if you still need a place to stay."

"Kicking me out?" He perks up the slightest bit.

"Harry. It's my day off. Don't you have anywhere else you can be?"

He shakes his head. "It's Sunday. Where else would I be?"

I want to say his own home, but... the obvious.

I pick up "Binds" from the coffee table, making sure he gets a good look at the front cover and the name on it, and move to the bedroom, pulling the curtain that separates the rooms closed between us. But with him here, this cheesy guilty pleasure is completely pointless. And still, all I can think of is Damien and how challenging running the store will be tomorrow.

8. What's in your bedroom?

Every once in a while, it seems like everyone in the world got together in secret to decide "this is our singular interest today." It's tarot decks and nothing else, and once those are gone, it's just as busy, but far fewer actual buyers.

Now here's the thing; when people come in to shop, they pick stuff up and buy it. Sometimes they decide halfway through browsing that they don't want it anymore and put it down in the wrong spot. It's annoying, but tolerable in small doses. No one is buying though, that's all they do, so instead of being a good saleswoman, I'm stuck rearranging the place as people are coming through. While reorganizing the charms, a woman comes up and asks about incense.

I'm pulled away for only the briefest of brief moments, and when I return the charms are all messed up again.

Then again, as I'm attempting to straighten them out, "Excuse me! Could I get some help over here?"

"Yes, of course, I'll be right there, darling."

"What's back here?"

"Please, that room is for appointments only."

"Ma'am, I'm ready to check out!"

"I'll be right there!"

And miss "I'm ready to check out" decides once I get to the register she doesn't want to go through with her order anymore.

Throughout the whole roundabout, my phone is vibrating like crazy. I don't even have to look to see who it is, and honestly, I'm a little relieved she's demanding my attention again.

Don't get me wrong, there's nothing I love more than *Witch's Brew*, but without a little help around here (Damien), I need to take any break I can.

Once the nevermind-buyer is gone, I put out a "ring me for assistance" sign next to the small bell on the counter and escape to the back room. I light a cigarette and check my phone.

> *-Hey*
> *-!*
> *-Are you busy today?*
> *-I got some stuff I gotta show you!*
> *-been reading alot from those books*

Inspiring, Maria, truly. I've got nothing going on tonight, right?

> *-I'll be over at 8.*

I slip my phone away and take a seat on the sofa against the back wall, sucking away at the much-needed nicotine, waiting for someone to ring the bell. Just as the embers tease my fingertips, I hear the ring for assistance.

Damien better get his shit together soon. I need more than a single five-minute break throughout the day. One more quick puff and I'm off with that pretty saleswoman smile.

* * *

An overpowering aroma of cinnamon overcomes my senses as I walk into Maria's apartment. Part of me assumes why, but I don't want to jump the gun on anything and say something that will make her defensive.

Her eyes are wide and bright as they meet mine, and an excited smile draws me in as she leads me through the narrow hall to the living room that's illuminated by moonlight and a handful of candles. There are also a few more plants by the windows than there were just the other night.

"Tea?" she asks.

"Thank you, no." I try to say politely. Cinnamon in my tea isn't preferred.

Instead of offering an alternative she drops onto a couch and watches me eagerly as I take a seat across from her.

"You really are embracing the culture, aren't you?" I ask, trying to manage the sarcasm in my tone.

"Oh yes! My boyfriend thinks I'm going a little nutty," she laughs, not unfazed, but clearly not having taken his comments seriously. "He says I'm just jumping on another trend. To be fair I do have a habit of that. But at least I know I have a habit, so that makes it better right? But I don't think this is just another trend. Like, this

63

feels really real to me, you know? Like in here." She puts a hand over her breast. "So I was reading that book right, for example, and let's start with the tea." She gestures over to the kitchen and the kettle on the stove. "I read that cinnamon was supposed to help with like psychic awareness. And I made some, right? And guess what?" She slaps her hands on her thighs and leans in, eyes as wide as ever.

I betray no sign of intrigue. If she is true, she won't retreat from my skepticism.

She waits though, and does a giddy bounce begging for an answer.

"You-" I begin but she cuts me off.

"I felt him again!"

It takes all of my power not to roll my eyes. "Mary, it doesn't work like that."

Thankfully she doesn't take offense, just gives a deep "hohoho" laugh. "I'm serious, Nyx! Last night, seriously, he came to me!"

"Thought you didn't let boys come over at night," I tease and her cheeks flush a deep red, clear enough even in the moonlight. Does that mean what I think it means? And with the cinnamon? Maria, you might even make me blush...

Her tone slows the slightest bit. "I wouldn't say it like that... I mean, it's just a spirit. I'm just trying to get connected with the... the um, universe."

For all she's trying to "get connected," as she puts it, the pause tells me she's not yet completely in. Aspects like that still feel awkward to her, hard to admit out loud even to me. Things like lighting candles, drinking tea, and the overall aesthetic are easy enough, but not admitting to others you believe in something truly foreign to the naked eye. For that, I'll at least give her some credit.

I try to adjust myself in posture and tone to sound more comforting. Like I'm talking to Jade.

Jade, now that's a girl I'd like to see again.

"Tell me what happened. How it happened. How you felt."

Her eyes dart from mine, down to the floor, up to mine, then back at the floor before settling on my mouth. Not direct eye contact, she's too embarrassed for that, but not totally avoiding me either. A good sign.

"Tommy had just left. We had a date night and he dropped me off. It was actually really sweet. We'd gone for a hike around the lake and had a picnic and everything for dinner and he brought wine and little plastic wine glasses and *OH!..* it was so sweet. But anyway, when he was dropping me off- shit, you know, you should really do something like that. You know, retreat into nature for a picnic? Nevermind, nevermind. Anyway, he's dropping me off and I tried to tell him about the spirit again and show him what I was talking about but he wasn't listening. So I asked him to meditate with me and at first he was okay with that because he thinks I never let him in and that is *not* true. I *always* let him in for a few minutes when he's coming to pick me up or at the end of dates like this when he's dropping me off, but he says that doesn't count because I 'always have to leave the door open like my parents are right down the hall,' and I tell him, 'well, they are Tommy. They're right downstairs. I rent this apartment from them.' Which always gets him on this long rant about how I

65

need my own space, and I always tell him, 'Tommy, I *do* have my own space, and I need you to respect that-"

"Mary. Please. The spirit."

She stares at me blankly for a half moment, all embarrassment from before now gone, then continues. "Oh! Right! So he leaves all pissy for some reason, but I have a principle not to go to bed with bad energy. And this spirit always has this positive energy about him so I'm like obviously gonna try to summon him or whatever."

This can only go well.

"I looked in the books you sold me for anything that had to do with like, psychic awareness and stuff like that. And cinnamon is one of the things that is supposed to do it. At first I, and don't laugh at me…"

I don't have to because she laughs at herself.

"I thought if I burned it like sage that would do it, and I don't know what I expected, like, is he going to show up in front of me in full form like something out of a movie? But the smell of burned raw cinnamon was just the worst and I felt like a complete dummy when I realized I could put cinnamon in my tea!"

I glance over at the kettle. It's still steaming, plenty of hot water in there, and there's another tea cup on the counter waiting to be picked up.

"Hold on, darling. You started with tea, then burned it, then went back to tea?" Now, I may not be the best storyteller, but I may look like Jane Austen compared to Maria.

She laughs again like I'm in the middle of an act. "Noohohoho! No, I guess I skipped ahead a bit. But anyway, long story short I've been drinking cinnamon tea a lot as I get ready for bed and it just makes me like… like… like I feel him ins-" she freezes.

Say it, Maria.

I lean in a bit more and let my voice drop low and airy. "How do you feel it?"

Her cheeks are so flushed she looks like a ripe strawberry, ready to be plucked from the vine.

"Well I… like you were saying. It'sjustapresence." She rushes out the words. "An energy, right? Not like a ghost like in a movie."

"Or a man in your room?"

Maria falls back in her seat and stiffens. Her fingers tighten around her tea cup. In the quietest voice I've ever heard from her, she whispers, "Maybe this wasn't a great idea."

Wonderful, Nyx. Got a little too ahead of yourself.

A few awkward seconds of silence pass between us. Her eyes stay locked on her tea, and from the look in them, she seems to be debating dumping it out. Maybe the thought extends to the books I sold her as well. The plants though? Maybe. But she comes off more as the person who would rather bring an ant outside than kill it out of guilt.

I look over toward the counter again. I hate cinnamon in my tea, but what kind of guest would I be if I didn't entertain my host's hospitality? Hey, might even walk out of here with a taste of "positive energy" from Maria's new friend.

She pretends not to notice as I get up from my seat and cross the room to the mug on the counter. I don't dislike the smell of cinnamon, but it's just something about it in my tea that I don't like.

I tried it in coffee once and it was just… just. But what's the harm in a little spiritual experimentation amongst confidants?

The first sip feels coarse going down my throat, like I'm drinking sand. *Good lord, how do you mess up tea?* I catch her watching me drink, but shies away when I return to the sitting area, next to her on the couch. I take another sip and set the mug down on the coffee table. One more and I'll start believing one can overdose and die from bad tea.

"Take my hands." I hold mine out for her.

She almost takes them, but then stops herself and puts her mug down first.

With her hands in mine, I ask her, "Now, where do you feel this presence the strongest?"

Her eyes dart to a door behind me. Through a crack I see her bed, perfectly made, with ten too many stuffed stuffed animals hiding the pillows.

Naturally, that's where she's feeling the most *positive* energy.

Crossing into her room feels…

Underwhelming.

Weak tea? Or was she exaggerating? No, that wouldn't be it. I've felt this home before and I know there's something special about this place.

"It's chilly in here," I comment as I pass through the bedroom doorway. I look to the open window. A warm breeze blows in but fades quickly.

Maria watches from the couch. I feel her gaze on the back of my head, watching me with those innocent eyes. I wonder what she's not telling me about her experiences with this spirit. What she *thinks* her experience has been. Talking about it like it's the ghost of a man coming into her bed at night, like a repressed erotic fantasy. *Tell me, Maria, do you touch yourself to the thought of it? Do you grind against your pillows when* he *comes around? Anything hiding in your nightstand?*

"What are you doing?" Her voice simpers into the room just as I open the drawer of her nightstand.

Empty except for lotion, oils, a sleep mask, Motrin, a crystal she bought from my store... But nothing fun.

I slide the drawer shut. "Just checking, darling."

The sound of her feet pattering on the floor draws close and she's in the room before I can turn around. "Checking what? Look, Nyx, I-"

I put a finger to her lips and put on my most charming smile. I whisper, "Just checking." For a moment, the look she gives me brings Jade to mind and my finger almost slides down her lips. But she pulls back an inch.

"Is there anything you were looking for?" She whispers.

I lie. "Connections to your spirit friend. Maybe an object that was dear to them when they lived here." I begin to pace around the room, pretending I'm studying the layout and her decorations. "Do you know who lived here before you?"

Almost too quickly she answers, "No. No, I mean, my parents leased this apartment to tons of people before I moved in. But no one ever died in here. At least not when we lived here. I mean, I mean maybe like a while ago someone did, but then... wait do you think someone was murdered here?"

I can't help but laugh. "This isn't *The Shining*, darling." I flick through the books on a little corner shelf next to her window. *Summer Snow*, by Daniel Cassidy. Of course, every girl needs a copy of that. "When we pass on, sometimes we return to where we were happiest. When we were happiest, sometimes." The sound of childhood I heard on my last trip here rings in my head again. "It could be anyone who's lived here, or even just had a strong connection with this place. Maybe…" Just a slight turn toward her adds all the drama I wanted. "A connection to you…"

Nyx, you are too much sometimes. It takes so much willpower not to laugh right now. Hell, I shouldn't even be messing with her this much. And it's a sign I've gone a bit far when she lowers herself onto the bed like her bones are about to shatter.

Overdramatic? Maybe. But, *know your audience, Nyx.*

I approach her again but don't sit down. I've done enough of the polite coddling tonight.

"Listen, Maria. I'll be honest with you. Whatever it is you say you've felt, I'm not picking it up. Do you feel it in here, now?"

Her eyes dart around the room. For a moment it seems as though she's going to nod her head, but it quickly turns to a shake. A lie.

"Thank you for the tea. I should be going."

As I turn to leave she jumps to her feet and takes my arm. "Wait! No, I do feel something."

There is a brief moment of silence in the world. A clarity I can feel in both of us, but, no. No spirits. She may believe it in her heart, but the heart can be deceptive. Based on everything she's said since first telling me about her spirit friend, I believe she only *wants* it to be there. All the teas, crystals, spells, and rituals wouldn't summon something that just doesn't exist on any plane.

"Darling, I-"

"I'm serious, Nyx." The tone of her voice cuts through in an impressive way. Who would have thought innocent miss 'like, I mean, like, yeah…' could stun you in such a way. "I'm not going crazy and I'm not just giving into another trend. I feel him in here. And I know you did too when you were here the other night, so I don't know why you're pretending you don't now! Or maybe he just doesn't like you because, and I'll be honest, you're not super nice, Nyx. I'm trying to be nice, I'm trying to be polite and a good host but all the time you act like you're so much better than me. And I look past that because otherwise, I think you're a really cool person. I want to be your friend and learn this witchy stuff from someone who's serious about it. And I know that if anyone can help me figure out what's going on in my house it's you, whether you talk down to me the whole time or not. Here's your stupid fee, now please do your job and help me out!" She hurls cash at me from her pocketbook.

The bills flutter down to the ground. I don't think I even told her I was going to charge her for tonight anyway. But, if she's paying anyway.

I kneel down and pick up the bills. Just a few fives and a one, but I can treat myself with it.

"Maria, you may have something here. In fact I know there's a *lot* going on in this house. But you are rushing to a conclusion that doesn't exist. Spirits don't come to you like this. It's not a movie. I

71

told you before, it's energy on another plane. Not a 'him' or a 'her' anymore. There isn't the ghost of a person coming to visit you every night. You want a man in your bedroom? Let your boyfriend in for once." With that, I tuck the bills away and leave the room, gather my things from the lounge, and make for the door, but Maria follows close by.

"Maybe you don't know everything then, because *I* know what is going on. And I am *not* letting *anyone* in my bed!"

"I said bed*room*," I quip over my shoulder. "But I respect where your head's at."

"That's another thing! You have to make everything so dirty! Not everyone's mind is always on sex, Nyx. Just yours."

Totally wrong assumption, but when is it ever worth the time arguing with someone like this? "Maybe because everything is better dirty. I'm sure your boyfriend and ghost friend would agree if you spread your legs for once." Crossing her doorway I turn one last time to see how she's fuming and add, "Maybe you could have 'em both together. Bet that'd be a lot of fun."

"Get the fuck out of my house!" Maria screams and the momentary victory-high I feel fades with the boom of the slamming of the door.

9. Late Night Rides and Messy Hair

She didn't deserve most of those words. She could have been less of a prude, yes, but okay, maybe I pushed a bit too far. But who is she to criticize me? She's the one who *begs* me to come over to help her deal with a very simple problem.

That girl is *so* sexually repressed.

She doesn't need my helping her to communicate with spirits or anything like that, she needs to get fucking laid! Let your boyfriend in for once. You've got a headboard. Hold on tight and let him have it. Might do you some good.

Either way, it's not like I'm going to lose sleep over this.

Not like I'm going to sleep now, either.

Monday nights are the only nights you'll catch me on Caroline Street. A deep meditation would probably do me more good right now, but fuck it. A drink won't hurt either.

There's a comfortable little place just past the bars all the college kids and thirty-year-old man-children who hit on jailbait go. If you've heard bad things about Saratoga, it's Caroline Street you've heard of. I wouldn't call it dangerous, but it is scummy. Not for a classy girl such as myself.

Old Fashioned might not be my kinda place either, but at least it's quiet. And they make their Whisky Sour wonderfully.

I order my drink from Frank at the bar, who nods to a trio of older guys down the counter. "They've had a few. Please don't play any games tonight."

From anyone else It would sound like casual misogyny – of course, the girl is going to be the one to start a problem when the guys have been the ones drinking. But I know Frank, and Frank knows me. And sometimes if the boys start acting up, I feel that gives me permission to respond in kind.

"Thank you for the warning. I'll be on my very best behavior, darling." I blow him a kiss and take my drink to the back where I can people-watch. Frank also doesn't mind smoking if it's in the back of the room. I light the cigarette in my cabriole, take a drag, then a sip of the drink.

It's a small crowd tonight. An old couple sits by the front window, chatting over drinks and apps. Three old guys sit at the bar. A pair of eyes from one of the old guys at the bar followed me to my seat. It's fun to play a game of "Is he thinking 'Back in my day' scolding of my style, or 'if everything still worked down there…'"

The other two men he's with are eyeing a girl sitting near the old couple with whom I assume would be her boyfriend, the other still stealing looks my way. Her irritated voice says something like, "Can we go? They're creeping me out." The boyfriend, who looks oddly familiar, glances at the three old men, then says something I can't hear that makes the girl scowl.

It's a scene that makes me think of Damien. If it were us there – although if they were staring me down I wouldn't ask my boyfriend to deal with them – Damien would probably say something stupid yet semi-charming like, 'What's the problem? I'd stare too if that's the best I could get of you.'

The girlfriend says something again, louder but inaudible, and clearly annoyed. Her boyfriend rolls his eyes and they land on me. He gives me a look of total exasperation like this is a nightly thing he suffers. It's a look that is clearly an attempt to gain sympathy, but tough luck, darling. I tend to err on the side of my sisters. And maybe if your girl's upset with you for something, don't look for a way out like that.

I'm careful with the look I give him back when the most satisfying outcome of this fight would be to see her give him a smack that would knock that pity-seeking look off his face. It'd be a great way to turn my night around.

Instead of giving him any sort of legitimate response, even a look of disapproval or a nod toward the girlfriend, I take another sip of my drink and study the couple.

His eyes go back to her and the pity-seeking look shifts to one of annoyance. Whatever this argument is, it's one they've been through a hundred times. The old men at the bar seem to have come to the same conclusion as me, as they stop stealing glances of pervert lust at the girl and start on me.

Oh well, they can dream. It'll be a good dream too, but I'm more interested now on the couple and the growing sense that I know these two. Have they come into the store before looking for something for whatever *this* is? Couples therapy spells aren't rare, but they're not common either. I just can't remember the last time I had an appointment for one, or who it was.

It's something about the boyfriend that has me sure I've seen them. Something in the eyes? No... that's not it. The 'I'm better than this argument' smirk he's hiding behind? No, not that either. The messy hair?

His eyes meet mine again and I realize I've been staring. Shit.

The girlfriend spins her head around, a long braid swinging and hitting her cheek but she doesn't notice. Seeing what her boyfriend's been looking at, she shoots back around and... there it is.

One good slap across the face and she's out of the bar.

The old men laugh at the boy, and one of them calls out the girl as she passes by them.

"Gotta be more careful, son," one of them teases.

Another adds on, "You're only supposed to look at the goods when she's not paying attention." He glances back at me and they all laugh.

Disgusting.

The boyfriend with the now even messier hair chuckles then drops his head into a hand he runs through his hair that almost completely covers his face. With his other hand, he picks up his glass before realizing there's only ice left in it. Through the long strands of hair, though faint, his smile drops and it looks like his eyes harden. There's no annoyance anymore, or pity-seeking, just pity for himself.

Deserved, I'd say. The girl was pretty. Beautiful, even.

Whatever you were arguing about, whatever you've been *arguing about, you should have taken it more seriously.*

Part of me expects to see him look up at me again through the hair in front of his eyes, come over here, and try to strike up a conversation as a rebound. But he doesn't try to talk, doesn't get up, doesn't even look away from the empty glass.

I take another drag of my cigarette, waiting for the next act of this show. Nights of people watching like this are never nearly half as exciting as this and I'm not done with my drink yet. Will she come back in for round two when he doesn't chase after her?

A stool pushes out from the bar. The screech against the floor derails my train of thought that I replace with a sip from my drink. When I put the glass down one of the old men is approaching my booth.

Please be going to the restroom.

"Pretty girl like you waiting on anyone?" His hand rests on the edge of the booth.

I didn't bother to give the old man a proper look earlier and I wish I didn't now. He's the typical creepy old white guy. He definitely came to the area for the track based on his high-end summer outfit and the over-use of gel in his combover that shouldn't exist with that little hair. If his presence in track season Saratoga didn't say enough about how much money he carried on him, the Corvette keys hanging out of his pocket like a dog whistle for other old white guys does.

His friends at the bar are laughing at the attempt and one of them pulls out a cigar. Frank the barkeep scolds him and says smoking is only allowed in the back, not at the bar. The man with the cigar eyes me quickly and jokes, "If you say so," but puts it away, letting his friend shoot his shot first.

"Mind if I take a seat? I don't mind keeping you company." Mr. Corvette doesn't wait for an answer before sliding into the booth.

I stand (or sit) my ground and keep looking forward, letting him know the extent of my disinterest. I take another sip of my drink. There's only a third left and I just know he's going to offer to get me another one. So, I finish it off.

My sleeve falls back when I raise my arm for the drink.

He falls back the slightest bit. "You know those tattoos last forever. Why's an attractive girl like you feel like you need to do that to your body to look pretty?" He forces out a laugh.

"To scare off men who hit on girls their granddaughter's age."

He laughs, seemingly genuinely this time. "That's a good one," he says and looks back at his friends.

The old couple at the front are gone now, but messy hair is still there. He doesn't seem to be listening, though.

Mr. Corvette continues, "Good thing I don't have a granddaughter. And I don't scare easy."

Alright, Nyx. How do you want to handle this one?

I flare my best customer service smile. "Oh, no? Girls like me can be a lot sometimes. We're quite a lot to handle. I don't think a man of your age has that much stamina."

His eyes follow mine down to my legs. I cross my right over the left to reveal a bit of inked skin. The look on his face tells me he doesn't mind tattoos as much as his generation tells him he should.

"Age just means experience. And I've got plenty, hun." He inches closer and I put up a hand between us, then knock back the rest of my drink.

"Not until I've had another."

Two more drinks soon arrive at our table. I let Mr. Corvette talk my ear off with some ego thing about what he does for work and his summer home, his interest rate, and refinancing. How he always comes here and stays in his fancy summer home and wins big at the track, big enough to pay off his summer home and take a girl like me out to fancier places than this bar. I nod my head with all the interest he wants to believe I have in what he has to say and perk up when he mentions his car. But my true attention is still on messy hair.

The bartender walks by his table and drops the check. For once, Messy Hair looks at something other than his glass, and at the sight of the check his face changes again. He glances around the room with worry now in his eyes.

It's fascinating to me how his night has gone.

"You know, my place isn't too far from here," Mr. Corvette slides a hair closer and his hand touches my leg.

For the first time in this conversation, I flinch and am pulled back into the scene in my booth.

Mr. Corvette's friends cheer again.

Letting him talk on and on about who knows what in exchange for a few free drinks is one thing. To be lingered at is another. But I didn't tell him he could touch. That costs more than a drink.

I raise my glass toward the bar and tap one of my rings against it twice. The men at the bar take it as I'm toasting with them, maybe that Mr. Corvette and I have sealed the deal, and they get excited. Another round of drinks is demanded. Even Mr. Corvette himself takes it as a sign that he's going to get lucky and moves closer, putting an arm around me and pulling me in. But Frank gets the message.

"Bar's closing guys," Frank tells the two old guys.

But they're not ready to go, because until Mr. Corvette and I are out of sight they've still got a show to watch, and they have just enough alcohol in them to push back.

As the three of them argue about closing, I get up close to Mr. Corvette and run my hand up his leg. Even for a guy his age, I don't think any blue pill would do more for him than my teasing.

"You know, I think I would like to check out that summer home," I whisper.

He moves in to do… something… to my neck. I don't know if it's a playful bite or a kiss, but I'm not having it. I back off as if I'm just teasing, not repulsed as I truly am, and say "Not here, darling. Let me just use the *little* girl's room first and we can get out of here." I wonder if he'll hear the inflection on "little" and realize how gross he's been.

"Just don't take too long, baby," he laughs through an old man cough as I slide out of the booth.

As a parting gift, I blow him a kiss and strut to the exit. The others are too distracted by Frank to notice me leave and messy hair is… gone.

I stop in my tracks and see the check is still there, untouched. I should tell Frank, but then my knight in shining armor with the summer home might realize the restroom isn't in the front of the bar.

I'll tell him another time.

Only when I'm at the door does Mr. Corvette realize where I've gone, but then it's too late for him.

I wait against the outside wall, just out of sight of the window, with a new cigarette burning between my lips. I'm waiting. They're still arguing about closing and hassling Mr. Corvette about fumbling the "pretty young thing" at the bar.

My ears stay focused on the conversations in the bar until I hear the old perv say, "Hey wait a minute, guys. Do you see my keys anywhere?"

This isn't my first Corvette, but this never gets old.

Don't worry, he'll get it in the morning. Frank knows where I park them and he'll make sure the old guy knows. And as long as I don't scratch the car, Frank will be more than happy to complain the keys were handed over freely in a drunken attempt at flirting with a *much* younger girl.

You can't be mad at me. He came at me first, and besides, he wanted to give me a ride anyway. Who cares how I get it?

My place is just a few blocks away, but that's no fun is it? Let's take this thing for a cruise.

I take off down Caroline, then turn right on Circular Street to head for the Interstate. A quick drive up twenty miles to Lake George and back should be good.

There on the corner of Caroline and Circular, though, is

81

Messy Hair, walking with his hands in his pockets. The show in the bar is over, but... I'm still interested. I pull up next to Messy Hair and roll the window down.

"Hey you," I call.

He turns his head but keeps walking without a word.

"Not a fan of paying your tab?" I tease.

"You come to collect?"

"Maybe. Frank's a good guy. I don't like when good people get stiffed."

Messy Hair halts and throws his head back. I put the car in park and lean in toward him.

"I'm Lo-"

"I don't care." I cut him off. "Why'd you stiff him?"

He turns, but backs away to the nearest wall and slouches against it in a posture that... well I'll be honest, there's some cool in it. Especially with that hair falling as it does in front of his eyes.

"I could call the police," I say. "I don't want to, but it's not a busy night. And you should be paying for two so that's like a quarter of his night's income. That's fucked up, darling."

"You're gonna call the cops from a stolen car?"

Hm.

"Fair. At least I've got a good reason to be here. What's yours?"

Messy Hair sighs deeply. "I lost my job."

"Huh." It should probably garner more sympathy, but he still has to convince me he deserves it. "Probably shouldn't be going out to nice bars then, should you? Is that why the beautiful woman you were with walked out?"

"She wouldn't have if you hadn't booted me from your store."

Our gazes lock. His is one of accusation, mine of confusion.

He continues, "You don't recognize me?"

"No. Sorry, darling."

Messy Hair pushes himself off the wall and steps closer to the car. He's too tall to lean into the window, so he kneels down. "I came in the other day asking for a job. You couldn't give me the time of day."

It's such a stupid excuse I have to laugh. "Oh! Ha! It's my fault your girl left you? Sweety, I don't even remember you." But as I say it, the memory starts coming back. Not that I'll admit it at this point, though. "Let's say I did, though. I have no obligation to give you a job. I have no obligation to save your relationship or pay your tab."

"No, but you *were* struggling the other day. Sure you're not obligated anything, but you're gonna tell me honestly you don't need help in that place? This time of year is busier than Christmas around here."

"I was doing just fine."

He shrugs and backs away from the car, then starts walking again. "It's only going to get busier. And hotter. Gonna be a lot of stress on just one woman."

I follow alongside him with the Corvette. "And I should hire someone that can't even be trusted to pay his tab?"

"I would if I had a job."

"What about a car? Walking home this late at night, could I even expect you to show up on time?"

"My girl took it. But yours is nice. It'd make my life a lot easier if I could get a ride home."

"I'm sorry. I have a rule to not take boys like you home."

Messy Hair laughs. Genuinely laughs. "Don't flatter yourself. I know better than to get involved with girls like you. You're 'a lot to handle,' right? I don't have that kinda patience."

"You're making a *strong* case to be hired."

"Oh, I thought we were talking about going home together. Totally different subject. That would be the *real* work."

I speed up and park a few feet ahead of him then get out of the car. I call over the roof, "What's that supposed to mean?"

He smirks, and… shit… I mean, I'd be lying if I said it wasn't a charming smile. A terrible quality when it's coming from an unemployed loser.

"I can see your type a mile away." He approaches but doesn't slow as he gets closer. "Typical witchy Pinterest girl. Even if you admitted you needed help you wouldn't hire me cause of star signs being off or some bullshit like that. And if we *are* talking about going home together, it's not a hook-up, it's a 'deep spiritual bonding with the universe' or something, huh?"

"You. Are. So. Presumptuous. Aren't you?"

He only shrugs again. "Am I wrong?"

"Well, regardless of any hypotheticals, I wouldn't *ever* consider taking you home. And not just because I'm already with someone."

"So am I. Which is another reason I wouldn't be going home with you. I just hoped you'd have enough kindness in your heart to help a poor soul home."

I didn't even realize it until now, but the Corvette is more than fifty feet behind us. And I'm actually following *him!*

"It doesn't look like you have someone anymore. I thought she walked out?"

"So you thought you could try your shot?"

"I already told you-"

"Yeah yeah," he waves me off. "Yet here you are following me."

"I just want you to pay your tab!"

"Return the 'vette and I'll pay my tab. Or..." he stops and turns so suddenly that I almost bump into him. He takes me by the arms to stop me from crashing. There's firmness in his grip, but not aggressive. I look up at him and it's the first clear look into his eyes I've had yet. Hazel, and I need to catch my breath.

He finishes, "Or, you could give me a ride to my place and I won't say anything to the cops about a stolen Corvette."

"Blackmail? Really? You must really not want a job then."

"I'm happy to negotiate if we're putting that on the table."

This man really is persistent. But would he really rat me out?

I consider it as his hands slide slowly down my arms. His thumb trails slowly behind.

"I'll think about it," I tell him, looking away from those hazel eyes.

"The ride or the job?"

The job, but first I ask, "Why do you want to work at my place so bad?"

Without missing a beat he says, "You look like you need my help the most."

…

I break away from his arms and walk back to the car.

"I'll consider."

"The ride or the job?" He asks again.

The car is a remote start. Just to fuck with him, I turn on the engine to get his hopes up. He follows me to the car and tries to get in with me but I leave the passenger door locked.

"Hey could you, uh…"

"If I see you again I'll let you know what I decide. Get home safe," I wink, and roll up the window.

10. Witch Puns

Tuesday, Dark Day at the raceway which means everyone that can't spend their money there comes to Broadway. Great for business, not great for my stress.

Wednesday. Slower. But still stressful, and hotter.

Thursday. The weekend has started early. The morning started off easily enough; I had my daily rituals completed in a timely manner and was able to peacefully sit outside and smoke for most of the opening hour, but as noon neared, customers started arriving. From one until closing, there wasn't a moment to breathe.

Nevertheless, I was able to handle it. A decent number of the customers were only window shoppers and out-of-towners looking to see what this town has to offer besides high-end chains and horse-themed shops. And at the very end of the day, just when I was beginning to worry that tomorrow would be worse, and maybe even break me, a shining light of insufferable hope made itself known.

-I'll be back in town tonight.
Want me to come over?

Damien. Thank god.

-Tomorrow's going to be
crazy.

If fate says we are to argue every time he comes over, at least this time he can't say I didn't warn him. Damien can have my bed *if* he's willing to put in the work, as any relationship should be.

Besides, I deserve some good bedside company after this week. My magic wand needs a break.

-I have plans tomorrow at 1.
Me and some of the boys.

-Can I get you for the
morning?

I wait a few moments, before typing something more, but the three little dots from his end appear, letting me know he's typing.

-Can I get you for the night?

-Do you deserve it??

-I'll take you somewhere nice.
Hb that?

Tempting… very tempting, Damien. At least it shows he's listening.

-Hmmm…
-Where are you thinking?

-Nové?

He should know by now I don't like Italian, and I consider recommending Wishing Well instead, but it's a fancy place, and he's making a semblance of an effort.

-It's been a while since you've taken me on a date. Anything else you had in mind?

It takes him a long time to respond. I assume he meant for me to say nothing but thank him for finally offering to take me out, not turn it into negotiations.

-I was just hoping if I took you out for dinner, I could have you for dessert.

A girl can dream of romance, but I'll take what I can get.

-I don't close until 9.
-And I have an appointment just after closing but it shouldn't take long. Make a res for 10?

-Cutting it kinda late.
-Yeah, i'll do that.

For half a moment I play with the idea of sending him a teasing dirty picture to make sure he *does* make a reservation, but also to let him know what he won't be getting if he doesn't. Just a little thigh in an otherwise revealing dress. But I throw the idea away. He should already know what's at stake, I don't need to give him any more motivation.

-Good. Can you pick me up? I'd like a drink with dinner.

-You got it babe.

A knock at the door interrupts my text back. I look up and who do I see but a messy head of hair and-

Fuck. Beautiful-

…hazel eyes.

Beautiful? Come on, Nyx, calm down. They're just eyes.

He sees me staring and knocks again. What a persistent ass. Fine, screw it.

When I open the door he almost falls through it.

"What do you want? I'm busy right now."

He peeks over my shoulder. "You don't look super busy." He's right, too. The store is totally dead, and if he were to ask me what I was busy with, I don't know if I'd have an excuse at the ready.

"Well, I am. It's closing time, so, sorry, no more customers." I should close the door. Why waste my time with him? But my hand doesn't move. In fact, the door opens a little more when his eyes fall back on mine.

"Good thing I'm not buying." He takes a step forward and I realize I've stepped back. Shit, it probably looks like I'm inviting him in!

"What do you want then?"

"Just wanted to check back in. You return the 'vette?" As he asks he drops his eyes down to the floor then kneels. Willow is rubbing up against his legs. Traitor.

"You pay your tab?" I glare at Willow. Dumb cat hisses at Damien every time he steps in here, but this guy? This bum who can't even pay for a drink, she's already in love with?

"I did, actually. Thought it'd be a good show of character for you."

"For me?" I put a hand to my chest in faux flattery, and

91

immediately regret it. *Does it look like I'm flirting? Fuck, he better not take it like that.* I fix my tone. "Why the hell for me?"

He stands back up with Willow in his arms, scratching the back of her neck. She eyes me like she's *trying* to annoy me. "I figured if I wanted a job, I should probably come off as a trustworthy person. Even to somebody who steals rich guys cars."

"Who cares? He's rich, he can buy another."

The ass holding my cat scoffs. "Okay, yeah. You gonna keep up the 'eat the rich' persona when you hit it big? Hey little guy, you're very handsome."

"Willow's a girl," I correct.

"A very pretty girl," he says and scratches the top of her head. Willow's rear end and tail stretch upwards in delight. She even nuzzles him.

That's it, the cat's going up for adoption.

"Are you gonna tell me why you're here?"

"I just did," he laughs.

Willow jumps out of his arms and scurries to the back room, making sure to give me one last instigating look before disappearing.

"You're serious about a job, huh?" I ask.

"Incredibly serious." We exchange a moment of heated silence before he adds, "Desperately... serious."

"Desperately?" I cross my arms.

Messy Hair rolls his eyes. "Look, I can't get a job anywhere else. I've worked most places around town but can't keep one held down. I can't go out of town 'cause I don't have a car. And now my girl is threatening to leave me if I don't get my shit together. So... please. This is my last chance."

It's honestly kinda sad. Not in a way that I'd pity him and give him a job because of his sob story though. "You make a real good case to take you on. I'd love to work with someone that can't hold down a job."

"Broadway jobs. These have been basically summer jobs, nothing anyone wants a career in. Jobs I could do in my sleep."

"And my store is one you'd commit yourself to? Put in thirty years and retire with a 401k?"

His lips purse to the side. "Look, I just need something to hold me down for a while, and you clearly need help here. I don't need a career, just something to hold me down until I figure shit out. So I won't be in your hair too long. Works out for everyone."

Hm.

I cross my arms and retreat to the register. I don't want to look in his eyes anymore. How he's been able to stay in my presence this long I just do not know. He follows me to the counter and I pretend he's not high on my priority list, cleaning up and reorganizing around the register. "Why not a job at the gas station up the road or something like that?" I ask, not looking up at him.

To my curiosity, he laughs. "I may be desperate, but I have standards."

"Something wrong with working at a gas station?"

"No, nothing wrong."

"But it's below you. Like you're above other people?"

"I didn't say that."

"Yes, darling, you did." There's nothing left to fidget with on the counter, so I cross over to the incense rack. As I do, his hand grabs my arm. Not in a hard way, in fact, it's just like the other night. Firm, but not hostile.

"Please," he says again. "Just need something to get by for a little bit then I'll be out of your hair."

He lets go of my arm and takes a step back.

But his eyes never fall away from mine.

Fuck it.

"Do you believe in any of this?" I ask.

"What, witchcraft?"

I nod.

"No," he laughs. "Not really. But I can act like I do. At least, I can know my stuff. Ask anyone I've worked for. I can pick up something new just like that." He snaps to emphasize his point.

"You are just one bad idea after the next, aren't you. Not even gonna try to lie and say this is your whole deal?"

"What'd be the point of that? Start a relationship based on a lie? That'd be my worst idea yet. How about this…" He scans one of the shelves he's standing next to and grabs a book, then flips through the pages. "How about I buy this from you? Right now. I'll take it home tonight, then tomorrow, I come in bright and early and help you out. First day's on me just to prove myself."

So. Fucking. Persistent.

"I'm gonna go out on a limb and guess your parents told you all you needed to get a job in life was to walk into the owner's office with a clean suit and a good attitude."

"Close," he says. "That's what my girl's dad said I should do. And here I am." He steps toward me again and I'm up against the wall.

My chest rises with bated breath. His eyes shake, almost stopping themselves from taking a peak down. If I'd known he'd get this close, much less in the store, I would've dressed modestly for once. At least he's not a creep that's just here to stare. Damien even wouldn't be able to take his eyes off my chest in a situation like this. He'd probably think we were about to mess around right here in the open. But not this man. He at least has enough respect to look me in the eye... even if I can't bear to look back.

"Fine. One day."

The tension in the air dissipates and we can both finally breathe.

"Thank you! Oh my God, thank you!"

I raise a finger of indignation at him. "But you'd better be an expert by tomorrow. I pride myself on not being some cheap cash-in for tourists. This is the real deal here, and even if you don't believe in any of it, myself and my clients do. Got it?"

"Yeah, yeah I got it," he says through a smile that lights up his eyes even more. "You're really doing me a solid, uh... shit, I don't think I got your name yet."

And here I thought he was stalking me. "It's Nyx."

"Nyx, huh?" He laughs.

"What's wrong with my name?" I'm this close to taking back my offer.

"Nothing! Nothing's wrong, it's... it's a cool name. I like it. I'm Logan." Messy Hair, or Logan, I suppose, extends his hand with the book, then quickly transitions hands to shake.

"Charmed," I shake his hand, and he gives me a look with a stupid grin.

"Was that a witch pun?"

My chest rises again, but he doesn't break contact. "One day. Off the books."

11. A long-awaited appointment

I'm stunned by Jade when she steps into my back room; a thin flowing green sundress, her hair shaggy with baby bangs, and her makeup all done nice and pretty. To round off the outfit, she has a pointed rose quartz crystal on a string around her neck. Definitely homemade by the type of string and the amatuer look of how the metal frame coils around the crystal, not one she'd bought here. She looks like she was arriving for a date in every way but her expression. There is despair in her eyes she's desperate to hold back.

"Welcome, darling," I greet her with open arms. She's clearly trying to hide whatever it is that's bothering her. I won't press too soon. "It's wonderful to see you again. Please, take a seat."

Leaving my embrace she sits at the table, and I glide across the floor to the other side, slowly taking a seat.

"I'm a fan of the necklace," I tell her, attempting to break this silence cast by her not-so-hidden sadness.

Jade looks down at the crystal and fidgets with it. "Thank you," she almost whispers. "I was reading those books you gave me... I thought it would help."

She's said enough for me to understand. I sigh deeply. "Jade…"

Her eyes perk up. She's not yet used to her name.

I continue, "I'm sorry it didn't work as you had hoped. Jenna, was it?"

Jade nods. "I thought magic would help, but I just feel so stupid." She sniffs and wipes away a tear before it can form.

Poor girl.

"Tell me what happened. Maybe I can help. Maybe I can help you help yourself."

By the dim glow of the red candles spread out around the room, Jade tells me her story.

"This last week has been… strange… between us. We went up to the lake with some friends to celebrate starting college. We rented out an AirBnB and everything, and brought drinks our friend Mikey swiped from his dad, and even a bit of weed. It was kinda a small place, like, the cheapest we could find, so I offered to share a room with Jenna. I mean, we've always been best friends so neither of us would think it's weird, and I mean, yeah it was fine at first.

"But all week, I guess I was being obvious. I've never shown how I felt around her, but when we would go swimming, I heard the guys talking about us, about me, so I tried to play it cool. Then the other night we had a fire and were drinking. Things got crazy, and Mikey put it out in the open, joking that I had a thing for Jenna. I didn't know what to say, but she saw I was embarrassed and… she kissed me.

"It wasn't real, just to make me feel better and get the guys off my case. But it felt real to me. If it wasn't for the drinking it would have been just that and we would've gone back to all just hanging out like friends, but I kissed her again, and she didn't say anything, so I thought she was really into me too. So, this morning I asked her if she wanted to go out tonight. Just as a way to get away from the guys. She said 'yeah' and we agreed to get dinner somewhere in town. I was going to tell her everything. While they spent the day on the water I stayed in and read more of the books and sincerely tried to do the magic it talked about. We didn't even make it to the car when she realized what was up.

"At first she said she loved my outfit and everything I did to get ready for dinner, even jokingly hassled me for not letting her know it was *that* kind of dinner. But once she said that, she realized I did mean it as *that* kind of dinner. Then she went cold on me. And I… fuck, I feel so stupid. I thought like an idiot if we touched, if I kissed her again, sober this time, she'd feel it, too. She'd feel how I felt when her lips first touched mine. How I've always felt about her. But she didn't. She didn't even say anything when she went back inside. I came right here after that."

Jade looks like she's about to crumble when she finishes her story. I let her have a moment to breathe. I can only imagine how hard that must have been for her.

"I'm so sorry, Jade. That was very brave of you, though. I want you to know that." I reach out my hands to her. The table we sit at isn't small, but small enough to take her hands.

"It didn't work," she sniffs back a tear. "The crystal didn't fucking work." She stumbles through the word "fucking" and tears the crystal from her neck. "I don't know what the fuck I was thinking. This witch shit, fucking crystals. All it did was make me look like an idiot!" Jade drops her face into her hands.

Well now, I'm not a fan of her words, although I can be empathetic to the cause of them. Moving forward though, I'll have to tread lightly.

"Jade, darling, you don't have to be embarrassed about this. Really, I'm sure by tomorrow it'll be like nothing happened. Maybe you just caught her unawares and she needs time to process." It's a bullshit excuse, we both know how Jade's friend Jenna acted when they were in the store together. As far as I could tell, she has no interest in Jade.

"No, she doesn't. Even when I told her about last week when I came around, she thought it was so cool until I asked her to call me 'Jade,' and then she laughed at me."

Typical. No one takes us seriously. It's one of the hard truths she'll have to accept about this life.

"Listen," I say with a tone of soft indignation, rising out of my chair and stepping toward her, trailing a finger along the rim of the table. "This is the life you chose. You can walk away at any time, but your name is in the book. My book. And not many names are." My finger runs off the table, along her hand, her arm, and up to her chin, guiding her to look up, into my eyes. "I said I would teach you this craft, and I will. *If* you really… truly… want this."

I watch as her gaze falls along my body. After letting her have her moment, I pull her chin back up.

"Is this what you still want?"

"Y… yes."

Good.

My hands fall to her shoulders and I step behind her. "Why do you think the magic didn't work?"

"I- I don't know. I gave my intentions before going out. Going for her, I mean… I guess. And the crystal I thought would help. The book said rose quartz was good for spells of love."

"But what did I tell you last week?" I begin to rub her shoulders, hoping it will key her in to the answer.

Jade's head falls back and her eyelids droop. "You said…"

"I said you need to clear your mind. You're a mess, darling, and not because of what happened at the lake."

She twitches in my hands, but I keep her firm and continue to rub her shoulders. "Your mind and your body should be one together. If your body is tense, your mind will be. And if your mind is under stress, so will your body. How much time did you take to meditate while you were at the lake? Did you ever have a moment to yourself?"

She exhales relief as I focus on a knot just beside her shoulder blade. "I tried. I'd sit by the water reading or meditating while the rest of them swam."

I almost laugh. "That will do nothing for you, sweetie. What I like to do; I have a spot in the middle of the woods, a little pool only I know of. That's where I go to meditate. No one around, no distractions, just me and nature, the moonbeams shining down on my body."

Jade hesitates, then turns to face me, looking up with

beautiful curiosity. "Could you take me? That sounds so nice."

This time I do laugh. Nothing loud, just a chuckle. "Maybe one day. But not now. I don't take anyone there. Besides, I don't think that's what you need tonight. No… I think we need to work on getting rid of all this stress. Come."

I take Jade by the hand and lead her to the cushions in the back of the room. In this spot we're lit ever the littlest bit more by the red candles, a glow that looks magnificent on her face.

"Lay down here, on your stomach. Good girl. Do you mind?"

She jerks back up at the feel of my fingers on the zipper of her dress.

"Don't want to get anything on it." I reach over to the cabinet next to us and grab a bottle of lavender massage oil.

There is conflict in her eyes. The bite of her lip tells me she wants it, but the innocent girl she is remains unsure.

"Don't worry," I console. "If you're uncomfortable, just say so. I just want to help."

With that, she lowers her head again. "Okay…"

Her back is so smooth, so soft. She shifts around, helping me move the fabric out of the way. I promise not to go too low, or anywhere uncomfortable.

Jade shivers when the first drop of oil falls on her spine.

"Too cold?" I ask.

"No, no it's fine."

I pour a little more, then begin to apply pressure. It's a shame, someone her age has so much stress built up. When I was eighteen… well, I suppose I wasn't like Jade. Not to be the "I'm not like other girls" kinda girl, but I cared much less about what others thought. I got into witchcraft young and took to it like a moth to a flame.

What I didn't have, which I envy Jade for, is someone like me. Someone to mentor her properly. She's so beautiful and innocent. I'm in awe of how her lips quiver as I press my hands between her oiled shoulder blades, and then trace back down her spine.

"How is that?" I whisper in her ear.

All she can do is moan back to me.

"After this," I tell her, "You'll find it much easier to clear your mind. With a clear mind, you'll have clear intentions. And with clear intentions, your spells will be more effective." I lean in again, pressing my chest against her back, using my body to massage hers, and again, whisper in her ear. "You'll be able to have anything you want." My hands run up her neck, thumbs behind her ears, and fingers meet in front of her throat. "Are you ready to take what you want?"

"Yes," she whispers back.

"Very good." I slink back, removing my hands from her neck, and unstraddle her backside. "Let's talk, then. Come upstairs with me. We'll get something to eat."

Jade takes a moment before jumping back onto her knees. She looks around the room like she has no idea how she got there and zips her dress back up. "Upstairs?" She asks. "What's upstairs?"

"Just my apartment," I laugh. "Nothing too scary. Come now, darling." I take her by the hand and lead her up the steps.

While Jade sits on my couch, looking as adorably out of place as ever, I brew some tea and heat up leftovers. I didn't expect company until later so all I can offer her is leftover Chinese.

"Are you having anything?" She asks when I only bring out one bowl.

I recline on the arm of the far end of the couch. "Oh, no. No, I have plans in a little bit. Date night."

"That's why you're all dressed up? You have a…"

She's trying to be respectful, not assume my sexuality. That is, if it goes one way or the other.

"Boyfriend. Yes."

Jade blushes. "Sorry, I thought you were into-"

"I am," I laugh.

"Have you ever had a girlfriend?"

"We're getting into very personal questions, darling." I'm sorry, I can't help myself. I must tease, I just must.

But I think I've gone too far. Jade is quiet again, eyeing her cup. So I ask her, "What is it you want, Jade."

"You don't have to keep calling me that."

"Oh, but I do." I give her a playful kick. "That's your name now, isn't it? The one you felt in your heart?"

She's about to speak, but I cut her off. "Don't deny it. It's a beautiful name for a beautiful woman. And better yet, it's fitting. Do you know what 'Jade' means?"

She shakes her head. "I didn't really think about it. The name just-"

"The name just came to you. Jade, or Jadis, is a literal witch, or enchantress. There are a thousand names that could have come to you but there is nothing more clear to me. There is nothing extra, you are through and through meant for this."

"Jadis?"

"Jadis. Now why did Jadis become a witch?"

Her hands tighten around the mug. Strife covers her face again to the point she has to put the mug down, and it almost explodes out of her, "I just want her to love me, too!"

It's an almost violent gesture, but I don't flinch. "No, you don't."

She shoots a glare at me. Her cheeks are red and stained with tears and running makeup. I can't help but nibble on my finger. It's an intriguing look, one that says we're getting somewhere.

"What do you mean, 'No, I don't?'"

"Say it again."

Jade takes a deep breath. Then, "I want her to love me-"

"No."

Her chest tightens. Her hands grip the hem of her lovely green dress.

"I want her-"

"No." I sit up and lean in. "Say it."

"I want-"

"Yes, you do. Don't you?"

Her mouth quivers. A girl with lips like that shouldn't have to want. She should just have.

"Don't you?" I ask again. "You just want. You *want* because you deserve it. You *want* because you *can*."

Jade's lips purse and her eyes harden. "I just... want," she finally agrees.

"Go back to the lake. With a clear mind, with clear intention. If you want, you shall have."

"I want." She says again.

What a beautiful woman.

12. Behave

"Appointment ran a little late, huh?" Damien asks when I step into his car. He takes my hand and kisses my fingers. There's a scrunch of his face but it quickly passes.

"Only a few minutes. Poor thing had a lot going on. Terribly stressed."

"Seemed like it when she walked out."

Jade had left maybe ten minutes ago. I took my time getting ready because Damien hadn't texted or called to let me know he was here. If I'd known, we could have avoided this next part.

As he pulls the car off the curb, he says, "She looked a bit…" Searching for the right words he shakes his hands beside his head like he's messing up his hair.

"I didn't sleep with her if that's what you're getting at."

Damien scoffs. "I didn't say anything like that."

"Yeah, well I know that's what you were thinking."

The car pulls out onto Broadway and we head north for the restaurant. Taking this road this late on a Friday night could add five, maybe ten minutes to a trip that should only take fifteen minutes total, if that.

"Look, all I'm saying, your hands smell like that oil you like having me use to give you back rubs, and she walks out of your place looking like you were doing cardio up there."

"My time with my clients is kept extremely professional. She's going through a very stressful period right now and I would do nothing to take advantage of her. That's absolutely repulsive that you'd think that of me."

"Oh, but if she wasn't going through a 'stressful period' you would?"

We pull up to a red light and I throw the door open. "Do you even want to do this? Do you want me here with you tonight at fucking all?"

"Nyx, don't cry," he says with such a dismissive tone.

"I'm not crying."

"Yeah, you are. Now close the door."

"No!" On the sidewalk beside us, people are slowing their steps to get a look at the scene. "Every time. Every fucking time I try to give you a chance you have to start some shit like this. It was just a fucking client."

The red light illuminating his face turns green. The car behind us honks, but he ignores it completely.

My right leg is out of the car.

"I'm sorry." He says. And in his face it seems true. "Come back in the car. I'm sorry."

The car behind us honks again. Damien then opens his

door and shouts, "Give me a *fucking* minute dude! Or go around! Fucking. Go. Around!" He slams the door again and as gently as before, pleads, "Come on, Nyx."

I bring my leg back into the car and shut the door.

He puts the car in drive.

I tell him again, "All we did was work through her stressors. We talked a lot, just trying to help her figure out her path."

Damien nods, feigning interest. Even though it's clear he doesn't get behind all of the witchy stuff, the least he can do, and does, is engage. "She someone getting into it for real or one of your 'aesthetic witches?'"

"Real. This girl's genuine. Just doesn't really understand much of anything yet. But I hope she does, soon. I hope she gets it."

"Cool, cool." He whispers.

The rest of the ride to Nové is defined by this awkward small talk skirting around the issue of Jade's walk of shame from our appointment. It's utterly ridiculous of him to have thought I'd try to have my way with her, just because he was probably eyeing her curves when she passed by his car.

Or maybe I'm overthinking it. Maybe he is genuinely concerned. And it'd be just as shitty of me to assume he's staring at other women like that if what I'm getting mad at is his much more serious accusations.

Walking into the restaurant gives me a much better look at my man. In the night's illumination of the car, I was impressed by his combed hair, trimmed beard, and button-up shirt. In the light, I see that the effort stopped at his waist. Ripped jeans and battered sneakers, and the shirt is untucked. Nové may not be the most high-end place in and around town, but it's much more highbrow than an untucked shirt.

I hide my displeasure as we're escorted to our seats. But after one bad thing, Damien follows it up with one good thing. He pulls out my seat for me and helps me scoot it in. It's one of those little things that he has never failed to do in our relationship, and for that, I give him credit.

"Can I start you off with anything to drink?" The waiter asks.

I scan the wine menu but think twice. "Just water for me, thank you."

He nods, but Damien leans in. "Thought you wanted something tonight?"

It's typical for dinners to go like this: He offers to drive, or I ask him to, so I can have a drink or two. I know I'm fine to drive after a glass, but I never wish to tempt fate when I let it out of my hands, even for a drop. Then once we get there, Damien orders something strong enough to get a buzz because he doesn't believe in lunch, and I have to stick to water.

"You don't want anything?" I ask.

"Not tonight. Go on, anything you like."

Okay, I think, *maybe he's truly making an effort. The kind of "do the dishes because you want to" effort.*

"I'll have the Chateau Montelena. A bottle please."

Damien's grin slackens at the request, but does not object.

"And for you, sir?"

"Water," Damien answers, keeping his eyes on me.

"Spring or tap?"

"Tap."

With the hostilities past us, the night is actually quite pleasant. The food is good, Damien behaves like an adult, the wine is delicious, and as the evening goes on and there is more and more distance between us and the argument in the car, we find ourselves laughing again. And when he smiles, I find myself smiling back at him. I'm truly having a wonderful time. And even if his shirt is untucked and wrinkled, he's still so handsome. Eventually, after dinner, while we wait for the waiter to come back with a dessert menu, I find myself holding his hand. It sounds ridiculous that I'd be so surprised by such a small thing, but I'd forgotten how long it's been since we've had a night like this. Since we were content in each other's company like this.

"What?" He draws back and pulls his hand away.

Shit.

I look over at the bottle of wine and it's almost empty. Fuck! How much of that did I say? Play dumb. "What's what? What's wrong?"

"It hasn't been that long, has it? We just took that trip like a month ago."

What's *he* talking about now? Does he mean...

"The Cape? Damien, that was *three* months ago." And he's right. The last night of the week we spent at Virginia Beach three months ago *was* the last real date we had.

"Are you sure?"

"Yes!" I have to lower my voice, although I'm not sure how well I'm doing with the alcohol in my system. "Fucking hell, Damien. This- this is what I'm talking about. I'm trying here, I'm putting all of my energy into this relationship and it only ever feels like you're trying to distance yourself."

"Me? Baby, *you* just threw this all in my face. I thought this night was going great and you interrupted what I was saying to complain that I'm not doing anything! How's that wine, by the way? It sounded expensive."

"It was," I tell him, pouring myself another glass.

Damien sighs and looks around the room like he's hoping someone is waiting by the wall or at another table, ready to jump up at his signal and give him some support.

"I don't know how else to say this tonight," he finally says. "I'm. Trying. I am, Nyx. I'm here. I did what you wanted, and then some. I'm not complaining about the expensive wine-"

"You literally just did."

"-or the fact that you're obviously drunk right now, or that all you've brought to this date was a bad attitude about everything. And I didn't want to bring up that we can't ever do a fancy date like you always say you want, because every time I come around all you do is put me to work."

"Every time you come around, all you want to do is fuck."

"Can you keep your voice down, please? People are staring."

"I don't want to keep my voice down." I shoot back, and then his next words sear through my bones and chain me to the chair.

"Keep your voice *down*," he says with such boldness. Such

intensity. Heat spreads between my legs. I instinctively bit my lip.

"That feel good, *baby*? Telling me what to do?"

"Fucking hell, Nyx." He knows. He knows if he's just the right type of dominant and I'm just the right type of intoxicated, he'll have a very fun effect on me. "Can't you just behave?"

My hands slide off the table and into my lap. That word, "behave." When he tells me to…

I gotta watch what I drink next time. This Chateau is fucking great for relationship counseling.

"Make me behave."

Damien calls for the check, and in a short five minutes we've moved the car down the road a mile or so and pulled off into an empty hiking trail parking lot.

For the first few feet we run, I try to lead Damien, but the alcohol is catching up to me and I begin to stumble.

"Let's just go back to your place," he demands.

I don't want to tell him that if we wait that long I won't be in the mood for him anymore. Even his suggestion makes me lose a little interest. I need him to keep up his dominance. "Don't you want me like this?" I ask, hiking up my dress to show my legs, and swinging my ass for him.

"You know like fuck I do."

I grab him by the collar with both hands. "Then fucking take me."

Damien picks me up in his strong arms and we find a thick tree. He bends me over, my hands supporting me on the bark, and he throws my dress up then pulls my panties down around my black boots.

I moan when his fingers rub against my folds and he wastes no time penetrating me. For the first time in a long time, it feels fucking amazing. The position can't last like this though, and we change it up. I fall to my hands and knees on the cool forest dirt, surrounded by all the loveliness of nature.

Damien mounts me, thrusting hard. After the first few pumps though, I notice that the intensity his tone earlier had promised isn't there. He's fucking me without any dominating passion. Or any passion at all. No words of endearment, not even his stupid "Oh fuck you feel so fucking good," just dull moaning.

When I pull off him, he doesn't even try to stop me. Just asks, "What's wrong? Not a good position?"

I pull my panties back up.

"I'm just not feeling it anymore. You were right, we should've gone home."

He licks his lips and breathes deep with frustration, then throws his hands up. "All right. Fuck it. Okay, let's go."

We both rise, fixing our clothes.

I just hate that finally, *finally*, I've been in the mood and it's just as dull as ever. On the walk back to the car, I tell him, "I think there's something we need to try."

13. Sex Magic

"Sex magic? Nyx, what the fuck are you talking about?"

"I'm serious. I thought you'd be excited by this. I *want* to have sex with you."

"Well I'd hope so! But what the fuck do you mean 'magic?'" At the word 'magic,' he laughs. "Look, I go along with a lot of your shit, babe, but you know I don't buy into it. You do you, but you're not going to convince me any of this is real magic like fuckin' Harry Potter." Damien backs up onto the walking trail in the woods and orients himself into the direction of his car.

He barely even reacts when my hand swipes across his face.

"I told you before to quit with that. Just because you don't believe in anything doesn't mean nothing's real."

Damien rubs his hand against his cheek. It's hard to tell in the moonlight, but it's surely turning bright red already. "Yeah, I'll believe it when I see it."

"But you won't give it a chance."

Turning away, back toward the car, he repeats, "Sex magic.

Babe, you know I'm down for kinky shit. You want me to tie you up, gag you, let's go. But when you do wanna get weird and we do shit like this," he waves to the trees around us, "You decide halfway through you wanna stop. What *would* be magical is if you stopped acting like you were the only one of us that mattered in this relationship."

"Fuck you, Damien. I offered because I thought you'd appreciate it. If I'd'a known you were going to be such an ass I'd've kept my mouth shut and let our sex carry on being pathetic."

"Pathetic?" Finally, he stops and turns to face me again. The look on his face is one of surprise and denial. "I don't know what you're talking about, it's been pretty great on my end."

I walk past him. We're only a few feet from the car and I just want to get home. "Of course it's great for you. All you need is a hole to finish in and you're good." I open the door to the driver's seat. "You couldn't tell the difference between my vagina and a sock." It comes out too quick and I immediately realize the insult doesn't have the impact I wanted, and if anything, just makes me look bad. But I can't let that show.

"What are you doing, Nyx?"

"I'm driving. Wanna make sure I actually get home tonight." I stare at him as he gives me a blank expression of disbelief. "You coming or what? I'm happy to leave without you."

Under his breath, but loud enough so I know he wants me to still hear, "You're a fucking psycho."

"You've known that from the start, darling," I say as I take my seat, then start the car.

He takes a moment to move while I adjust the seat, then concedes and gets in the passenger side.

"I would've taken you home," he says.

"After driving around for however long it takes me to get on your good side."

Damien scoffs. "I don't know. I really. Don't. Know, Nyx. Every minute it's something different with you. You're mad at me, you love me, you're mad at me, you're horny. You're *not* horny, but you wanna be horny, and when I get confused you get pissed. What. The. Fuck."

We pull out onto the road. This ten-minute drive is going to feel like an hour.

"I *want* to be horny, and I *am* horny. Is it a crime to want to have good sex with my boyfriend?"

"What's wrong with the sex? You keep complaining and say we need to try this fucking sex magic shit but what the hell is so wrong with the sex we've been having?"

What does it take for a guy to get it?

"Passion, Damien. I want *PASSION* in it. When I haven't seen you in a week I want to know that you didn't come over just to have sex with me. When you take me out somewhere fancy I want to know it's because you want to take me out. And I don't want the sex to be us fucking, I want you to make me feel like you actually love me!" I reach over to his glove compartment to check for a cigarette. Thank fuck he has some. Or they're mine that I'd left behind, I'm not sure.

"I do love you! Jesus! Nyx, the fucking road!"

I look up in time to avoid a little animal in the middle of the lane. Jeez, I'd blow my brains out if I'd hit it.

117

"Then act like it when we're having sex. That's what sex magic is. *That's* why I want to do it. That's the whole point. It's sex with the focus on us not as bodies mashing together. It's a spiritual thing. Like, actual intimacy. Sex for the purpose of pleasing each other on a deeper emotional level. There's intention to it. None of the 'oh fuck, oh fuck, Nyx you feel so fucking good, UH UH UHHHH!" I mimic his voice and cheesy sex noises.

"Okay okay, I get it."

"Do you?"

We come to a red light and challenge each other in a stare.

Damien's the one that breaks first. "No. Not at all."

I roll my eyes, and the light turns green.

"I mean, I kinda get it. I still don't see how it's magic, but… fine. Let's go back and try it."

"Not tonight."

Damien throws up his hands in annoyance, then laughs. "I can't win, can I?"

"Nope." The cigarette is still between my fingers, unlit. I'm starting to think that he doesn't have a light in here.

As if reading my mind he pulls one out of his pocket and lights me up.

"Thanks."

"Don't mention it. Can I at least stay the night?"

"No, I'm mad at you." I take a drag of this much-needed cigarette and roll the window down. And when I say roll, I mean it in this old car. "You can come over tomorrow night after work."

"Can't tomorrow. Going back out of town."

"Dad?"

"Yep."

"Just come back tomorrow night. Your dad's like an hour away."

He sighs deeply. "I gotta stay the night. We'll be working late."

Sure. Working late with his dad, again. I get it, family's important and all that. Especially when you've got a good one. And Damien's dad has always seemed like a good guy. He's one of the few dads of boyfriends I've had who hasn't looked at me either like a total creep, or like I'm the creepy one. His father has always treated me well. Plus, he's an older man, mid 60s who still works a blue-collar job. It's hard to be completely annoyed at Damien for leaving me to work with him.

"Fine. Just let me know if you'll be around next weekend."

Three years. Three fucking years and we see each other as regularly as when we first started dating. Maybe even less frequently. Harry's mentioned before that his ex Sylvia and her famous boyfriend are already talking about marriage and how long have they been together? Less than a year I suppose. How often has Damien brought up marriage with me? I don't think I could even count on one hand.

"I'll see if I can come around."

There are no hints of playfulness in my tone when I tell him, "Be there. Sunday night. There'll be a new moon on the fourth." We pull up to Witch's Brew and my apartment. "If you can't, don't come again."

"Hold on now-"

Leaving the car running, I open the door and step out, then take another drag of the cigarette.

He rushes to get out to catch me as I cross in front of the car toward my door. "Hold on, Nyx." Damien takes hold of my arms, but I pull away and walk past him, and search for my keys. "What are you talking about?"

I'm done explaining myself tonight, just as you're probably sick of hearing his bullshit.

"Us, Damien. If you can't make time for me, I'm done. I'm not going to argue with you about it anymore, I just want to go upstairs and go to bed. In a week, maybe I'll see you and this will just go down as a bad night. If not…" Willow is on the other side of the door, looking past me, giving Damien an evil glare.

You're on my good side again, Willow. Good Kitty.

"If not then that's it, huh?"

I see his reflection in the door's window. He's standing a few paces back with his hands in his pockets. Just like me, there's no desire to argue in his face.

I know I shouldn't. I know I should just go inside and let it end here for the night. But I turn, and let myself be vulnerable to him. There's no doubt that the dread I have for the last few things I've said are evident in my eyes. Three years. Three years of both wonderful and terrible memories. I want to say the good outweighed the bad but in a moment like this it's impossible to remember all the good. And I want there to be more good memories. I truly do. When I say I want him to love me, it's because I love him back already with so much of my heart.

"Don't let me down, Damien."

He nods with his eyes to the sidewalk.

The embers of the cigarette begin to warm my fingers. It's already almost gone and I've barely had a moment to smoke it. Such a waste.

"Good night, Nyx," and he saunters to the other side of his old car with the roll-up windows and my cigarettes in the glove box.

14. The New Employee

It seems as though Damien and I are on a bit of a hiatus. No call or text last night after he left, which I didn't entirely expect to receive. And nothing this morning. Instead, I was greeted by another man.

"Good morning!" Logan beams then looks me up and down. "Purple, that's a new look."

"What?" Is this guy trying to antagonize me right out of the gate?

"No, I mean, every time I've seen you it's the, you know, Wednesday Addams look." He motions around my outfit, then adds, "Modern Wednesday, not the original."

I give him a look to say, *what the fuck are you talking about?* And I genuinely can't tell what he's getting at. Is he making fun of me? Trying to be endearing? Just spilling his thoughts as they come up?

"May I come in?" He asks.

Willow sneaks up between my feet and we both look down at the cat.

"Hey there," Logan says, kneeling down to her level. "Good morning to you too. Happy to see me again?" He reaches out a hand and Willow approaches, nuzzling his palm.

"It's just a trial day," I say, stepping aside to let him in.

I still can't believe myself. Never have I had an employee before. Not only is the idea of dealing with payroll an absolute nightmare, but one, no one has ever applied for a job here, and two, never before would I have considered someone who isn't a believer in witchcraft even if I'd had inquiries. At least Damien I didn't have to pay. But, I can't see him coming to help out any time soon.

Hopefully, after next week we'll be back to normal. He'll be caring and attentive again. He'll stay around for more than a night, and maybe even help around the store.

Logan steps in and looks around like it's his first time in the store. In one hand is the book he bought yesterday. Sticky tabs of varying colors stick out of it from front to back.

"You weren't kidding about doing your homework."

He looks down at the book and grins. "Oh, yeah, no, I just put those in to mess with you. I haven't made it through the table of contents yet. Can't read for shit."

I take a deep breath in and feel my cheeks go red.

Then he laughs. "I'm kidding. I'm almost done. Didn't want to let you down on my first day." Logan fingers the small pendants in one of the crystal bowls. "Aventurine, right?"

"That's what the label says."

He smiles again and regurgitates information I know *isn't* on the label next to the bowl. "Good for healing the heart and emotional tranquility."

I nod, cross my arms, and tap a finger on my bicep. Okay, maybe he read a few pages.

Logan then picks up one of the pendants. "When I first saw the name in the chapter on crystals, I thought this was going to be like, 'good luck charm on grand quests' or 'helps the bearer gain the spirit of adventure,' haha."

"You know, you've got a bad habit of ruining a good thing."

He puts the pendant back down and rifles through the other bowls. "You are not the first person to tell me that. But at least I know my stuff. Like this one…" He picks up another pendant and shows it off like a kid finding a cool rock in a creek, then his grin slackens seeing the label held up between my fingers. "How'd you do that?"

"Just wanna make sure you're not cheating."

"That's not what I asked," his grin begins to return.

I shrug.

"All right then, keep your secrets. I've seen enough magic shows to know there's always a trick. Okay," he studies the pendant. "Agate. Easy one."

I flip the card around. "Agate pendants - $3.49"

It's his turn to shrug. "Lucky guess," he says. "But are you going to quiz me on this stuff all day, or should I get to work?"

"We open in thirty minutes. There's still some time to test you." To be sure we're not interrupted, I lock the front door again. We're right in the sweet spot of the season where people *will* try to come in early if they see a living soul in a store. It doesn't matter what time it is, even if it's the crack of dawn and I just came down to get a drink of water. If they see me, they think we're open.

"Locking me in, huh? What happens if I get something wrong? Gonna put a curse on me?"

"Something tells me I should do that regardless to keep you from making stupid comments."

Logan huffs, "Alright, I'll do my best then."

I curl my finger, instructing him to follow. We wander around the floor, and I challenge him on different wares and what their magical properties are. To my delighted surprise, while he's not right all the time, he knows a lot more than I expected from him. His knowledge of gemstones, incense, herbs, teas, candles, and things such as those, is vast. Much more vast than that one book could've provided.

Eventually, I ask him, "Have you worked somewhere like here before?"

He shakes his head, then picks up a baggie of a tea blend I made and gives it a sniff.

"So, your girlfriend, she's a witch."

Logan laughs again. "Ha! She a-..." and he stops himself, but a grin remains. It's easy to tell that he was about to make another poorly conceived comment about witches but is finally starting to learn better. "No, she's not into this kind of stuff."

"Then what is it?" I ask, partially curious, partially cautious. "You didn't learn all of this from that one book."

He puts the bag down and picks up another one, a simple caffeinated honey camomile blend, and inspects it. "You are correct. I didn't get it all from that one book. Wikipedia helped."

I purse my lips. He has got to be fucking with me. By the sounds of it, with the pop quiz I gave him, it's like he was up all night studying for a college final. But for a retail job? No way, there's something he's not telling me.

"How about some tea," I offer.

Logan pulls out his phone and checks the time. "Shouldn't we be opening soon?"

We.

What a strange thing to hear. Not *you*, not *shouldn't you be opening*. It feels almost dirty and sweet. I now have someone in here with me, someone who is knowledgeable of the craft. Someone who is eager to be here. It's sweet, and I should be grateful. But there's still the nagging in the back of my mind. Why couldn't Damien ever show these qualities?

"The customers can wait a little while. Come," I take him by the hand and lead him into the covenstead.

Unlike when I have my appointments, I turn on a small lamp, but let the morning sun streaming in from the front window illuminate the room. It's not as cozy a feel as when it's candlelit, but that's not exactly the atmosphere this conversation needs. I tell him to wait in there while I go upstairs to brew the tea, and when I come down, I'm pleasantly surprised he's seated instead of poking around and touching everything in sight.

"Here you are, darling," I say, handing him his cup.

"Darling?" He snorts.

Every time. He leans toward my good side and has to throw himself right back to the bad.

I take a deep breath and smell my tea. "Is there something wrong with that?"

He takes a sip with a little shake of the head. "No, not at all. Just didn't think we were official yet."

I roll my eyes. He can dream if he likes, but as long as he keeps it to himself and doesn't disrespect my craft, I think I can tolerate him.

"What are your beliefs?" I ask Logan as I take my seat across from him.

"What do you mean?"

"You've made it clear you don't believe in witchcraft, but you must believe in something."

"Oh, like that. Yeah, um, I mean I'm Christian, try to go to church on Sundays, but forget to most of the time. Don't worry, I won't try to burn you at the stake if that's what you're worried about."

"And you are okay with working in a place that goes against your beliefs?"

"I don't really think of it like that." For the first time this morning, the humor fades from his tone. "I don't believe in magic and all this, no offense to you obviously, but having that belief, lack of belief, I wouldn't think it goes against what I *do* believe. And at the end of the day, I'm not here to convert people to witchcraft."

"But you will be selling my goods, books that teach differently than yours. Your contribution here would lead people down a different path than what you would consider is a true one."

He puts the cup down. "How about I ask you a question?

In today's day and age, how many of your customers believe in what they're buying?"

The aesthetic witch, I think. And although it's one of my own criticisms, my blood begins to rise at his mention.

Logan continues. "I mean, I know there are people from all religions that get involved with this kind of stuff, not because of some magical properties, but they like the aesthetic, or some aspect of it. Yoga, let's say. Meditation and all that, I'm sure you believe that it goes hand-in-hand with witchcraft. Every middle-aged mom I know who goes to church will go to a yoga class right after. Or astrology. Personally I don't believe in it, and using the stars to read fate or whatever is considered going against God because only He decides the plan. Right? *Or…* and not saying I agree with this, that's one of many ways we can read and understand God's plan. Maybe this stuff is real, maybe it's witchcraft, maybe it's all just another tool God gave us to understand the world around us. The only thing I know I believe to go against my beliefs is Satanic shit. There are things we know and things we don't. I know there is good, God, and evil, Satan. I don't think there's much grey area, but there are things we don't understand."

"And if my stuff here is Satanic?"

Logan tosses up his hand and smirks. "Then that's on me, I should've asked sooner, and I'd've wished you well."

"Just like that?"

"Just like that. Even without church, I know better than to fuck with that." He chuckles. "Get a few good years on Earth just to suffer eternally by the literal Devil? Nope. I'm good. But you don't believe in that anyway, do you? So I have nothing to worry about here."

I take a moment, considering pushing this further. But, he's right. I don't practice Satanic stuff, nor would I want to "fuck with that" as he put it, for similar reasons.

"But now what about the people that do buy into it? My customers that do believe, do understand. This is the only time you'll be permitted in this room. At all other times, it's for my appointments only, where we do practice."

"If I had a Jewish friend that needed help at his store where he sold Hanukkah things, I'd help him out. I don't have to believe in it, but I can have respect for a friend in need."

"But we are not friends."

"No," he agrees. "But you're someone that needed help, and I needed a job. In my book, you're my neighbor. And from what I've read so far, your values preach respect and courtesy towards others as well."

We share a moment of silence. His hazel eyes pierce into mine, challengingly.

Finally, I say, "I don't share your beliefs. You put your trust in a god, I put mine in nature, a whole we all exist in. But, you're right, we do share a value of respect for our neighbors. And I respect that you are both knowledgeable and firm in your beliefs. What is it the Bible says about the lukewarm?"

"To not be one."

I nod. "That is also something I agree with. While I would prefer to employ someone who believes in witchcraft, I would not want someone who sacrifices their own beliefs for a paycheck. Even if it was the other way around. I would not want an aesthetic witch working here if they caved once challenged." I take a deep breath. "If you can accurately represent my store while you work here, I won't ask you to concede your own beliefs. I won't ask you to do anything that goes against your faith. But if it gets to the point where it interferes with my customers or the way I run this store-"

He cuts me off. "No Satanic shit, right?"

I nod again, "No Satanic shit."

"Then I go back to what I said before. I know enough to know that I don't know everything. Until I see that this does go against my beliefs, I'm here to work."

I raise my cup of tea to my lips and sip. He watches intently, waiting for my response. We should be wrapping this up soon, we're already well past our regular opening time, but I'm still undecided on him. I mean, either way, we've still only agreed on one day. This whole conversation since he first entered could have just been a well-rehearsed ploy, and once he starts working I'll see the real him and ask that he never steps in my presence again.

Or... he could be a great help for the rest of the summer.

"Go and unlock the door," I tell him once the cup is empty.

His smile returns and he rises from the chair.

"And once you do, grab a broom and start sweeping. Just tidy up today."

"A regular broom or a flying broom?" He asks.

"They all fly," I respond in a tone which is impossible for him to gauge if it's a joke or not.

131

He gives a half smile and a drawn-out, "Right," then is gone from my covenstead.

* * *

The Saturday crowd steadily pours in, and the new addition immediately catches the eyes of my regulars. He probably would have gone unnoticed, if not for the fact that he insists on greeting everyone that walks in with a big friendly smile and a "Good morning!"

Throughout the morning, a few of the patrons came up to me asking who he was and were just as shocked as I was at myself for bringing someone on. But it was Harry who had the best reaction.

He came up to me at the register and asked, "You've got Damien working here now?"

If I'd had a cup of tea in my hand I would have drank some just to do a spit take. "You think that's Damien?" I ask.

Harry glances over at Logan who's tidying up the bookshelf. "I… I mean I thought so. I never see him around so it's kinda hard to tell."

"No, that's not Damien. Damien's away this week. I needed help and that man over there wouldn't stop bothering me about a job."

"Why'd he have to bother you about it if you needed it?"

"Harry, is there something you came in here for?"

"Yes, actually. Aria's birthday is coming up and she's getting into this stuff now."

I grab for him one of the first expensive things I see, a

decorative garden figurine of a garden fairy with a watering bucket.

The morning turns to noon and nothing's broken yet. There's been no big controversy with Logan so far. And even though he showed me he knows what he's talking about, when a customer approached him with a question, I would step in. We're taking baby steps here.

When afternoon came around, though, just about all that could be tidied up, was. And honestly, I can't remember the last time I'd seen the place so neat. In all these years, mostly summers, I never had time to stop and give the place a deep clean. I mean, sanitary, always, but now the store looked like we just prepared for a grand opening.

"The place looks… surprisingly decent, Logan."

"Surprisingly decent? You don't like giving out compliments, do you?" He teases.

"I'll give them when they're earned. Do you need to take a lunch?"

"I'm all set," he says, picking up an amber crystal. "Been snacking on these all morning."

I don't even know how to respond. He said it with a straight face and a part of me thinks he might be serious.

"Jeez, calm down, I'm kidding. But, no, I'm not hungry yet."

"Okay… well, do you think you can hold down the register on your own for a bit? I need to step out." I pull my cabriole out of a slim pocket sewn into the inside of my gown.

"What's that?" He asks.

From another pocket, I pull out a cigarette and lighter. I can feel the judgment radiating from him. "I don't like tobacco-stained fingers."

"I don't think the stains are gonna be the problem."

"Logan, I thought we agreed on a 'you do you, I do me' kind of basis?" I step toward the door and halfway exit it. "We're still busy. No time for a lecture anyway."

Logan shrugs, clearly holding back his tongue, then retreats to the register when the door shuts.

Here now is the real test of the day. Can Logan handle himself when I'm not in the store? I look down between my legs at the feel of Willow brushing against me.

"Where've you been all morning?" I ask between drags.

Willow nuzzles my calf.

"Still think he's a good choice?"

Willow pitters a figure eight around my feet. I take another drag.

The clouds above us part and the warm summer sun beams down. A calm sense of joy spreads through me.

"Yeah, we'll see I suppose."

Willow jumps up into my lap, and paws at my chest.

"What do you want now? This? You can't smoke this, Willow. These aren't good for cats."

She ignores me and continues pawing me for attention.

"All right, all right." I put the cabriole between my lips and hug Willow, gently scratching her neck just the way she likes. "You jealous you're not getting enough attention?" She responds with a meow. "I'm sorry, girl. Been a little busy."

But not anymore, I think to myself. With Logan lightening the load a bit, I might be able to give Willow a little more screen time in this story.

When the attention quota is met, Willow hops off my lap and rushes back to the door.

"I'm not done yet," I tell her, holding up the cabriole with the still-burning cigarette.

Willow doesn't care. She raises up her paws and presses on the door.

I put the stick back between my lips. She can beg all she wants. I finally have a break and I'm going to enjoy it.

As it turns out, I don't even have to get up to help her. The door opens and I hear Logan's voice. "There you are! I was hoping you'd drop by." He picks Willow up and she throws her front paws over his shoulder.

"Are you big into cats or something?" I ask.

"Not at all, but this one is just so cute. I think I might take her home."

"You can have her. You're the only person she seems to like. Half the time she doesn't even want to be around me."

"Really? A shining ball of sunshine like you? Noooo…"

This close. I am *this* close. But I also find it hard to argue.

"I take it back," I say quickly. "Willow's my cat. She's also a witch. You two wouldn't mix well."

The cigarette burns out, signaling my return to work.

"Take your lunch now if you want one. There won't be time this afternoon until closing."

He takes off with a nod and cheesy salute guys do for some reason. And once he leaves, business really picks up again.

Or is it the same as it's been all day? Has Logan really eased the stress that much? With him gone, I'm stuck behind the counter, unable to move. Almost instantly everything on the shelves gets rearranged by customers picking things up and putting them down somewhere else when they decide they don't want it or have found something better. Dirt piles up quickly in front of the freshly swept door.

At least the cash is flowing in.

But I've had a taste of sanity I didn't know I needed, and now that I know what it can be, not having it is a fucking nightmare. I want to wring my own throat for not giving Logan a time to be back by. I just need to step out of this room; have a cigarette, have a cup of tea, something to destress.

And where's Willow now? I should find a spell to turn her into a person so she can start pulling her weight around here too.

As the floor fills with browsing customers, the line to check out gets ever longer, until it's wrapped all the way around the counter, and threatening to go into my covenstead. But I can't even pull away to ask them to move because when I do:

"Excuse me! Can you help me find this?"

"Hey, Nyx! Where do you keep this?"

"Nyx! I need to set up another appointment."

"Nyx!"

"Nyx!"

"Nyx!"

A heavenly (heavenly? Pull yourself together, things aren't *that* tough) voice enters. "Here, let me help you find that." Logan puts himself between a customer and the counter, then calls the back half of the line. "Hey everyone, if we could, can we move the line over? That's where Nyx does her black magic, and I don't want anyone getting cursed."

A few faces contort in dejection and the line shifts away from my covenstead.

Logan hops around the counter and takes on the next customer for check out, then says to me, "Sorry I took so long. Was on the phone with Kat."

"Who? Nevermind. Yes, take over, I need to breathe." Without another word, I'm gone.

As soon as I'm out onto the main floor, another customer corners me, but before she can speak, Logan calls for her attention. "Hey there! What can I help you with?"

I dive into my covenstead and close the curtains.

Today is definitely busier than ever, it's not just Logan.

I pull out a cigarette, one of just a few left in the pack, and light it. Once the nicotine hits, relief washes over me. I can breathe again.

I take a few minutes to myself, not even finishing the stick. The chatter from outside is muffled by the curtain, but enough gets through. If I leave Logan alone out there, they'll eat him alive.

Okay, Nyx. Just make it to the end of the day.

The next few hours up until closing are a free-for-all, as I warned Logan before. But once the door is closed and the sign is flipped to "closed," we both breathe a sigh of relief.

"Fuck," Logan exclaims. "And here you thought you could handle it on your own."

"I could. *Can*," I correct myself. "Me and my 'black magic' got it covered." I lock the door and stomp back to the register to count the day's earnings.

"Maybe, but aren't you glad you didn't have to do it on your own? Come on," he says with a grin. "You're glad I was here today."

I slam down on the button to open the drawer a little too hard. "Yep," I say bluntly. "Worked out real great. You can go now. Goodbye, Logan."

His posture stiffens, not yet having picked up entirely on my tone. "Uh, yeah. Okay, I'll see you tomorrow then, huh?"

"No. Trials over. I changed my mind." I say this all without looking up from the money laid out on the counter.

He takes a step forward, and I shoot my head up, glaring at him. He freezes in his tracks. Slowly, very cautiously he says, "I thought today was going well. We seemed to make a good-"

"Black magic, Logan?"

Silence hangs between us for half a minute.

Blood boils in my cheeks. "What the fuck was that? Who the fuck do you think you are, saying shit like that in *my* store? To *my* customers? Saying they're going to get cursed? Do you have any idea how that sounds?"

He opens his mouth to speak, but I go on.

"Half of those people thought you were serious and are now terrified of me and that room, and the other half think it's a

138

fucking joke. Now *I* look like a fucking idiot!" I slam the drawer shut, just as hard as I mean to this time.

Willow jumps up on the counter, serving as a barrier between us.

"Nyx… I just-"

"Get out," I say. "Just get the fuck out of my store."

Logan steps backward toward the door, and only when at the door, turns and tries to pull it open. It's a force of habit locking it at the end of the day, I didn't even think about anyone being here past closing with me, and I wish no one ever had to, especially not him. He flicks the lock to the side, crosses the threshold then says, "I'm sorry, Nyx."

Willow runs to the door as it closes behind him, and paws at the glass as he walks away.

Fucking traitorous cat.

15. The Point in this Story Where We Discuss Demons

Willow wakes me, pressing against my cheek with her paws.

I thought I put you outside?

My head pounds from too much alcohol, and I bet if I look outside, I'll see a very fancy car down by the front of the shop. But no one came home with me so I don't have to worry about fucking up that bad in my sorry state of rage at Logan.

I turn over to hide from Willow, but when I do, I put my face right in the light. A lot of light.

Way too much light.

Fuck! What time is it?

I bolt upright and reach for my phone. It's almost 11 o'clock. I should have been opened nearly two hours ago!

I jump out of bed, almost tripping over a book laying on the floor. Willow follows close behind me, watching like an eager child ready to play. I grab the purple robe I wore yesterday off of the arm of the couch and throw it over my head. My hair's a mess, and yesterday's makeup probably doesn't look too great, but screw it. It's part of today's look. I can clean it up when the store is at a lull.

Wait, I stop myself before reaching for the door.

It's Sunday. The store isn't open on Sundays.

I put a hand to my pounding head. Frank was right to not let me drink at Old Fashioned last night. But he should've known I'd get it on my own if I couldn't hang out there and people-watch in peace. Instead, I drank too much of a special potion of vodka, whiskey, and whatever flavor bitters I had in my cabinet, and got carried away reading that smutty Daniel Cassidy book.

For the life of me, I can't remember what the chapter was about, but I do know Damien better be open to experiment when we get our relationship back on track.

But, okay, I rushed out of bed too soon, and I have the day to myself. I can recuperate, relax, and get ready for this next work week. I'll clean up today, make a nice, homey dinner, and tonight go to the pool in the woods. By tomorrow morning, it'll be like yesterday never happened.

And that's when I hear it downstairs.

Someone's moving.

Someone's moving a lot.

Willow paws at the door. I open it a crack and she rushes out and down the stairs. The speed in which she runs fills me with dread. The laziest cat in the world only runs like that for one person lately.

I run down after her, ready to kill.

Why the fuck is he in my store?

142

With each step closer to the shop I hear louder and louder voices. Multiple. The place sounds as busy as ever!

I rush through my covenstead, pull back the curtains, and see it, a fully operating store with all of the regulars, and Logan behind the counter. I'm completely stunned. He's taken over! Logan's broken in and taken over!

"Since when are you open on Sundays?" A familiar face asks.

"I… I'm not. I'm sorry, Shannon, we're not supposed to be open." I don't kick her out, but I brush past her, crossing the room to Logan.

He takes a customer's cash for the register and spots me and the murder in my eyes coming for him as he puts it in the drawer. With that stupid cute grin, he says, "Hey, I was getting worried about you."

Under my breath, just loud enough for only him to hear, I quietly shout, "What the *fuck* are you doing here? Did you break in?"

He laughs. Actually laughs, like I'm not about to rip those hazel eyes out of his face.

"No, I didn't break in. The door was unlocked. I thought you opened it." Then, to the customer. "Here's the change, have a great one." Back to me, "I only meant to come by and apologize. I was outside that curtain for like fifteen minutes shouting at you."

"I could've been taking a walk."

"There's an Audi outside that's definitely not yours. I can put two and two together."

Shit. My face goes pale, and he reads my expression.

"Don't worry. Your friend from the bar came by and took care of it. He'll need the keys though, as soon as you can."

Another customer walks up to check out. Like it's his instinct, he begins the transaction. The process is fluid. He doesn't even need to check the tags before putting in the right codes and prices for the register.

"After a while, people just started coming in. I didn't know you were usually closed today, that's on me."

"It's all on you," I interject, and he shrugs it off.

"Well, stupid me thought it'd be better to actually work, rather than let these people grab and go while you were passed out with a hangover."

"I don't have a hangover."

Logan drops his head in an expression of, *oh really?*

I roll my eyes. "Do you ever not have something smartass coming out of your brain?"

"Probably not. At least for the 'smart' part of that."

Someone calls to me from across the room. I take a deep breath.

"Logan. Sundays are my day off. This is my one day of the week to breathe. And you shouldn't be here. Go... go do whatever else you should be doing today. Go to church or something, just don't be fucking here. And don't come *back* here."

Again, he grins and chuckles. "It's past 11. Church is over, Nyx. Besides, aren't I doing God's work? Helping out my neighbor?"

"UUUGGGH." I look down and see Willow crawling under his arms, rubbing her back against his forearms.

"Look, if it's your day off, take a day off. I'm fine here," he says as if this is negotiable. "Besides, I've got Willow to help me out."

Again, the customer calls me over for assistance. My hands clench.

"I don't *want* your help, Logan. Go home. Don't you want to spend the weekend with your girlfriend?"

His grin wavers, but doesn't entirely fade. "Nah, she's out now."

"Then, fucking I don't know. Do something on your own. I don't care! Just go!"

"She's gone, Nyx." Logan's tone is completely flat. "I didn't tell her what happened last night, she just left before I got home. It's over."

Silence passes between us while he checks out the next customer. Even they respect the quiet and keep their eyes down throughout the exchange. What breaks the silence over the store's natural murmuring is the customer in the corner by the window, shouting my name.

"We'll talk about this later," I say under my breath as I walk away.

With the grin returning, he asks, "So there *will* be a later?"

I ignore the comment and follow the sound of my name. There in the corner is a woman with a wide-brimmed hat, deep scarlet, almost black in color, which contrasts sharply with her blond hair.

She turns around, and Maria shows her face.

"What do you want, Mary?"

"I didn't know you were open on Sundays," she says lazily, looking around the store.

"We're not."

"Your handsome new employee says otherwise."

I pull her attention back to me with a snap. "Eyes off. I don't believe Tommy would appreciate that."

"I don't think he'd care anymore. That's over."

Pressed against her chest, she holds a copy of "Summoning Spirits: The Complete Guide for Wiccan" which isn't a book we carry.

"Where did you find that?" I ask.

Peppy as ever, she answers, "Online. I thought you might enjoy it." She holds the book out for me to take.

"Why would I ever want that?" Engaging with spirits, listening to them, is one thing. But summoning? Never in a million years. When people pass, they're best left to the peace of the afterlife.

"Because *I* read it, and I found it very enlightening." She speaks intently, with a high pitch like she thinks she's speaking to a child. "I just thought you might like it because it has a very different outlook on the ghost in my apartment than you do. And the magic it shares…" Her voice drops low. "He's more real than you'd think."

"What the hell is wrong with you, Maria? Have you been taking anything? There is no ghost in your apartment. Whatever you think you're feeling is in your head."

Undeterred, she gasps, "Oh! So all of this here is just a bunch of make-believe?"

"Maria, this is not the kind of day I want to deal with your shit. You wanted my help with your dead boyfriend and I was honest. Don't fuck around with this."

I feel the energy of many sets of eyes on me. Am I speaking louder than I mean to? How many people are watching us right now?

I continue, "Look, I could not be more serious about witchcraft like that." I press the book back into her chest, hiding the cover and Satanic imagery from the view of prying eyes. "Please, heed this warning. Do. Not. Take. Anything from this book. I'd rather you come back for an appointment and we can talk more about why this is a horrible, terrifying path you're walking. But please, not today. Give me a call when you're free this week and you can come over."

There is conflict in her eyes, a flicker of something I can't quite read. But her condescending expression remains. "Thank you, Nyx. But I'm busy this week. My new sisters are getting together."

"All week? Maria, who are these people?"

"Just some girls I met that are genuine. They actually believe me. They're real friends."

"Real friends wouldn't let you do this."

"Why don't you come over to my place instead? Maybe we can change your mind." Maria leans the book forward toward me again.

"I will be free, literally whenever you need. Just please don't be tempted by that."

Maria laughs, "Why are you always so dramatic?" She mocks my words, "*Don't be tempted, you're walking a dangerous path,* haha, ease up a bit, *darling.*"

Who is this girl? Just a few weeks ago she was innocent and eager, a bit wayward in her thoughts, but showed signs of hope. And she was kind. It was impossible to feel any bit of malevolence in her energy. But now she radiates with it, coming here just to taunt and mock.

This is a very delicate situation. One I don't know how to navigate.

"If I come, will you hear me out? At least let me inspect the house again to make sure there's nothing evil impressing on you?"

She raises her hand to her mouth, covering a laugh. "Nyx, do you know what kind of spirit this is?" She leans and whispers, "Do you know what we do together?"

I stumble back and take her by her free hand. "Join me in the back."

Maria pulls away. "So now you believe me?" She asks with an evil smile.

We can't talk about this in the open. Like Logan's black magic joke, this line of questioning will either freak people out or make them think I'm crazy. I take her hand again and pull her into the back. She doesn't fight it this time, just holds on to her hat. It's better, people seeing this act, than hearing us talk about demons.

As we cross the floor, Logan catches sight. "Everything okay, Nyx?"

I point to him and order, "You stay there. We're not done yet." I catch a glimpse of a smug look as Maria and I enter my covenstead, the curtains falling into place behind us and shielding our conversation from unwanted ears. The candles flicker to life.

"Sit down," I tell Maria as I take my spot at the table.

She ignores me, and instead asks, "How much are you going to charge me for this session?"

"Will you just take this seriously?"

Whether out of fear of my intensity, or a force pulling her down, she takes her seat, keeping the book in her lap.

I tell her, "No, I don't believe you when you tell me you're interacting with the ghost of someone who's passed away. That doesn't happen in real life like it does in the movies. What you're talking about without realizing it is something evil. With what you're saying, I worry that you may be inviting something malicious into your home, masquerading as a peaceful spirit, taking advantage of your innocent assumptions. You left a relationship because of this thing. Doesn't that sound manipulative?"

Maria stirs in her seat, clearly uncomfortable with being called out. "My sisters say it's for the best."

The candles burn a little more brightly.

"Who the fuck are these sisters? Where did you meet them?" I take a breath. My heartbeat is racing. "What have they been telling you?"

"They're a coven I found," Maria says flatly.

"Where, Maria?"

"And I don't want you to call me that anymore. They call me Hunith now, or Hunni for short."

I drop my head into my hands. "I am not calling you that."

"Why? Because I didn't find my name with you?"

"Did you choose that name for yourself, or did they?"

149

She leans forward, onto her hands as if she's about to push away from the table. "Why does it matter?"

"Because *you* find your own name. I wouldn't trust someone who chooses it for you. Names have power, Maria. If they chose one for you there is a purpose. And you're dealing with a coven that is pushing you toward black magic! Don't you see how wrong this is?" I find myself standing now, towering over her as she cowers in her chair. "So tell me, who gave you that name?"

"I did!" She shouts back at me. Maria corrects her posture in the chair, pulling herself out of her slouch and fixing her hat. "And they respected it. They actually take an interest in what I'm going through. They've listened to me. They don't make me feel like an idiot for all of this. I thought of all people, *you* would understand me when I first came here for your help. They actually helped me. I was meant for this spirit, and they are helping me connect with him."

I stare down at the table in utter disbelief.

"Maria... I rarely say this. But I think a therapist would be more helpful than witchcraft right now."

She doesn't say another word before storming out of the room. Maybe she left with one last "Fuck you," but I didn't hear it.

She leaves me alone in the quiet room. Even the noise on the floor has died down to nothing.

How the fuck am I going to deal with this?

You're not, Nyx. It's not your problem. This is her beast.

No, but it is my problem. I could have prevented this.

I pull the book out of my lap, feeling lucky she didn't feel me snag it out of hers.

The book is old, very old. Not Necronomicon old, not old like you'd find hidden in a cabin in the woods, leather bound and wrapped in barbed wire with a note that says "Do not read this book" old. It's a paperback, maybe fifty years old. Saying she found it online was an obvious lie, unless off of another witch's personal shop. The pages are all worn, many creased or ripped, with a fair amount of handwritten notes; favorite spells highlighted, or elements added and taken away to personalize them. The first few chapters are all background and lore, nothing inherently bad. In fact, good stuff to know to avoid. But after all that, thankfully the pages that look less flipped through, are incantations for summoning. Some in English, some in a language with characters I've never seen before. And there are pages that look like they were once filled with images, but have now been scratched out, yet the text remains. And to be completely honest, I'm glad the images have been covered with ink scratches. I don't want to know what's supposed to be there. It turns my blood cold just thinking about her reading these parts, and the room seems to be getting colder.

I need tea.

Fuck it, I need a cleanse.

16. Willow Gets Her Way

"I'm sorry, everyone," I announce to the few customers still in the store. "We opened today by mistake, and I'm sorry, but I have to close."

There are a few audible groans, but no one moves. In fact, after a moment, they all go back to shopping. Maybe one woman put down the items she hoped to purchase and left.

Logan appears at my side.

"Hey, is everything okay?"

"No, everything is not okay. And darling, you being here is only making it worse."

His hazel eyes harden, looking down on me. I didn't realize how tall he was until he gave me that look.

Logan then turns away from me and addresses the crowd. "Everybody out! We need to burn some sage. Nyx found a bad energy. Needs to be cleared or all of this stuff is gonna be useless."

I grab his thick arm - *thick? Nyx, what the fuck are you talking about?* - and pull him back to me. "What are you doing?"

He continues, "Come back tomorrow for 10% off everything." Then to me, "You can take it out of my paycheck," and he stands in front of me, hiding my annoyance from the rest of the room.

Still, though, nobody moves.

"If you don't leave, Nyx is going to fire me. Wanna see me tomorrow? Get the fuck out." He shoos them away, and at his threat, which will come true regardless, they all begin to shuffle out.

"You can't talk to my customers like that."

He spins around, his chest in my face. "Why not, you're going to fire me anyway, right? I should've gone further and told them I'd curse them if they didn't leave."

"Do you just get off on pissing me off?"

"No, but you get this funny little crinkle in your nose when I do."

I cover my nose. Was he trying to flirt? Not even twenty-four hours after getting dumped and he's already making a move on someone else? And *me* of all people? "Why are you looking at my nose?"

His grin wavers. "I-... No I mean, it's just a thing you do. That I noticed."

We stand there awkwardly, glancing at each other and quickly away.

"Do you want me to lock the door?"

"Yes." I blurt out a little too loudly.

He nods as he takes a step back, then turns fully and walks toward the door. "Look, I am sorry about yesterday. Really, I didn't mean to come here today to start a whole big thing."

All things considered with this morning, "It's fine… thanks for cleaning it up."

"What was that?" He tilts his head up a bit as he locks the door.

Did I say that too quietly, or is he being an ass again? "I said thank you for cleaning it up. The people, I mean. Sunday is my day off. I don't really get many chances to breathe here."

He flips the open/closed sign over, then draws the blinds over the door and window.

I take a step back toward the curtain. He's definitely trying something.

At my withdrawal, he stops what he's doing. "I'm not trying anything," he assures. "Just thought you wouldn't want people walking by and seeing us in here thinking you're open."

It's an accurate assumption. It doesn't matter how late or early in the day it is, or if there's a bright neon sign that says "CLOSED." If someone sees you in a store, they'll bang on the door until you open.

But now it's just the two of us in here. Alone.

"I need to do a cleanse of this place. The week can't start with this kind of energy." From under the counter, I grab a box of matches, and then a white sage smudge from a nearby shelf.

Logan watches me as I light the sage and begin my smudging of the room. Really, I should be focusing on my covenstead, but I don't feel right letting him out of my sight.

"Also," he speaks up again, "Sorry about the whole discount thing. Couldn't really think of anything else to get them out."

"You threatened to curse them."

"*I* did, yeah. Didn't really want to throw you under the bus again."

I shrug. "How kind."

As soon as I'm turned away, I hear his footsteps slowly approach me.

"Look, I know I've got a bit of a mouth. Kat hated it too."

"She sounds like a bright woman."

He chuckles, and I think, *is there nothing this guy takes seriously?*

"Well, she bailed on me. So I guess we all have our moments."

"So humble, aren't you?"

Somewhere behind me, a fan turns on and I realize he wasn't walking toward me.

"You really going to let the smoke just linger?" He asks. "Or are you just trying to avoid me?"

"Why are you still here?" I bring the sage down into its bowl.

"Why haven't you kicked me out?" He asks in reply. "Because you said there'd be a later, right? Well, it's later. So let's talk. What was going on with that girl? She's been here before, hasn't she? Always that annoying?"

"My business with Maria doesn't concern you."

"But that's why you're smudging. Which, by the way, she was in that corner and your spooky ritual room." He points to the corner, then the covenstead as he addresses them.

I drop the smudge and dish down on the counter harder than I mean to. "Can I ask you a question?"

"Sure, anything. What's up?"

"Your girlfriend left you. Why do you still care about working here? You don't have to anymore. Go back to being a slacker."

Logan laughs. "Okay, harsh. The break-up is still a fresh wound."

"You're not acting like it."

He shrugs. "How should I act? Sulky and downtrodden? Get shitfaced and try to rebound with the next hottest girl? Or should I go out and try to get myself back on my feet?"

"And *I* am getting you back on your feet?" I ask with my hand placed over my heart.

"Don't flatter yourself. Remember, I just came around to apologize."

"You've made your apology."

He leans on the counter. When did he get so close to me again?

"Yeah, I have." He says. "So now is there something *you'd* like to say?"

I stumble over my words at his sheer audacity. "I- uh- hold on, what?"

He gestures for me to get words out that are a mystery to me. "Maybe something along the lines of, 'You're forgiven Logan, here's your work schedule, I'll see you on Monday or whenever we open again.'"

I cross my arms. "I'd really like to smack you right now."

"I'm surprised you haven't already."

So I do. Not too hard, I try not to be a violent person, but a good *SMACK* enough to leave a faint red mark on his cheek.

Logan barely reacts, and even retains his grin when those hazel eyes pierce me again.

"Feel better?" He asks.

I bite the inside edge of my lip. "A little bit."

"Alright. So when do you want me back here?"

"Tomorrow." The word comes out so fast, that neither of us realizes what I said until it's out, and the look on his face tells me there's no taking it back. I open my mouth to stop him from whatever stupid thing he's going to say next to gloat. I even raise my hand to cover his mouth, but he pushes off the counter and struts toward the door.

"All right. If you want me around that badly, I'll see you tomorrow. Eight A.M.?"

I want so badly to shout at him to fuck off, but the stubborn words that come out are, "We open at nine," like I have a stupid need to correct him.

"Nine it is," he says, unlocking the door, walking out, and letting it swing shut behind him.

Just to punctuate the moment, Willow meows from her hiding spot next to the door and grimaces at me.

"You did this, didn't you?" I accuse.

I swear, she grins at me like the Cheshire Cat.

"I'm putting you up for adoption if this goes bad."

17. The Summoning Book

The evil book rests on the center of the table in the covenstead. A horrible energy emanates from the thing. I don't even want to touch it again. Just thinking about it makes my hands clammy and irritated.

I have to dispose of it.

But first, it has to be cleansed.

A book is only a book. No object has evil inherent in it. It is the acts of those who use such objects that imbue the evil. One must only be around this book to know that it has been used before for misdeeds. How Maria - Hunith, if she's going by that now (though that's a ridiculous name) - didn't feel this energy is beyond me. It's something to investigate, as well as this coven she's found.

I take a step closer to the table. An invisible fog makes itself known to me. The air is thicker, musty, like stepping into a mold-filled basement. My throat clenches with my step.

In the blink of an eye, I exit the room and return with an evil eye pendant around my neck, and the roll of sage I'd used earlier.

The pendant vibrates in the presence of the book.

Fuck. This.

I light the sage. I light it far more than I should have, but I feel an extreme desperation to clear this room as soon as possible. The smoke gently rises from the smudge, up toward the ceiling in little wisps. I circle around the table, moving in an inward spiral direction toward the book. Each inch closer is like wading through mud. The book is pushing back.

No… that's ridiculous, Nyx… it's just a book.

The room dims. I shift my gaze toward the candles that are now almost burned out. *When was the last time I replaced them? Have they been burning all morning?*

No, I only lit them when Maria came in.

And they burned brightly.

I inch another step closer on a new lap around the table.

This is *a bit silly, isn't it? This is my day off and I'm fretting over a stupid old book. I could occupy myself with a much better one. "Binds" is upstairs. And it's due for another steamy chapter soon. I should just relax with that book instead and… indulge in the fantasies. Damien isn't here, but there's a toy in the nightstand.*

I catch myself standing still, back against the wall. One hand is holding the smudge lazily at my side, the other grips my robe just in front of my crotch.

And between my legs… I'm already getting wet.

The book is putting up a fight. Whatever force, whatever spirit lingers on it has no intention of being cast away.

I hold out the sage firmly in front of me.

"This is my domain, and here only I have authority," I begin. Never had I needed to cast a spell over an entity, and in the moment, I can't think of any spells or rituals one can do on their own. This is a gamble, but if I'm strong enough, it could work. "You have entered my home, a place of peace for nature's sisters and caretakers. You have no place here. You have no say here. I cast you out. By my own authority, I cast you out of this book."

It's a weak spell. I say it with all of my heart, but it's rushed and weak.

I push through the fog, sage directed at the book, repeating, "This is my domain, and you are not welcome. I cast you out."

My fingers stiffen and turn cold.

"This is my domain, and you are not welcome. I cast you out."

The evil eye vibrates, and I hear a faint *tick* as it cracks.

"This is my domain, and you are not welcome. I cast you out."

The smoke of the sage disappears. The burnt face loses its glow entirely. That's when I stop and turn it around. The smudge looks untouched as if it was never lit to begin with.

The evil eye pendant drops off my neck, onto the floor.

Fear floods into me.

Icy hands run up my legs, between my thighs, trailing higher and higher.

My mouth goes dry when the hands reach me.

Air escapes my lungs and both pleasure and terror fill my being.

The smudge drops from my hands and rolls across the room.

My legs fail me.

Fingers like icicles penetrate me.

Slowly, as if time forgot how to work, I fall backward like I'm sinking in water. I fall for an hour until I hit the ground.

With the thud of my head against the floor, I'm thrust back into consciousness, control. I throw myself back, away from the table, away from the book as fast as I can.

The hands withdraw, painfully tearing out of me with a fury, and leave me sweating, panting, gasping for air.

I don't know if I can deal with this book on my own. But I don't know who can help me. And I don't have the strength to exorcise this spirit now. I thought I needed a cleanse before. Now I can't wait another moment to get to the pool.

18. The Greene Witch

"Are you feeling alright?" Logan asks, restocking the tarot decks.

He wouldn't believe it even if he had been in the room with me. "Right as the rain, darling."

"You look it," he retorts sarcastically.

I couldn't sleep all night. I didn't even feel safe leaving my apartment for hours, until determining that the book lashed out because of my actions against it. Until I knew how to exorcise it, I wouldn't touch it. The book would stay where it is, covered by a black cloth on the table in the covenstead, surrounded by selenite crystals. My home, and Witch's Brew, are safe. Yet, I still don't feel it. And Logan's calling out of my appearance doesn't help.

"Sorry I didn't get all dolled up for you today." I shoot back.

"Hey, I never said it was a bad look."

I roll my eyes.

"But really," he continues. "You seem more high-strung than usual."

If I were him I would think I actually look very relaxed for the state I'm in. I'm sitting comfortably behind the counter with Willow in my lap. And the view isn't half bad.

The view of having someone do the shop's work for me, I mean. Not specifically *who* is doing the work.

"Logan, sometimes I begin to think you're trying to be nice, but then you say stuff like that and I just think… what is missing in your brain?"

He laughs, and, finishing the re-stocking, moves on to his next task before opening. "Nothing's missing. All accounted for up here. You're just very defensive. Too many spirits whispering evil thoughts."

If only you knew.

I stroke Willow's neck and back while trying to think of a comeback. But his mouth opens again, spilling words that catch me by surprise.

"I just noticed the selenite crystal basket looked a little empty. Unless someone came in after we closed yesterday, I was worried a high-strung witch had a need for them. Especially after that whole thing with whatever-her-name-is."

I straighten myself in my chair. Willow shifts uncomfortably, trying to stay in my lap when I move.

"So, what's going on?" He pries further.

I lift my chin. "Strength. I put out the crystals to be blessed with strength to deal with you."

Logan rubs his chin. "Weird."

"What? You think you're easy to deal with?"

"Not in the least," he laughs at himself. "But amethyst would be better for that. I'd think you, of all people, would know."

Willow kneads my lap.

Logan waits for a response that's not coming. At least, not the response he hopes for.

"The floor still needs to be swept before people come in," I say.

He gives another one of those stupid little salutes and stops what he's doing to find the broom.

Logan interests me. I want to believe I can trust him with my store. He has a truly deep and surprising knowledge of the craft, and how I like this place, after only a few days. And he has a charm about him that I feel other people would be hesitant to resist if it weren't for his compulsion to turn everything into a joke. And too, I don't even think I can blame this on a defense mechanism. It's just how he enjoys acting. Yet so far, I am the only one concerned with it. It seemed as though yesterday morning, everyone that came in was eating him up. They barely acknowledged me when I told them to leave. But Logan? With the promise he'd be here today, they did exactly as they were told. And promptly.

But let us be honest. Is he really that attractive?

On second thought, let's not get into this now.

"I need to go," I say, stepping up from my chair. Willow hops from my lap and follows close to my feet as I grab my hat off of a hanger on the back wall and walk toward the door.

"Go?" Logan halts his sweeping. "Like out for a smoke? We haven't been working *that* hard yet."

Although I do produce a cabriole, I tell him, "No. I need to see a friend about..." How would I even tell him about the book? So instead I just say, "Something. Just stay out of the covenstead." I turn around the open/closed sign and raise the shades on the door window.

"I don't even know what that means."

"The back room," I clarify, stepping out and onto the sidewalk. "You stay here, Willow. Make sure he doesn't break anything."

Willow bounces back and scurries over to Logan.

He bends down to pet her and I hear as the door closes behind me, "I prefer hanging out with you anyway."

* * *

Nissa Greene lives in a beautiful little cottage an hour outside of town. Driving up to it is like something out of a fairy tale. A dirt road breaks off from the state route, and following that for about a half mile leads to a one-story home with vegetation crawling up almost every inch of the walls and wrapping around the windows. A burgeoning garden welcomes visitors from both sides of the dirt road; a mix of flowers, herbs, and vegetables. Nissa is one for abundance and life, not organization.

Before I'm even in full view of the cottage, I see Nissa stepping out of the cottage and waving at me.

And what have we here? A man emerges from behind her and wraps an arm around her waist. If it weren't for the eclectic, overgrown yard, it would look like they were posing for "Better Homes and Gardens."

I step out of the car and they both come to greet me.

"Nyx! Oh my god, I can't believe it's you," Nissa says, absolutely beaming.

Behind her, the man gives a warm, "Welcome. Brian. Nice to meet you," and holds out a hand.

"Pleasure." Then to Nissa, "Thank you for making time for me, darling."

"It's nothing. What else would we be doing on a Monday morning? Come in, come in," she beckons. "I was just baking for the farmers market this weekend."

"I can smell it," I say, taking in a whiff of something sweet coming from the cottage.

Nissa takes me by the hand and we all go back inside. Once in, Brian gives Nissa a kiss on the cheek and excuses himself from our company. He exits to the only room in the house that looks like an average middle-class home, while the rest looks like a hobbit hole.

"Come, come," Nissa says again, bringing me into the kitchen.

"You really went all out with the cottage-core aesthetic," I comment, inspecting the cast iron stove, plants hanging from the ceiling, and the overall greens and browns of the counters and walls.

She giggles with pride. "Brian let me do the decorating. Lots of the ideas came from Pinterest, so I can't take all the credit. But don't worry…" she flicks a switch and a ceiling light turns on. "We're not living in the stone age." She flicks it back off and lets the sunlight command the room.

Nissa had always been one of the more, let's say... eccentric... sisters. There isn't a doubt in my mind that they only pay an electric bill because Brian had to put his foot down on certain amenities. If the Amish accepted witches, she'd join them in a heartbeat.

Nissa opens the stove and the sweet smell of strawberries and cream emerges. It's like watching a Disney princess, the way she takes them out, takes in the smell, and smiles at her delicious creation. "We're bringing strawberry shortcakes to the farmers market this weekend. Just had to be sure I got the recipe right. You're welcome to try them when they've cooled a bit."

"Thank you, Nissa."

"You can even take some home with you if you'd like!" She offers. "Whatever Brian and I don't eat tonight we're bringing over to the church dinner."

"That'd be lovely."

She giggles at being able to provide for others.

"Nissa..."

She raises a finger to her lips, sensing the hesitation in my voice. "Not yet. It's been too long to jump right into business." Nissa takes a kettle off of the stove just as it begins to whistle and leads us into a little nook filled with plants and books, enough books to make my old neighbor Silvia jealous, although these might not be her genre. Many of these she'd bought from me, and practically all of them, I'm sure, are reference books on her practice. There are probably more texts in here than there is actual information on green witchcraft. How many times she's probably read the same thing over and over I couldn't guess.

Taking a seat, I pick up the closest book. "The Magic Garden." Not one I sell at Witch's Brew, but it looks like something I should stock.

"That's been a real eye-opener," Nissa says, watching me study the cover. "We've never had better tomatoes."

We both take seats and she reaches over, handing me a cup of tea.

"How's the store?" She asks.

I blow on the tea then inhale and let the aroma fill me. "Good. It's been a busy summer so far, but I'm managing."

"Have you seen Angie around lately?"

I shake my head. "She doesn't come around much anymore." Not in years, actually. But that topic's not something I want to dampen this home's energy with right now.

"Have you heard from her at all? Piper?"

Again, I shake my head, but slowly this time. *No, Nissa, none of them. And you know this.* "Not in a bit."

"But the store's doing well?"

"That it is, darling."

Her giddy smile returns. "Good. I've been praying for your good fortune."

"I'd say my daily rituals do well for that, too." Since when is she one for prayer?

Nissa smirks. "Nothing wrong with a little extra help, though, is there?"

I return her smirk, and glance down at her fingers, noticing an unfamiliar ring. "How long since that happened?"

"Last year. We only dated a few months but we knew right away. He doesn't practice with me, but he lets me live how I like. Brian doesn't ask for much and he gives me all the support I could ask for. I think he thought the farmer's market was just a hobby when we first met, and he'd have to support us."

"It sounds like he was expecting you to be his stay-at-home wife."

Nissa shrugs. "I wouldn't have complained if that's how it turned out. More time for my gardening without the stress. But we do well every weekend. Enough to comfortably afford this place."

"How does he feel about all of this?" I ask, looking around at all the plants. It's hard to see someone so cut-and-dry being cool with an atmosphere like this.

She nods to a room off to the side. "Brian has his office if he needs to breathe, haha."

"Congratulations. On everything. I'm happy for you." I sip at my tea.

"It was a really small service," she rushes to say. "Out of town. Brian's from New Hampshire, so we did it over there. Really just immediate service."

I didn't want to be the one to say anything, but after knowing each other since middle school, joining a coven together with Angie and Piper, one would think I'd at least be told about it.

"That's great," I say, trying to sound sincere. "That's just how I'd want it. And the ceremony? How did his family feel?"

"We kept it traditional."

I raise an eyebrow. "So do they not know Brian married a witch?"

Nissa's guarded tone drops and she laughs again. "I think the green dress gave it away. And I kept my name."

That, at least, makes me smile too. I'm glad she didn't completely hide herself from his side.

"Did he take yours? Hyphenate?"

"Nope. He's keeping Roberts for professional reasons."

"Nissa Roberts, though…" I let the name roll around in my mind. "Yes. You made the right choice, darling. Nissa Greene is much better."

Nissa rests her head against her fist and stares. "You're still doing that, huh? Calling everyone 'darling?' I thought you'd forget about that after high school," she says, getting out of her chair. "Let me get us those shortcakes." She pitters gently out of the room, almost gliding across the floor with her soft footsteps.

"I think everyone thought we'd forget about all of this after high school," I raise my voice to reach her in the kitchen.

She returns with two small dishes of little pastries, and offers me one of them, then takes her seat again.

"Thank you." I take a small bite.

Nissa begins again, "To be fair, I almost did move on. If not for the girls, I probably would have gotten bored of it and found another personality. High school was just so…"

"About the aesthetic," I say for her. Because, yes, it was. For the rest of them. This isn't to sound all, 'I'm not like other girls.' It's just the truth. I was the one who discovered it for us, and Nissa was along for the ride until we joined the coven. She didn't even stop using the name 'Kate' until we were out of school.

171

"Maybe a little," she admits.

"You don't have to be embarrassed, darling. Everyone's like that when they first get into it. That kind of person is probably ninety percent of my clientele." An exaggeration, sure. "All they need is a little push through the door. A little direction. You know, I offer a lot of one-on-one's with women to help them on their journeys. You should come around sometime and meet these girls."

"You've joined another coven? Or started one?"

While she nibbles at her shortcake, I explain the appointments I hold in the covenstead. I tell her first about Jade and the slow progress we're making with her, then I give her the background on Maria. Just about the first few meetings though, when she first came around looking for my help.

"It sounds like you have your hands full." She says it like her next words would be an offer to help, but the offer doesn't come.

I put my dish on the coffee table between us, along with my tea cup. "I do. But I can manage it. Actually though… this business with Maria is why I wanted to stop by."

Nissa nods contemplatively. "I had a feeling it wasn't for my shortcake."

"No, but that was delicious. But you see, Maria's brought me a problem I don't know how to deal with on my own."

Again, I wait for a response from Nissa, but she says nothing.

So, I continue. "I'm worried she's become mixed up with some… I don't want to sound overdramatic… She brought me this book that was given to her by a group that feels malicious. And there was something wrong with the book. Really wrong with it. When I tried to cleanse it I…" At the thought of the memory, my blood goes cold, and I can almost feel those icy fingers running up my inner thighs again. "I think, whoever these people are, they're trying to use Maria to summon something evil."

If it were anyone else, even Jade, I'd expect nothing less than a dismissive scoff or an outright balk at my claim. But Nissa only nods along with what I say, taking in every word.

Her silence, though, makes me feel crazy.

"I know you try to avoid this stuff, Nissa, but I really need help. I'm scared for this girl."

"Does she know about any of this?"

Relief comes over me like a long-awaited spring rain.

"I tried to tell her but she doesn't believe me. After the last time I went to inspect her home, I think she just came by the store to gloat."

"Gloat over what?"

"It's like high school. She feels like she's upping me because she's got a cool new friend group to hang out with. And now this cool new clique is manipulating her. She could be in really serious danger. And I really need your help." I find myself by her side, holding her hands pleadingly.

"Oh, Nyx. I wish you came by more often," she says with a faint smile.

"I'm sorry. The store just keeps me so busy. And now this," I say, trying to keep her on track. "I need to cleanse this book, Nissa. And I can't do it alone. It won't let me."

Nissa pulls her hands away from mine and places them on her stomach. "I don't think this is something I can help you with, sister." The word is tactful; meant to be encouraging, but only feels cold.

Should I tell her what it did to me? Or does pushing that only serve to guilt her into it?

"Please, Nissa. I... I don't have anyone else who can help me." Tears well in my eyes. "And I'm scared. I don't even want to be in my own home while that book is there."

"Then get rid of the book."

"I can't until it's cleansed. Maria doesn't know I have it yet."

"Have you reached out to Angie or Piper?"

Explaining that history to Nissa would be harder than everything with Maria. "I can't," I tell her outright.

"Why not?"

"Because they've moved on. They're out doing their own thing now and want nothing to do with me." A half-truth.

Nissa rolls her eyes, then scooches over, making room for me on the couch. "I'm sure they would help you if they knew you needed it."

I wipe my eyes. "They wouldn't. Not in the way I need them to. Why can't you do this with me?"

"Nyx, I don't do stuff like that. That's not my kind of practice. And I," she hesitates. "I just can't get involved with that now."

I push off the couch and pace around the room. "I'd prefer not to be involved in this either. But I am. And the one person who can help me *won't!*"

"Now, Nyx-"

"No 'Now, Nyx,' Nissa." I feel myself shaking, almost violently. "I'm sorry I didn't come around sooner just to hang out or grab a drink or do some gardening with you. I'm sorry. But I will if it makes you feel better and you help me with this."

Nissa retains her composure and it only drives me crazier, like nothing I'm saying means anything at all. She says, "I understand, an open invitation isn't an invitation at all. Would you like to have dinner with Brian and me soon?"

Angrily, I accept. "I'd love to."

"Good. I'll let you know when we're free. I promise."

"Thank you."

"You're welcome."

"And then will you help me?"

Nissa scoffs. "Ha, no… No, I still can't do anything except give you advice."

Advice? Fine, I'll take advice.

I stop my pacing and face her.

"First," she begins, "Work with this girl, Jade. Be honest with her about what's going on, and teach her."

"I couldn't bring her into this," I argue.

"Why not? It sounds like she wants to be a part of this with you. You've pushed everyone else away, why not let her in?"

"Who have I pushed away?"

Nissa gives me a challenging look.

Alright, fine.

"Take your time with her. Find somewhere safe for the book, and teach her."

"Okay," I say with some chagrin. "Now, what's the other thing?"

"Second, You need to let your man fuck you good. You are way too worked up."

Believe me, Nissa, I'm working on it.

Nissa wraps two shortcakes in parchment for me to take home, with string to tie it together. The whole way out the door and to my car, she insists over and over that she's not upset with my lack of presence, and that she does in fact want me and my boyfriend to come to dinner with her sometime soon.

It's only when I'm in my car, driving away, do I realize that Damien and I started dating after Nissa and I fell apart. And these shortcakes won't last until this weekend.

Her sight is a strange, strange gift.

19. Just A Goodbye Kiss

Jade is waiting inside when I arrive back at Witch's Brew. I see her from the road, standing by the counter next to Logan, laughing at some dumb joke he probably just made. Logan, for his part, is leaning against the back wall, with a fair amount of distance between the two of them. The rest of the store is almost empty. Only a handful of customers walk around.

I stand outside on the sidewalk, the wrapped pastries on a paper plate in one hand. Nissa gave me two of the pastries, somehow aware that Logan was here when she did so, even though I never once mentioned him. Although, if she has the gift of Sight, why did she not see Jade? Was this yet some poor attempt at forcing diplomacy between Logan and I? An offering of a sweet treat to sweeten our relationship?

Working relationship. Naturally.

When I walk in, Logan perks up and jumps to his feet.

"This isn't the Army," I tell him. "You don't have to go to attention when I walk in a room."

He still gives me one of his smartass salutes. "Aye aye, Captain."

I'm going to have an aneurysm working with him, I just know it.

"Jade," I save my last surviving brain cells and divert my attention to the radiant woman laughing at his imbecility. "Would you join me?" I hold out my arm for her.

"Whatcha got there?" He asks, eying the pastries as I put them down on the counter.

"Don't touch them," I snap back. "They're for myself and my guest." I give her arm a little tug in the direction of the covenstead.

"It's nice meeting you, Logan," She says, taking my arm.

Logan nods with a charming smile and I tell her, "Oh, don't enable him, darling."

He laughs, with a shake of his head, and his eyes fall on me just as we pass through the curtain to the covenstead.

As we enter, the chill envelops me. The book has been awaiting my return, and now it mocks.

"Do you feel that?" I ask, pulling my arm in tightly.

The rest of the building seems so quiet, I can hear her breathing next to me. "Feel what?" She asks.

I turn, taking her hands in mine, and face her. We're nearly chest to chest. Hers rises with anticipation or fear at what I'm about to tell her. "I need your help, Jade. Do you see the book on the table there?"

She looks without hesitation, and when I know she's seen it,

I guide her back toward me with a finger lightly on her cheek.

I continue, "This may be hard to grasp, but that book is a vessel to something evil."

"What is it?" She asks, and I'm relieved she doesn't dismiss it as a joke.

"I'm not sure yet. But I believe the universe brought us together for this reason. The book needs to be cleansed. And you have to help me do that."

Her eyes fall back to the table. Around the book are the crystals, as well as candles around the edge of the table, and the Algiz and Eihwaz runes written in salt; Algiz for protection, and Eihwaz for strength. It may have been a bit of overkill to put all of that out, I'll admit.

"Jade, focus on me."

She snaps back. "I don't feel anything. What am I supposed to feel?"

"Not feeling anything is good. For now, you will have nothing to do with this book. Do you understand?"

She opens her mouth. What for, I cannot guess, but I interrupt her.

"Do you understand, Jade? Don't ask questions, I only need you to trust me."

Jade nods.

"Good girl." With that, I cross over to the cabinet against the back wall and scrounge through its contents to pull out a grey cloth and twine to wrap the book in. My athame, my ceremonial blade unrolls from the cloth. For a moment, I picture stabbing through the book as if it were a heart. Once wrapped and tied, I take one of the candles and dip the hot wax onto the knot. It's just a little extra safety.

"Wait outside for just a moment, darling. And please tell Logan to come in."

"Um…" She bites her lip. "Yeah, okay, Nyx." She does as she's told, and a moment later, Logan enters the room.

"Thought I wasn't allowed in here anymore," he teases.

"You're still not," I say, making my way over to him. "But this is important." I place the book against his broad chest. It smacks with a thud against the muscles under his (too tight) shirt. Does he only get shirts too small for himself? "Hide this for me," I demand of him.

"Hide it? What is it?" He takes the book in both hands and then begins to flick at the wax.

I smack his hand away. "Stop that."

"Jeez, I've never had a boss so handsy with me before."

"I can be plenty handsy if you don't get your act together."

…

His stupid fucking grin begins to spread.

"Stop that."

"Hey, it's all good. I know what you meant." He begins to lean in, and says softly "Just as long as it's not in front of the customers." But it's a feint, and he steps away to wander around the room.

"You are such. A. *Pig!*" I throw my hands onto my hips. "You can't ever let anything lie, can you?"

Without looking at me, wandering around the room looking

for a hiding spot, he says, "Me? Of course I can, I love letting things lie. Usually, if I can lie with them but that's only after the third date because I *am* a gentleman."

"Oh my god, you're disgusting."

"All right, you got me," He laughs. "I meant three drinks."

"It's like you're actively trying to get f-"

"Hey, aren't you not supposed to know where I'm hiding this?"

He stops me completely. I have a need to scream at his annoying behavior, but again, he's right. And he has to be the one to hide it.

I search for the right word to storm out on, but all that comes out is a grunt and I retreat.

Every second of him alone in that room drives me crazy. Jade should have been the one to pester me for a job. It would've been perfect, too, since it would have been pretty much just for the summer, and when she begins college soon, she could still help out on the weekend. At the very least, she'd still come around.

I find myself biting the inside of my lip with anxiety.

"Why did he have to do that?" Jade asks.

"I don't want to know where it is for the time being. And I don't want to be tempted to use it."

"I could have hidden it if you don't like Logan."

I wave away the offer. "No, darling, I don't want you to have anything to do with that until we're ready." Off to the side, a customer calls for my attention. "Just a moment, Jade."

Jade stays to guard the covenstead while I assist the

customer. The woman is trying to decide which tarot deck she should go with.

As I step away, though, Logan steps out of the covenstead. I keep a watch on him and Jade from the corner of my eye while helping the customer. The way they stand together is not at all like how he is with me. While I find Logan is over-casual with me, the casualness with which he has around Jade is totally different. There is a clear, respectable distance between them, and his lean is more away from than toward her. I can't hear what they say to each other, but he says something, she responds, and they both exchange a laugh and glance my way, then laugh again. Even around me, Jade doesn't come off that gleefully expressive; always restrained and unsure.

When the customer has decided on what to buy, a task that has been mostly just her talking to herself, I escape back to the corner where Logan and Jade are hanging out.

"Something funny over here?" I ask.

Logan's eyes drift from Jade to me. "Just talking about how wonderful of a boss you are. So caring and understanding and all that."

"Hm. Back to the counter," I order. "And Jade, let's go upstairs. I want you to fill me in on everything that's happened since we last met."

We practically rush through the covenstead to get to the stairs up to my apartment; Jade pacing in front of me, and I give her a little pat on the butt to hasten her up the stairs.

As she hops up the stairs, she asks, "Are you sure you have time for this? You don't have to be downstairs?"

182

"I don't like Logan all that much, but I trust him enough to not burn the place down. And it seems like a slow day. He'll manage. Besides, you are much more important." She enters the apartment first, and a heat wave hits us when she opens the door.

The July sun is cooking my room without any air conditioning running. The stark change in temperature from the cool store and covenstead drenches us in sweat.

"Fuck, I'm an idiot," I curse myself. "Do you mind?" I ask Jade, lifting my robe. "I'll put something else on, don't worry, darling. This is just too heavy."

She shakes her head timidly. "Not at all."

"Thank you," I sigh, removing my robe.

Jade respectfully shies away at my naked upper body while I find a smaller top to put on, but I can feel her eyes stealing looks at my bare flesh.

"Don't worry," I laugh. "We're sisters now. You don't have to feel uncomfortable around me."

"It's just…" She begins softly. "Uh. A lot of ink?"

The first thing I grabbed was a bra, and I clip that on as I turn back to face her. "I've got a good artist in Wilton. Part of why I care so much about the store. Gotta fund my addiction."

Even as I approach her, it's like an invisible force is casting her eyes away from me. "Hey," I tell her. "This doesn't have to be weird. Nothing's going on, right? It's just hot in here." Sure, wearing just a bra and shorts doesn't leave much to the imagination, but my nipples are covered. Isn't that what everyone gets so uptight about?

"Here, take a seat. I'll get you a drink. Kombucha okay?"

183

Jade nods, her eyes still on my bare flesh.

I laugh. "I thought we were working on you and your friend. What's her name, Lily? Emily?"

"Jenna," she corrects.

"That's the one." I open the fridge and pull out a mason jar of my homemade kombucha. Pouring two glasses, I ask, "And what happened when you saw her again?"

She swallows hard and stays quiet.

"Jade?"

"I um… I couldn't do it."

I take my seat next to her and hand her the glass of kombucha.

She goes on, "It was already pretty late when I got to the cabin, but everyone was still up, hanging around the fire. I didn't really feel like throwing myself back into that yet, and kinda worried Jenna would have told everyone what happened. They hadn't even called or texted the whole time I was away, so, yeah. She told everyone.

"So at first I went back to our room, but something came over me and I knew that wasn't where I was supposed to be. Instead, I went down to the water. I snuck around the cabin so they couldn't see me until I was already down by the beach, and even then there were some bushes between us. I thought about that pool you told me about and thought I could try some meditation like that. And you know, it really felt like that. Like I was separating myself from the rest of the world, just letting the universe fill my mind and ease my stress.

"Nyx, It was really such a wonderful moment. I mean, it was until they spotted me. Mikey and Dale thought I was skinny dipping so they both rushed out and, yeah," she laughs, "Definitely not into them. But they joined, and then Jenna came behind. It took her some convincing, but eventually, she stripped too and got in the water. I guess it was too dark to see that I was in my underwear.

"So everything was fine then, like, back to normal enough. The guys were all kinda drunk or cross faded but Jenna was sober. And she had definitely told them what happened by then because they started making jokes again about me getting a chance to check out Jenna's boobs. She tried to change the topic, but I... I'll admit, something came over me.

"I swam over to her and planted a kiss square on her lips."

She paused for dramatic effect. I was leaned in close with amazed anticipation. Here was this shy young woman actually taking what she wanted for once. "And?" I pressed. "And how was it? Just a kiss or was it, you know, more?"

Jade went shy again, blushing, and fell back a few inches. "I mean... I don't know. It was a kiss."

"Yeah, but was it..." I pull her face in and kiss her, imitating passion. "Was it like that? Or more daring?" I go in again a little rougher, licking her teeth. When I pull away, she's completely in shock.

"Well?" I ask. "Come on, give me details! Did you win her over or what?"

Jade tries to pull herself together. Why this is so difficult for her, I have no idea. If she can't get the words out she should at least be able to show it.

"The uh... the second one." She finally answers.

185

"That's my girl!" I shout, throwing my arms around her. "You're taking what you want! I'm proud of you."

Shy hands eventually hold me back, gently laying on my skin. "Yeah," she chuckles. "Yeah, I guess I did. But Nyx, that wasn't it."

I pull away. "There's more?" I ask with a devilish grin.

Jade blushes further, like a bright red cherry ready to burst. "Not *that* much more. Okay, sure, I went in a little aggressively. There *may* have been tongue. But kissing was it."

"Then what's 'more?'" I ask, mostly seriously. A good amount of me though is just glad she had the tits to go for it.

"Well, once it started… she didn't pull away. She actually pulled me in closer. Like…" Jade is the one to lean in this time. The kiss starts off lackluster, but her tongue finds its way into my mouth until we're interlocked.

After a few seconds, I'm the one to pull out. "Wow…" I say. "Maybe if it worked out so well *we* shouldn't be the ones recreating it."

"That's about as far as it got," her voice lowers. "It was a fun night, and we were all cool after that, but I still can't get a read on Jenna. The next morning it was like nothing happened. It wasn't awkward or anything, but it wasn't like, 'Hey we're dating now' either."

I put my hands on hers. "I think you're at a great start. You meditated, you were true with your intentions, and you were headstrong with what you wanted without disrespecting a friend." I wipe my lip of her saliva. "And it seems as though you showed her a good time. You'll have to keep me updated on this situation."

"The meditation helped," she says. "And I was thinking, maybe you could take me to that pool in the woods sometime."

I push back a lock of her hair that fell in front of her face when she reenacted the kiss with Jenna. "Maybe. It's important for us to have our private places of meditation. For now, there are other places around here to explore that are strong in magic. Which, by the way, is why we're here today. The gossip is fun, but there is work to do." I stand to fetch one of my own annotated handbooks.

"Like what? You didn't invite me here just to give me another massage?"

I spin back toward her with a grin. "Seems like that kiss really brought you out of your shell, Jade."

"Maybe I do feel a little more sure of myself. What I want."

"Ha, good girl." I return to finding the book. It's hiding on a small shelf by the base of my bed. "Today's lesson. Spells."

* * *

The hours fly by. Jade and I practically read through the whole book together. No practical exercises or anything, just learning the fundamentals and basic teaching of spellcraft.

Eventually, when the room cools down I put my robe back on, and Jade pretends to be upset, which gets us talking about my tattoos. And she asks the same thing they all ask: Will she need to get any? Do they all mean something?

No, and no. I just like them. A handful have meaning, but

most are just musings of my artist who needed a canvas to work on.

We're torn from our lesson by a knock at the door. My first thought is Damien, having come to surprise me. Then my mood drops all the way to the basement when Logan pops his head in.

"Hey, Nyx, I'm taking off. Just cleaned up."

"Taking off? What time is it?" I reach for my phone but he answers.

"7:30."

"Shit," I say, pulling myself out of the bed, then helping Jade. "Sorry, darling," I say to her. "Guess we were having too much fun. Didn't mean to keep you for so long."

Jade fixes herself and scampers over to the door. "No, that's my bad. I should have been home already. Just text me when you're free again, okay?"

"Of course. It'll be soon, I promise." I give her a kiss on the cheek and watch her hop down the stairs.

Logan watches the goodbyes from his spot up against the wall of the stairway. When she's gone, he asks, "So, is she your girlfriend?"

"She's a friend."

"Coulda fooled me."

Instead of a response, I close the door on him. Just before shutting, the door hits his foot and bounces back open.

"It's 7:30." He says again.

"I heard you before."

"Okay good, I was worried you missed me while you were ogling her."

"*I* was ogling? Says the one that kept making her laugh like a schoolgirl."

"She looks old enough to be one. I wouldn't fuck around with jailbait."

"She's 18."

"Oh," he says, eyes wide with fake surprise. "So all bets are off."

"Oh my god, Logan. Don't-"

He raises one hand to stop me. The other stays behind his back. "Don't worry, she's not my type."

"Yeah?" I ask, now a few feet backed away from the door, with Logan still in front of me. "What is your type then?"

He shrugs, and says with that stupid grin, "Oh you know, tatted goth girls that like to degrade guys like me. The more piercings the better. As long as my parents are disappointed when I bring her around."

I cover the half dozen cartilage piercings in my left ear.

We're almost all the way across the living room, drawing a little too close to comfort to the bedroom. "Is there any particular reason why you're up here?"

"Yeah, there is. I said it's 7:30. We're past closing."

"And?" Another step backward.

His concealed hand moves out from behind his back. "And…" In it is the dish of shortcakes, and hanging on his wrist, a plastic bag with a big yellow smiley face. "You left these on the counter. But also, I was worried you lost track of time up here. I ordered Chinese."

We both stop moving, not yet crossing into the next room.

"You..." I'm not sure how to feel. Thankful or creeped out that I'm on his mind that much.

"Don't worry, I paid for it with money from the register."

Aaaaand we're back to square one. I snatch the dish from his hand.

"I'm kidding, obviously," He laughs, putting the bag of Chinese food on the coffee table. "But I did lick both of the cupcakes."

"They're strawberry shortcakes."

"Oh, so that's why they tasted like apple fritters. You gonna eat them both?"

"You're done," I say, already pushing him back toward the door. "Good-bye. See you tomorrow, Logan."

From the top step, he squeezes in one more tease, "What, no goodbye kiss for me too?"

The door slams.

20. Logan Needs to Go

I keep Logan at arm's length for the rest of the week. I feel gross having let him in my room. It felt bad enough letting him enter the covenstead, but if Damien found out some guy had been in my room like that, bringing me dinner, closing in on my bed? Well, at least on the bright side Logan probably wouldn't be so eager to make his stupid flirty jokes around me.

Oh you know, tatted goth girls that like to degrade guys like me. The more piercings the better. As long as my parents are disappointed when I bring her around.

What an asshole, saying that like I'm beneath him. Who'd be disappointed by me? And who does he think he is, lumping me into that stereotype? And worse, if he's just looking at me as another one of his type. Did his ex look like me?

No, quit it, Nyx. You're not going to become a stalker over some ex like he's your boyfriend.

Screw this. Tomorrow I'm firing him. It's a waste of time giving him this much space in my mind.

* * *

Logan walks in the next morning, bright and early at 8:30, a half hour before opening. He strides in with a cup of gas station coffee.

I'm ready. I can do this.

"Mornin' Nyx," He says, holding up his coffee. Willow runs up to him and rubs up against his leg.

Just kick him out, I tell myself. "Tuesdays are the track's 'Dark Days.' Be ready for the crowds."

He nods. "Noted."

"So just-"

"Keep the place neat?" He asks, putting his coffee down on the counter, settling in.

"Yes." Fuck.

"You got it, boss." And like that, he gets to work and I still have an employee.

Tomorrow. Tomorrow I'll do it.

* * *

But Wednesday comes, and Logan comes with it. Coffee cup in one hand, a cat toy in the other.

"What's this?" I ask when Willow jumps up to snag it out of his lowered hand.

"It's coffee. Do you want me to bring you some tomorrow?"

"I don't drink coffee. But I meant the toy. Willow doesn't need that."

The cat stops playing and gives me a look as if to say, *oh yes I do*, and returns to playing.

Logan watches her play, and says, "I don't know, she's always messing around by the counter, getting in the way. I thought she could use a distraction. Plus I'm trying to stay on her good side."

Can no guy ever get their priorities right? "You should focus on staying on my good side instead of stunts like that one the other night or trying to bribe my cat." *Yes, Nyx, it's coming. Oh, it's coming. Just gotta deliver the blow.*

"Her name is Willow," Logan asserts, "And I'd love to be on your good side sometime if you let me."

"Don't try anything stupid today and we'll see if you can get on it later."

Nyx...

What the fuck was that?

That stupid. Fucking. Grin. "Plans later. Sorry." He passes by me and walks over to the counter, putting his cup down. "But you've got me for eight hours to do with what you will." He turns around to face me again. "So how can I get on that good side?"

I grit my teeth. Or bite my lip.

Logan crosses his arms, propping up his pecks. His hazel eyes taunt me.

I take a deep breath, and meet him at the counter, looking up at him.

"I really should fire you."

"Nah..."

"Nah?" I mimic his coy tone.

"You'd miss me too much." His arms tighten, pressing against his sleeves so I can see a perfect outline of his upper arm muscles.

"I would celebrate never having to see you again. I'd throw a big party and invite all the customers. Give them a big discount to show how happy I am."

Logan scoffs, "They wouldn't show up if you fired me. We both know I'm the looks of this place."

"At least that leaves me to be the brains."

"So you think I am, then?" He tilts his head down toward me.

"You are what?"

"You're the brains and I'm the looks."

This time I do bite my lip. "You are just so full of yourself, aren't you?"

"Maybe a little bit. But just because you haven't said otherwise yet."

"Someone really needs to put you in your place."

"Yeah? Why don't *you*?" He pushes off the counter, standing another inch taller over me.

"Because that's what you want, isn't it? Just some hot tatted goth girl your parents would be disappointed in. That why you wanted to work here so bad? So you could stare all day?" I breathe in, puffing my chest to test him, my robe exposing just enough for a good tease.

His eyes shake, but don't break away from mine.

"Or was that just all talk?" I pout.

Logan's sturdy expression turns to faint amusement. "Still my type, I just prefer them not to be taken."

The comment snaps me back to reality. To Damien. *Fuck! What the hell am I doing?*

He smirks, thinking he's victorious in this battle and it sends me over the edge. I reach around him, grabbing his coffee cup, and take off the lid.

With still more to say he adds, "You coulda texted me if you wanted one."

Without responding I gather up saliva in my mouth and spit in his cup.

"Nice." He says flatly. "Not how I usually like my coffee, but," he takes the cup from my hand and raises it to his lips. "Fuck it." And pour the coffee and my spit into his mouth.

And when he does, I feel heat between my legs.

Logan brings the cup back down and returns it to the counter. Through the whole ordeal though, his eyes stay focused on mine. "Am I on your good side yet?" He asks.

My heart races in my chest. "You're getting there."

"Should we get to work?"

"Yes."

* * *

Thursday starts out a fucking nightmare. As if yesterday wasn't torture enough getting through the day, Thursday is fucking dead in the store. For the first hour, no one comes in. For the second,

195

only one person. But by noon it's dead again. And the whole time, Logan and I are both very aware of yesterday's comments. At least today he's wearing something that actually fits and he's not trying to show off his muscles.

"I need a smoke break," I tell him just before one.

"I don't blame you," he says, leaning on the counter playing with Willow. "This day's got me beat. Just one thing after the next."

"Need one?" I hold up a cigarette in offering.

Logan smiles politely but shakes his head. "Those things are so bad for you."

"Hm." I flick the cigarette between my lips. *Surprised there's no witty comment this time. Maybe he's learning.*

I take my time with the cigarette and enjoy the summer warmth. Saratoga as a whole seems to be quiet today. But when someone walks by I invite them in. There just aren't many takers.

Halfway through the cigarette, I chide myself over the realization that one, Logan is still here, and two, I didn't even think about firing him this morning. Track season isn't even close to over, so, yeah, it'll still be busy moving forward. But if there was a time to do it, it'd be now while I have time to get someone new working here by Saturday. Someone like Jade.

But shit, I've been texting her all day and already know she's not available on weekends. I need someone, if I let anyone continue working here, that doesn't have a life. Or, as Logan was so kind to remind me, Damien. If he would put in the effort.

This Sunday he will. Just a few more days, a new moon, and some real love making, and we'll be right back on track. That

Daniel Cassidy book "Binds" can only keep me held down for so long. Suppose I'll have to read his other stuff but I heard this one is as kinky as it gets.

The door opens next to me.

"Hey, Nyx, I don't know if you noticed but it's kinda dead today," Logan announces.

"Very observant," I say through a drag of the cigarette.

"I try. But look, if you don't think it's gonna pick up, I'll just take off."

What?

I perk up and for some stupid reason put out the cigarette on the sidewalk, nearly snapping the cabriole. "Why?" I ask, with a little too much concern in my voice for comfort.

He looks back into the store, then back to me. "It's dead, Nyx. I mean you haven't paid me yet, though I hope you will eventually, but if you're not making money today I'm not gonna drain you."

"It could pick up."

The look in his eyes says he wants to make another witty comment, but instead, he says, without a hint of humor, "Nyx, I'm offering to get out of your hair for the day. Do you want me to go or not?"

Fuck, I wish I didn't put out that cigarette.

"I don't think we actually discussed pay."

"Nyx." He holds it in but a little laugh escapes him. "You're really bad at putting your foot down."

A strange thing to say, because it's true, but it never had

been until he threw himself headfirst into my life.

I take out a new cigarette. "Just stay a little while longer. Just to see if it picks up."

"All right. Cool."

"Cool," I agree.

And somehow, up until the end of the day with maybe a dozen customers total, he's there closing with me. Before we lock up we agree on eighteen an hour, checks paid bi-weekly.

For now, there are no more thoughts of firing him.

For now.

The worst part is though, as I'm reading "Binds" tonight and another steamy scene comes up and I let myself get carried away, it's not Damien's hand I imagine caressing my loins.

What the fuck am I doing?

21. The Part Where a Little Too Much is Seen

The new moon comes.

I've spent all morning preparing my apartment; clearing it of any lingering negative energy from previous nights spent with Damien, as well as meditating and clearing my mind of those bad memories. It's been so long since I've had a good orgasm, and just thinking about the incredible experience we're about to have has me wet and craving Damien all day. It's so bad I need to take breaks even from my meditation to read more of "Binds" and relieve some of this tension.

But as the sun sets I feel like a fool. What kind of place is my apartment for such a magical event? All my work is for naught when I decide to instead prepare the covenstead.

The energy from the book still lingers, though dull now, like the feeling of leaving the refrigerator open after leaving the house. The sexual nature of the spirit forcing itself out of its bonds does nothing to settle my heat while I work. And working, I am.

The table in the covenstead is perfect for a sexual fantasy. A large mahogany center table that weighs at least a thousand pounds. Trying to move it would take more than myself and Damien. Someone with muscles like Logan could probably do it all on his own without even scratching the flo-

No, Nyx. Stop. Don't even think about him today. This night is for you and Damien.

But this table takes up a good amount of space in the room. Sure, we could do this on the pillows by the back of the room where I give my massages, but if we're going to be that half-assed about it we might not even do this at all. So, could the table work?

I clear the table of the cloth and everything on it, then prop myself on it, lying down. The table has a sturdy base so far, just climbing on it. I shake around a bit. Not even a wobble. I turn and bend over the edge of the table, thrusting back and forth as if Damien was penetrating me from behind. I feel like a fucking idiot, but it works. Still not even a wobble. This thing is tough. I back up, sitting upright on my knees, and begin to bounce. Nothing. I bounce harder, really riding him. Nothing. I slam my hands down on his imaginary chest, caressing his muscular chest, grinding my wet lips against his thick cock, giving him the time of his life, looking into those hazel eyes. The table starts wobbling.

I bring one hand up to my crotch and rub my soaking-wet pants. I want him here, now, on this table inside of me, surrounded by burning red candles. I want his hands on my body, running up my side to my tits so he can play with them. I want to feel his teeth biting at my nipples while I soak him in my juices. I want to play, want him to drip the hot wax on my body. I want him to tease me, making me beg for more.

Fuck, we haven't had sex like that in forever. I used to squirt when we first met. I don't think I've ever done that even on my own in years.

No use thinking about that now. It's all in the past.

Before I feel too silly, even though I didn't finish the fantasy, I dismount from the table. I'll need to change my pants before he gets here.

Oh, who am I kidding? I'm not waiting for him to undress me. I'll be ready for him.

My phone vibrates. Damien, maybe? The "break" is over so he can text me any time today.

Any. Time. Damien…

-Are you around?
-I need to come by.
-Emergency.

Maria.

Nope. Not doing this today. You can try again tomorrow if you want but this is *my* night.

My phone continues to vibrate while I set up the covenstead for a romantic evening. Will Damien use the candles on me? Hopefully.

But my phone goes off, over and over and over again. Fuck, if I wanted a vibrator I'd use the one in my nightstand. This might be a risk, but I turn my phone on "Do Not Disturb." I send Damien a quick text letting him know the door will be unlocked at nine and for him to let himself in, then put it upstairs.

Outside, the last bits of sunlight fade from the sky. It's a little past eight.

He's coming. Oh, he better be coming.

With the table all set, and the candles placed, I run upstairs for a quick shower. After all my mediations and statements of my intention, I feel the magic surrounding me. Every fiber of my being is jittery with anticipation for this evening. The hot water does nothing to calm me, so I turn the heat down, and let the cool water satiate me. It's fractionally more soothing.

When I step out of the shower I check my phone. It's just before nine, and no text yet from Damien.

So, he just wants to go for it. That's fine with me. As long as he's here.

I throw on a black robe and make my way down to the store to unlock the front door. Willow follows close behind me. I tell her, "You stand guard, okay? Don't let anyone in except Damien."

Willow meows her agreement as I flick the lock to the side. Then, I draw the blinds and return to the covenstead.

In the glow of the candlelight, I disrobe, then fold it up and put it on one of the cabinets.

Any minute now, he'll be here.

I mount the table, laying down, resting my head on a pillow. I spread my legs, awaiting Damien's arrival, and begin to touch myself. I'm already gushing, swimming in a euphoric state of anticipation. I feel like just seeing his face again will make me cum, and everything after that is just pleasure for the sake of pleasure.

Out in the store, the door slowly creaks open. Willow meows invitingly.

He's here. I rub my clit with more vigor.

A soft whisper from outside. "Nyx? You there?"

My body reacts to the sound of his voice. The orgasm builds up, ready to enrapture me.

"I'm in here," I try to whisper back through bated breath.

His footsteps approach.

My nipples harden. Fuck, I need him on top of me, inside of me.

A strong hand pushed through the curtain, pulling it slowly to the side.

I'm on the edge, holding back my moans.

"Nyx?" he asks again.

The littlest bit of juice squirts out of me when I see the skin on his face, his eyes... his hazel eyes.

"What... the fuck... is this?" Logan asks.

My eyes widen with terror. I close my legs, trapping my fingers inside of myself. I try to pull out but the movement keeps me going, so I freeze, ruining my own climax.

"Get out!" I yell at the top of my lungs.

Logan stands like a stone in complete shock, then throws the curtain back between us.

"I'm sorry!" He shouts through the barrier. "I just needed-"

"Get the *fuck* out, Logan!"

203

I hear him race through the store and pull the door open, but it doesn't shut.

Throwing myself off the table, I stick my head through the curtain and see him standing there, gripping his hands like there's something stopping him from leaving.

"What the fuck are you doing, Logan? Leave!"

He half-turns, and says back to me, "I'm really sorry! Promise I didn't see anything. I just needed to get something."

"Fuck off! Get out of my store!"

"All right! Yeah! Bye See you tomorrow morning!"

"Fuck you!" See me tomorrow? What? "I'll see you in the morning! Now fucking leave!"

He's out the door before I even finish my sentence.

Willow perches up on the counter next to me and gives me another one of those Cheshire Cat smiles.

"I bet you think that was real funny, don't you?"

Don't you?

22. An Old Fashioned Gentleman

I sit in bed staring at my phone. Text after text after text sent to Damien.

9:46 p.m.

-Damien!
-Where are you? Are you coming or not?
-Damien!

10:04 p.m.

-Damien I'm fucking serious call me back

10:11 p.m.

-Why tf haven't you called yet? You said you'd be here!

-Something really
embarrassing happened
-Damien
-Damien
-DAMIEN!

10:37 p.m.

-If you don't call me back
now, don't call back ever.
I'm fucking done with
you!

10:41 p.m.

-Fuck you Damien

11:01 p.m.

-Please call me!

By nearly midnight there is still no word. Maybe I shouldn't have told him not to call at all.

Sitting alone in my bed, I feel so much embarrassment that Logan saw me so exposed. And I know I should be grateful that a pervert like him didn't take advantage of that, but the fact that he saw me, that he was here at all! What was he doing, sneaking in here at nine at night on a Sunday?

Did he mean to break in? Steal from the register? He probably knew I was thinking about firing him and decided to cut his

206

losses, taking what he could. Oh, that piece of shit!

If Damien was here he could have beat the shit out of him. If he caught Logan and all his muscles by surprise, that is.

But, Damien's not here. I have no idea *where* he is.

So, I call him again. The phone rings six times and then goes to the automatic voicemail. I call again. Voicemail. Again. Voicemail.

Fuck, he should at least be answering out of annoyance by now!

An idea hits; I want to beat myself for not thinking of it sooner. Location sharing. Maybe he was on his way and got in an accident. Now I'm just a horrible girlfriend for not even considering that. I pull up the tab that shows his location. It doesn't take long to load, and centers in on Saranac Lake, a good two hours away. I zoom in and thankfully, it's a familiar address, his dad's address. At least it's a sign he's not cheating. Damien's dad is a real conservative God-fearing type. He's not my biggest fan by any means, but he'd for sure take my side over Damien's if he cheated, and everyone knows that.

So, what the hell is going on?

I send another text, then call again to no answer.

Once again, I check the location to make sure it is up to date. The text under his name and the little blue dot says "Active now."

That son of a bitch!

Never in my life have I been so close to wanting to actually curse someone. I could do that. I could set up the covenstead and use the power of the new moon to curse him for humiliating me like this.

No, no I couldn't do that. That's an abuse of the natural

world. An act of unjustifiable selfishness. I can't be one for revenge. I don't even fully know *why* he didn't come.

Maybe it is something serious. Maybe something happened with his Dad and sex isn't the first thing on his mind.

...

But it's sex with *me!* Relationship-defining sex! And I told him, I threatened him! If he didn't show up tonight, then that would be the end of it. No more putting up with his half-assed, fuck-me-when-he-feels-like attitude.

"It's over!"

I breathe.

What should feel gratifying, having said it out loud, only feels empty. I don't want it to be over. We were together for three years. I wanted to do this tonight because I believed - still believe - we could fix this. Why am I the only one that feels this way?

If I'd looked at his location and saw he was at someone's house who I didn't know, at least I could think he was cheating on me. I could have something solid to hate him for and sleep peacefully knowing I'm better than giving in to self-loathing and self-pity, that the thoughts spent on it were beneath me. But it's nothing. He's given me nothing.

I call him one more time, telling myself that this time he'll answer, even though I know he won't.

Willow sneaks up the stairs and pushes her head through the crack in the doorway.

"What do you want?"

She sulks across the room, acting like she's guilt-stricken, but I know better.

"You were supposed to be my guardian. Why'd you let him in?"

Willow meows, then jumps up on the bed.

"Why am I even talking to you? We're not friends tonight."

She nuzzles against my chest, holding her butt up high, a request to have her back rubbed.

"No, you're pissing me off tonight." I push her to the side and slink off the bed. I pick up a pair of worn sweatpants and a tank top from the foot of the bed and change into them. Willow begins to follow, but I point at her accusingly and she freezes. "No. You stay here and think about what you did. I'm going out. Alone."

I grab a tin of hand-rolled cigarettes from the shelf underneath the coffee table, and for the rest of the night, until I can get my head clear, I wander through the park down the road.

I wait… and wait… and wait… for a phone call that doesn't come.

Even at three in the morning, with half the pack gone and my clothes stained from lying in the grass, not a sign in any way that Damien has any interest in reaching me.

But at 3:15, my phone vibrates. Just a quick little *BZ*. Not a full ring. So, not a call. I give myself a small victory by not immediately checking to see what he said. Instead, I wait a minute or two then cave and pull out my phone.

Unfortunately, it's not the man I'm most pissed off at the moment. It's the man I'm second most pissed off at.

Logan.

-You doing okay?

I drop my phone back onto the grass. Not dealing with him tonight. Or tomorrow. Or ever again. I gave him enough chances.

-Look, that was embarrassing
for both of us.
-I mean, didn't mean to make
you feel embarrassed. I had no
idea. And I promise I didn't
see anything.

That's a fucking lie. Not trying to be full of myself here, but Logan couldn't take his eyes off me.

-Hey, I'm making my peace.
It's not polite to ignore me.

-I could be sleeping.

Well, that was a fucking idiotic thing to say.

-Well then wakey wakey. But I
know you weren't, so we might
as well talk this out.

-I was. It was a very

peaceful sleep until you woke me up. Why would I even want to talk anything out with you?

-Because I think talking it out over a drink would be more fun than lying in the grass.

I bolt upright at his last text. Is he fucking stalking me now?

I look all around, to the fountains, the ponds, the old casino building. Then from somewhere to the left, I hear a shout.

"I was here first by the way." Logan's sitting on a bench by a grand stone staircase on the other side of the pond as me. I feel like a fool for not noticing him sooner, even though it's only a very dim light shining on him.

"How long have you been there?" I shout across the pond.

"Wasn't really keeping track of time. But a while."

I pick myself up, wiping the grass from the back of my pants. He doesn't move an inch. "Why?" I shout. "Do you have literally anywhere else to be other than around me?"

"A million other places. Just not tonight."

"Why not tonight?" I slowly make my way around the pond. "Didn't get enough of me yet?"

Here comes the witty response. I can already hear it, something like *I could never get enough of you.*

Instead, it's more sincere. "Only because I didn't get to explain myself."

As I draw closer, he rises off the bench. There's no humor in his face. No smug I-saw-your-boobs smirk. If anything, all I see is remorse.

"What happened was..." he waves his hands around looking for the right word. "Wrong. I guess. Look, I didn't know what was going on, but I probably should have been louder coming in. I'm sure you thought I was someone else when you told me to come in."

I cross my arms. At least he's not so cocky he assumes I was expecting him.

"Why were you in my store tonight?"

The corner of his lips pull back in the makings of a grin, and waver. It's a dumb joke, I know it is. It's rolling around in his head, and he's fighting with all of his might not to say it.

"Left something behind," he finally says.

"Couldn't get it in the morning?"

"I thought it was urgent."

"What was it?"

"A drink."

"Huh?"

He points past me. "Old Fashioned is still open. Should be for another half hour maybe. Get a drink with me and I'll spill everything."

I take a step back, appalled. "Are you asking me out? Like, you see me naked and think *now's* a good time to do it?"

Now the grin makes itself known in full. "You're always so quick to assume I'm flirting with you. It's past three in the morning on a Sunday night. Something tells me my boss isn't letting me into work tomorrow, so I don't have to worry about coming in late, and I don't like having a guilty conscience so I'd just like to talk. Hand to God, nothing's gonna happen. If it feels like I'm flirting... I mean I probably am but not in a serious way. We both know I don't have a filter, but I swear I'm just trying to be a friend right now."

Every fiber of me says I shouldn't believe him. But...

Oh, fuck it. What is there to lose?

This might be the dumbest thing I do all night, but I put my hand on his outstretched arm, and let him lead me back to the bar.

* * *

"So, why the wallowing?" Logan asks as Frank brings two drinks to the corner booth we sit in. For myself, an old fashioned with chocolate bitters, as Frank knows I like. For Logan, straight whiskey. Neither of us hesitate to take a first sip.

By this point in the night, it's just the two of us in the bar. Unfortunately, that means there aren't any nice cars to borrow if I decide I need a little fun. But also, on the plus side, none of the creepy old guys looking for a sugar baby.

"Who says I was wallowing?"

"You had four cigarettes while you were lying there. I don't think it was all on account of me seeing those leg tattoos."

"Thought you said you didn't see anything." I take another sip, giving him a challenging eye.

His eyes go heavenward in humored defeat. "All right, I saw a little. But nothing those super thin clothes you wear don't already show."

"Oh, so this is my fault?" I pose, trying to refrain from a threatening tone.

"It's neither of us's fault. Besides, I could barely tell what they were with your clothes on, and if it makes you feel better, I still couldn't really tell with your clothes off."

It does make me feel a little better. Sure he froze, but if he's honest, it wasn't to stare, and I can appreciate that.

I stir my drink with the mini straw. Logan watches me intently, most likely hoping I'll say something to let him off the hook.

How bad could this hurt?

After another quick sip of my drink, I scoot to the edge of the seat and pull up my right pant leg. "This side is ivy," I display the tattoo that wraps around my calf, up and around my waist.

Logan peers down at my bare leg, and traces the vines upward with his eyes. With these sweatpants, only up to just below my knee is revealed. "How high up does it go?" He asks.

"All the way."

"And the other leg?"

I look around to see if Frank is watching, or even around anymore. For now, he's gone. Great. But hopefully not for long because at this pace we'll both need another round soon.

For a moment, I consider contorting myself so I can put my foot on the table and pull up the other pant leg. But that's too much all at once. Instead, I scoot back in and around to the center of the booth, and bring my leg up, foot resting on his lap.

"A snake. Also all the way up."

This time, it's not just his eyes that inspect me. He places his hands gently on my calf, feeling it like there would be texture to the skin of the inked-on snake. The calluses at the base of his fingers scratch against my flesh, but it's by no means unpleasurable. When his fingers get a little too close to the cuff of the pants, I swing my leg back under the table.

"Any reason behind that?" He asks.

"I wanted to do a dragon at first. Specifically the one from The Hobbit."

"Love that movie."

"The book version," I correct.

Logan shrugs. "What's the difference?"

Aren't guys supposed to be the Lord of the Rings nerds? Or at least, general fantasy nerds?

"The movie version wasn't a dragon," I explain. "It's a wyvern, two feet and wings. Dragons have four feet and wings. Also, the book version is more of a wyrm than the bulky look of dragons the mainstream shows off. It's more snake-like. Long neck body and tail. Would've looked really cool."

The whole time I speak, Logan has this huge, but gentle smile on his face. "You're kinda a nerd," He laughs.

I fall back in my seat, wanting to roll my eyes again as if it were supposed to be an insult, but I know it wasn't. He said it with endearment. Instead, I defend myself saying, "It's one of the most read books ever. You don't have to be a nerd to know that. And besides, I'm a witch. It's mythology, that's like a big part of my history."

"The Hobbit?"

"No, not The Hobbit. Faerie stuff and ancient lore."

Logan finishes off his drink. "So that's what I'm getting into, huh? Should I be expecting any little gnomes to be running around the store soon?"

"Myth can be just as important as actual history. The guy who wrote the Hobbit knew that. There's nothing wrong with having a little fun with it."

"If you say so." He pushes his glass to the edge of the table. As if on cue, Frank comes out of the back.

"All set for the night?" Frank asks.

Before I can speak, Logan reaches over and slides my glass to the edge as well. "One more," he says. "I'm not working tomorrow." Then to me, "Unless something changes."

"Gonna pay this time?"

The more I look into his eyes, the more comfortable I am in this booth. He gives a quick jerk of the head up toward Frank and I'm in.

"We'll see after another round."

Frank takes the empty glasses away and promptly returns with two new ones, and three shots of vodka, his own nightly tradition. "You're my last two of the night. Here's one on me."

We all clink glasses and knock it back. As he leaves, he puts a hand on Logan's shoulder and grips tightly. Logan winces but shows no pain someone with weaker arms would. "Don't fuck around with my girl," he says and exits to the kitchen again.

I bring the new glass up to my lips and sip.

"What the hell was that about?" Logan asks.

"Pretty sure it's my turn for questions."

216

"You can have two, but come on. What the fuck?"

I sigh and put down the glass. "He's protective. An old friend's brother."

"Uh huh…" Logan says, unbelieving.

"My high school friends and I got into shit a lot. He wasn't super cool with it and thought we were the problem, being a bad influence on his sister and stuff like that. Until some shit went down, that I'd prefer to not get into, and saw it was his sister that was the problem. I think he felt guilt or some kind of responsibility to us for letting that shit happen and blaming us, so since then he's always been like a big brother to me. While we all stuck around at least."

"Real bad shit?" He asks before taking another drink. He shivers as he swallows.

"Bad enough. So, my turn. Why were you in the park?"

Another swig of his drink, and I catch up with a swig of my own.

He says, "Remember that girlfriend I had?"

"How could I forget? She's the reason you wiggled your way into my life."

He smirks admittance. "It's been a real awkward week living with her since the break-up."

Oh, don't tell me he's sleeping in the park now.

"Before you ask," he says, reading the look on my face. "Yes, I have somewhere to sleep tonight. I'm not some bum about to give you a sob story so I can crash with you."

"Great, because that wouldn't happen."

"Yeah, I figured. Well, I am still living with her. It's my name on the lease. But I wasn't going to kick her out or anything until she found a new place to live. So I just don't *want* to be home some nights. And tonight seemed as good a night as any to just sit out in the park and clear my head of… obvious things."

"I'm sure she wouldn't be thrilled either if she knew what you saw."

"Yeah, no. I'm keeping that under wraps."

Good, I think to myself.

"And on that note, question number two. Why were you in my store at all tonight?"

He shrugs. "Just trying to catch you at a good time to talk about work-related things. Like, pay, for one."

"At nine at night? Look, you lie, you drink. I'm sure Frank would be more than happy to get you to spill your guts."

Without hesitation, he downs the rest of his drink like it's water.

"Be careful," he warns. "After three drinks I can't help but lie. And I count that shot as a half."

"Funny," I say through a smirk.

Again, I ask, how bad could this hurt?

I follow suit and down the rest of my drink. It burns my throat, but I push through and smack the glass back down on the table. "I have the same rule. So why were you there?"

Logan leans forward, with his bulging arms crossed on the table. The gears of absurdity turn in his head. His eyes wander my exposed arms, chest, and neck, landing on an old, faded verse just under my collarbone. "Some light reading," He says.

I purse my lips, feeling tense all over my body.

"Drink," I tell him.

"That wasn't a lie. But for you..." He slides the glass to the edge of the table and on cue, Frank comes to take the empty glasses away. "You're the boss."

Frank returns once more with two more drinks, and Logan quickly begins to consume his.

"All right! All right!" I laugh, pushing his hand down before he can finish half of it. "Don't ruin the fun early."

"Wouldn't dream of it. Really though, that wasn't a lie."

"Oh, yeah? I may have other lines around here you could read." *All right, Nyx, tone it back a bit.*

Logan chuckles playfully, but, for some fucking reason, doesn't bite. "Actually," he says, "I was looking for that book. You know, the one you wanted me to hide."

I sit up a bit straighter. The movement makes the alcohol in my blood hit my brain like a bat to the head. When was the last time I ate today?

"Why were you looking for that book?"

"One of your friends, that blond girl was looking for it. She caught me outside earlier and asked me if I knew where it was. You were trying to get rid of it, weren't you? She said it was hers and seemed really beat up that she lost it. I just figured it would help everyone. 'Specially cause you seemed pretty spooked about having it around."

"Logan." I slap my hands down on the table a little too hard. "First of all, don't listen to her. That book is evil." I say it sincerely, but the alcohol running through me makes it sound silly. Even Logan cracks a bit, which only makes me smile more. "I'm serious. Stop laughing!" I laugh. "The book issa fucking demon or something."

His smile widens and his face goes red. He's trying so hard not to laugh at me and I can't blame him. I have no idea what my face is saying but I can feel the heat in my cheeks and I can guarantee I look like I've got front-row seats to a comedy show.

"Oooo, terrifying. I'm real scared, Nyx." He takes another drink, and winks.

"You should be," I try to warn, pointing hard at him, and when my hand falls, it falls around my drink. My instincts kick in and I bring it up to my lips.

Through a hard laugh, he says, "How about tomorrow morning, I come by with a priest and we get rid of that thing."

"AAAAAHHHHH…" I breathe in, followed by other strange drunk noises. "I already tried to exorcise it."

"But have you tried the power of Christ?" He eyes sternly. "That'd be my first guess."

I roll my eyes. "I'll stick to my own methods. *Thaaaank* you."

Frank strolls by and takes the glass from my hand.

"Hey wait," I pout. "I wasn't done yet."

"Yeah, you are," He argues. "Come on. I'm closing." Then to Logan, "You picking up the bill, chief?"

Logan reaches for his wallet. "Yeah, yeah, just a sec."

"No!" I shout a little too loud. "Frank, put it on my tab." I then lean in toward Logan and fail to whisper, "This is a business expense. Tax *wriiiiiiite* off. Ha! Seriously, Frank. Bill me."

Both of them having ignored me, Frank takes his card.

"If you remember this in the morning, you can add it to the paycheck I'm never gonna get."

"You've still gotta earn that, darling." Then, in a teasing voice I already regret, "You've still gotta get on my good side."

Logan downs the rest of his drink. "Which side is that? Ivy or snake?"

I bite the inside of my lip. "Between them."

He takes a deep breath in, his muscular chest expanding. But his poker face gives nothing else away. "I think your friend was right. It's time to take you home."

Frank returns one last time with the check and Logan's card.

Logan puts his wallet away, and is the first to rise, helping me out of the booth.

Through my stumbling, I hear Frank whisper to Logan, "Don't try anything."

This time, Logan puts his big hand on Frank's shoulder. When they stand next to each other, all of Frank's earlier intimidation is diminished. Logan says back to him, "Wouldn't dream of it." No squeeze like Frank did, just a tap on the shoulder, and his attention returns to me. "Up we go, come on, boss."

He pulls me up and the blood rush sends everything black for a second.

"You okay?" He asks.

I nod clumsily while the words 'yes, completely,' try to find their way past my lips.

"Can you walk?"

I shake my head, nod, and shake and nod. "I can try."

We make it five feet out the door before my legs decide it's time for bed, and I find myself thrown over his right shoulder.

"Hey!" I shout. "You can't do this!"

"How else are you gonna get home?" His voice is so stern, so clear, like he didn't even drink anything.

"I. Will. WALK! I will *not* be carried like this!"

A hand hits my ass.

I scream the loudest laugh I've laughed in years. "What was that?"

"You're being a brat," He says calmly like it's no big deal he just touched - no, slapped! - my butt!

"*You're* being a brat!" I say, trying to reach down and hit his ass in return, but my arms won't reach. "That's it! You're fired!"

"That's fine. As long as you get home in one piece."

"I'm serious! You're not coming in tomorrow!" I keep slapping away at his back.

"That's a shame. I just got a bunch of new tight shirts so you can keep staring."

Quietly, curiously I ask, "You did?"

He laughs, "I fuckin' knew you were staring."

We travel a few feet in silence until I think to say, "Dress code! After tonight, we're having a dress code."

"Isn't your dress code nothing at all?"

"Ohhhh... I hate you."

"Keys," he says.

"Left pocket," I respond without thinking.

He reaches over my ass and I feel his fingers dig around in my pocket. Moments later, my front door opens.

"Okay, put me down here."

But he keeps going. "We both know you're not walking up those stairs."

We cross into the covenstead, and an image flashes through my mind of him throwing me down on the table, just as I was earlier and tearing my clothes off. We pass through, and he's carrying me up the stairs, through the door, and we're together again in my apartment.

My heart races with every step we take closer to the bed. Every time his foot hits the floor I hear a *THUD* in my chest. He lifts me from his shoulder, and I fall into my bed.

Logan stands over me, breathing heavily. His chest rises and falls. The veins in his arms pop. I couldn't have been that heavy for him. It must be something else.

"Congrats, Logan. You've taken me to bed."

He smirks but doesn't move.

I scoot back in the bed, letting my legs spread a few inches apart. I try to think of something seductive to say, but nothing comes to mind in time for Logan to speak, and it's not what I wanted to hear.

"Goodnight, Nyx," he says.

My legs fall back together. Dejected, I ask, "What?"

Logan crosses the apartment to the kitchen, grabs a cup from one of the cabinets, and fills it up with water from the sink.

When he returns, he says, "Thanks for tonight. The last hour or so, I mean. I'm glad we could get everything worked out and behind us." He hands me the glass of water. "You might wanna start drinking. You're gonna feel like shit tomorrow and I can't run the place on my own. I'd rather have you around."

I take the cup but don't drink from it. "You're leaving? Is this because of Frank?"

He smirks again and raises his right hand. "Hand to God. Remember, I wasn't trying anything. Just wanted to be a friend tonight. Maybe tomorrow you can fill me in on why *you* were in the park, huh?"

I bite the inside of my lip. Is he actually leaving me now? Isn't this what he was getting at this whole time? All that flirting? Was it even flirting at all or was that just... me?

"Yeah... yeah, okay." I quietly agree.

"I'll see you tomorrow, Nyx."

"8:30?"

"You got it, boss."

23. The Sight

Logan arrives at 8:30 sharp. Today, with two cups of coffee. He walks in casually, but as if someone smudged him when he woke up this morning, cleansing him of all of his energy. Willow greets him all the same, and when she does, a little life returns to his eyes.

"Good morning, Logan," I strain to say through a killer hangover. I should have drank more of that water before going to bed. Or, at least *tried* to stay up a little longer to let my liver do its job.

"Hey there, Wednesday Addams. You look the part now today more than ever. Except… this." He points to his hair and I know exactly what he's talking about.

Instead of hydrating as I should have, I impulsively and hastily dyed the right side of my hair white. Why? Not even I know. It just happened. Didn't even know I had white dye. Or any dye, for that matter. It's just how I woke up. At least I cleaned up afterward and didn't leave a mess.

"I guess it's not just lying I start doing after three drinks."

"Guess not. Here," He hands me one of the coffee cups.

"It's just black. I didn't know if you wanted any spit in it or not."

I accept the coffee and hold it in both hands, smelling the brew. It does a little to clear my head, just taking in the smell. "Thanks."

"Don't mention it." He takes a sip from his own, and for a moment, no words pass between us. Eventually, he puts his cup down on the counter and gets to work around the store, first making his way to the clothing rack to rearrange and take inventory.

I keep my head down, counting the cash in the drawer to make sure the baseline is right.

We both go from one task to the next in almost complete silence. Willow darts her little head back and forth the whole time from me to him, waiting for someone to break the horrible monotony.

Logan is the first to crack. At the sound of his intake before he speaks, my heart leaps and I spin around, but what comes out isn't any revelation. "It looks like we're low on these figurines. Any in the back I can grab?"

I bite the inside of my lip. "Yeah! I mean, yes. Do you need me to show you where they are?"

"No," he says politely. "I'm sure I can find them." He exits to the storage room on the opposite side of the counter from the covenstead.

Part of me says I should follow him. Just in case he moves something around and leaves it in the wrong place, throwing off the whole organization, of course. Or… just to be in there… just in case.

He comes out a few moments later and holds up a box of little stone fairies sitting on mushrooms. They're the most adorable

226

decorations. I've kept one or five for myself upstairs. "Found 'em," He says.

We're just a few minutes to opening.

"Hey, Logan…"

He keeps taking figurines out of the box to put on the shelf but turns his eyes toward me. "Yeah?"

I don't know. What did I need him for, again? I look at the shelf next to me. Oil diffusers.

"Oil diffusers. Can you grab a few more?"

His eyes drift to the shelf. "Looks like it's pretty stocked up."

Fuck. "I have a feeling it's going to be a good day for them."

Logan cracks a smirk. "Sixth sense kicking in?"

"Sure. Yeah. Just a hunch." It's not convincing, but he doesn't argue.

Follow him. Follow him in!

My feet stay frozen to the ground, even as I lean forward. Willow, on the counter, tilts her head down at me judgingly. "Fuck off," I whisper to her. Just as one foot breaks free from paralysis, Logan returns with a small cardboard box.

"Didn't know which people will be rushing in for, so I just got a bunch of them."

"Thanks," I say, taking the box. My fingers graze his in the exchange.

What all happened last night? Did I say something I don't remember? Was it too much? The wrong thing? Did I piss him off? I refuse to fall into this misunderstanding trope.

227

A minute until opening.

I should have fired him.

"Logan," I say again just as he returns to stocking the figurines.

"Yeah?"

The back of my lip is almost bleeding from how hard I'm biting it. I said something strong last night over drinks. Something about the tattoos on my legs. Something definitely too flirty. Maybe it pushed him away. I mean, he didn't stay the night...

"I just..." *Come on, get it out!*

He stops what he's doing, and steps a little closer. I was wrong about the smudging. His energy is strong. Intense. It's the warmth in the store. With every step toward me, it gets hotter.

"What can I do for you, Nyx?" The way he says it, so much softness in his voice, yet so boldly.

The hangover pounds against my skull.

My throat tightens up.

"I just... I think I need a smoke." I rush past him and pull my cabriole from the inside of my robe. Willow rushes out behind me, slipping through the door as it closes.

I light the cigarette when I sit down in my chair in front of the store window, and take one long drag. It eases the pounding in my head, but not by much.

How did this happen?

You've never been this hung up or petrified around anyone before. Especially for a guy? This is ridiculous!

Someone walks by and waves with a "Good morning, Nyx!"

I raise the cabriole in a wave back, but my mind is too far away to say anything.

If only he'd say something to let me know where his own mind is at. Or even if he refuses to, for once I'd appreciate his crass humor, a dirty joke, a flirt for the sake of reaction. He can joke about me being a devil worshiper to anyone who walks in for all I care, just as long as things go back to normal!

Willow hops up into my lap and paws at my chest.

"Quit it, Willow." I give her a little push, but she stays fast and keeps pawing.

It wouldn't be so annoying if it was Logan touching my breasts like that.

Get a fucking *GRIP*, girl!

But that's just what I need right now, isn't it? I was supposed to get fucked good last night, but the only pounding I got is from too much whiskey. And that's probably why Logan didn't stick around, I was a slobbering drunk mess.

I just need to get fucked. That's why I'm being so weird today. I'm deprived. It's not Logan. I'm not into him like that. He's just an objectively attractive man and I'm too fucking horny at the moment. All I need is a release.

He could give you that release.

"Logan, can you help me get something out of the storage closet... yeah, it's just up there..." And he stands tall above you, trapping you two together where no one can see anything. He could do anything he wanted to you, so you might as well get on your knees...

Nope!

229

Stop!

Not happening.

I remove the cigarette from the cabriole and smush it on the ground. I need a distraction, not release. I need to stay focused on work and not let my mind wander.

Without making any form of contact with Logan, I trudge back into the store, through to the back room (where *nothing funny* is going to happen) and grab a blackboard sign, then carry it back outside. I write on it an announcement that we will be open for tarot readings today and walk-in appointments for all your witchy needs. I'll hopefully be occupied in the covenstead, and Logan will stay on the floor.

For good measure, I send Jade a text, letting her know how I'm operating today.

> *-It'll be a good chance to get some hands on experience with spell casting and potions, if that is to come up.*

She responds almost immediately.

> *-I'll be over as soon as I can!*

Good girl. That will be a big help today, not being around someone who radiates strong sexual energy.

When I enter the store again, it feels almost impossible to ignore Logan further, just out of courtesy.

"Will you be okay on your own in here today?"

Logan's sitting behind the counter, coffee cup in hand. He looks around the room, then back to me, and says, "Wouldn't mind having you around, but I'll manage." His hazel eyes threaten to pull me closer; into his arms, onto his lap, my mouth on his.

I hold back a smile by biting the inside of my lip.

"Well... good," I say, and rush into the covenstead.

You're just horny, it's not him, I remind myself.

And then there in front of me is another reminder of last night. The covenstead is still set up for lovemaking. And it was Logan who showed up instead of Damien.

On the night of a new moon, Logan was here with me. And a part of me wanted him.

A part of me still does.

One part of me really wants him, is already wet at the thought.

I send one more text out:

> *-Don't let anyone in the covenstead.*

...then rush upstairs, lock the door, throw myself onto my bed, and hike up my dress. I press my phone to my clit just as Logan texts back, and the one quick vibration makes me quake.

There's no time to find my wand, so I toss my phone to

the end of the bed, turn over to bury my face in my pillow, and use my fingers, sliding them deep into myself, picturing Logan on top of me. I see us in the covenstead, surrounded by candles, my legs wrapped around his neck as he thrusts, slamming his body against mine, rocking the table.

My eyes roll in my head as I play with my clit, imagining his tongue caressing it, his mouth sucking on it, his teeth nibbling at it. I want him to give me that good pain, forcing my legs wide apart so he can fuck me however he wants. I want his hands around my throat while he sucks on my fingers. I want him to fuck me from behind, pulling me up from my hair. I don't want to be able to breathe because I can't catch my breath the way he ravages me.

Like a spring I cum, spraying the bedsheets with my juices, and my body shudders.

My legs spasm as another stream of cum sprays out. I struggle to catch my breath with my face pressed into the pillow.

I fucking needed that. This should make things easier.

After a few moments of enjoying post-orgasm bliss, I struggle out of bed and fix myself. I can't go back downstairs looking like I just had the most intense orgasm I've had in months, maybe years. And the bedsheets. The bedsheets have to change before Logan comes back in here.

Not that I'd invite him. Just… he keeps finding his way in here.

Jade is waiting for me downstairs when I return to the covenstead, reclining, but not lying, in the cushions against the back wall. She looks like she was expecting her girl Jenna to find her there, the way her hand plays with the belt around her green romper.

"Hey," I breathe out, exhausted. I'm still in the process of recovering from my private time.

"Hey," she smiles back. "Everything all right?"

"Yes darling," I cross the room wiping sweat from my brow and sit by her head.

Jade scoots in and puts her head on my arm, so I run a hand through her hair.

"Something you wanted to tell me?" She asks.

I take a deep breath in, and let it out slowly. Should I tell her about Logan, what happened last night? I suppose, who else would I open up to?

"I wasn't planning on it, but something did happen. And I just don't know what to do about it."

Jade adjusts herself and sits up straight. "Do you need anything from me? You seem stressed, maybe I could give you a back rub this time." As she says it she reaches for the oil.

Odd of her to offer, but, if she feels she owes me, "Thank you, darling. But let's take a rain check on that. I'm trying to get appointments today so you can learn. Witchcraft isn't all about massages."

She smirks in defeat. "No, I know. But it was nice."

I brush her soft cheek. "Another time. Trust me, I'll hold you to it."

"So, what happened then?" She asks, gingerly putting the oil back.

I explain to her in detail what happened last night; the

background with Damien, the preparation I did all day, how I set the room up, and how Damien never showed up. I leave out the part about Logan and blame Willow for ruining the atmosphere. Now, with the time that's passed, it's not as aggravating in my memory as it was in the moment. And to seal my feelings about it, Jade asks, "Have you told your... your boyfriend?" The word comes out with a hint of disgust which I don't blame her for.

"No!" I scoff. I don't mention he still hasn't texted or called me back. Instead, I fill in the rest of the truth. "We're done. I told him if he didn't show then we were over, and he never showed."

"Well, what happened?" She asks eagerly. "Was he ignoring you? Did he call? Was he stuck somewhere or..." Her voice lowers as if she's about to say something dirty. "Was he cheating on you?"

I wave away the comment. "It doesn't matter. Honestly, I could not care less. Damien blew it, and I've already moved on. I'm free as a witch should be, and I plan to enjoy my freedom."

Jade shuffles giddily. "Good," she says promptly with a grin. "You deserve that."

"Oh, thank you, darling." I lean over and give her a kiss on her blushing cheek.

"So..." she begins again. "Is there anything you want? To do, I mean. Now that you're 'free.'"

It's like she's reading my mind. I tilt my head in and purr, "Do you have a little of the Sight in you?"

"Hm..." She looks up at the ceiling with a faux-guilty lip bite. "You might be a little easy to read."

"What do you see? In here." I tap the side of my head.

If she truly has the Sight, that could provide an incredible asset to figure out the book situation. And a wonderful sister to have.

"I think," She pauses and studies my face, my hair. "I think you've got someone on your mind. And it's driving you crazy."

"Go on." I finger a lock of hair out of her face and behind her ear. What she said isn't a clear indication of the Sight, but it's a start.

"And," she licks her lips. "I think that you're happy about your ex not showing up because you wanted this other person anyway."

My heart begins to beat faster again. "And what do you think this other person wants?"

She puts a hand on my cheek. The Sight is strongest when paired with physical touch, so I don't push her away. "I think this person has been craving you since the moment you met."

My heart could leap from my chest. *Please, please let this gift be real.*

I ask her, "And what do you think I should do about it?"

"What you told me already. Take what you want." The words come out so softly as though they're drifting on a cloud, and her eyelids hang low in concentration. What she says, bringing my thoughts out into the open feels so relieving, I could kiss her out of gratitude!

Just then, light floods the room. We both pull away from each other and spin around to face the curtain. A couple stands across from us, and Logan calls in from behind the curtain, "They're here for a tarot reading."

Jade goes pale for some reason, but I jump up and take their hands to welcome them in. "Good morning, hi, welcome. Please, take a seat. I'll be right with you."

Logan lets go of the curtain when they pass through, but I throw my head out between the slits.

"Hey!" I whisper-shout to Logan's back. He pivots and looks at me with an expressionless face.

I bite the inside of my lip, unsure what to say.

"Anything I can help with, boss?" He asks politely.

I shake my head in tiny jerking movements. "No. Nothing."

"Alright. Well, if you need anything."

"No, I… I just wanted to say…"

He waits a moment, hand resting on the counter.

"I'm glad you're here today."

Logan finally smiles back at me. "Glad to be here with you."

24. Letting Jade In

Throughout the rest of the day until closing and into the week, Jade nearly becomes a full-time employee, joining me in my appointments with clients. She picks up quite quickly on simple things like tarot and palm reading, although when given the chance to display her clairvoyance, she often pulls back. And while with each day she understands the theory of spellcasting better and better, Jade takes a backseat to the practice. And through much of it, she comes off distracted in the queerest way.

As we finish up a tea session and prayer with one client, someone I was delighted to run into as I haven't seen them since high school, I confront Jade. "Are you feeling all right?" I ask her.

"Fine," she acknowledges, though it's obvious something's eating at her.

"There's an energy in the room, isn't there?"

She lifts her head the smallest bit without looking at me. "There must be," she says dismissively.

"I feel it too," I tell her, glancing around the walls. "It's that book. It's still in here somewhere. Gnawing at us."

"The one Maria brought?"

"Yes, darling."

"Do you think…" she asks gingerly, fixing herself in her chair. "Do you think I'm ready for it now? You know, I get it a lot more. I might be able to help cleanse it."

"I don't think we're there quite yet. I'm impressed with how far you've come so quickly, but Jade, I really must stress this. That thing is dangerous. And until your mind is completely cleared of distractions, I worry of the harm it could do to both of us."

With an almost antagonistic tone, she says, "It's only a book. What's the worst that could happen?"

I take a deep breath. The ice of the spirit seeps into the room.

"I don't want to talk about it here," I whisper to her.

Losing all hostility, she eagerly asks, "Should we go upstairs?"

"No, it's a lovely day outside. Let's not waste it." I take her hand and bade, "Come. The park. We can talk there."

Her smile dampens to a pout.

"Oh, darling, come on," I encourage. "We've spent all week cooped up inside. Some sun would do us both good."

"What about your pool?" she offers.

It throws me off at first, thinking of a literal pool. "Oh! Yes, right," I laugh. "Not yet. I don't know if I'm ready to share that place yet."

"Not even with me." Her chest tenses.

238

"Jade, darling, you're the very first person I would bring there. But just not right now."

She playfully rolls her eyes. "Okay, but one of these days I *do* want to see it."

I take both of her hands in mine. "And you will. I promise. Now come." We pass through the curtain to the main floor.

Logan sits behind the counter wearing a big black pointy witch's hat like something out of an old movie.

"Where'd you find that?" I ask.

"Found it in an old chest with a broom and a vial labeled 'eye of newt,'" he snaps back.

Jade leans in and whispers, "Do you actually use that stuff?"

I avoid the question and tease Logan, "You know what happened to the last person who worked here?"

"What's that?"

"She's sitting on your lap."

Logan looks down at Willow, who's nuzzled quite comfortably in his lap.

"So be careful," I warn him. "I could always use another cat."

"Doesn't Willow sleep in your bed with you?" He says without missing a beat and gives me a wink.

"Only after she got fixed."

Both Willow and Logan squirm at the comment. Yet, he still has more to say. "I think I'd still take my chances."

* * *

"When I tell you that book is evil, I don't mean the words on the page or the paper that binds it," I warn Jade between drags of a cigarette.

She sits next to me on a park bench. The summer wind blows by us, carrying the smell of the mineral-heavy spring water Saratoga Springs is well known for. Jade inhales a cigarette of her own and stifles a cough.

"Then what can be so bad about it?" She struggles to ask.

I flick the ash from the end of my cigarette on the cabriole and Jade mimics. "You know you don't have to smoke. That's not a part of all this, it's just a bad habit."

She takes another drag, this one much smoother.

So, I continue. "Did you ever meet Maria?"

"Maybe," she says, blowing out a small cloud of smoke.

"She brought it to me. And one thing I will never teach you is black magic, or anything Satanic. You don't seem like that kind of girl, so I'm not worried about that with you. But it's a terrible thing to be involved with. That alone made me want to keep her from that book. But more than that, I felt something with it. Something horrible, something evil. A spirit that had attached itself to the book. And when I tried to cleanse it..." my heart begins to race at the memory of that day. "Spirits like that don't wish to be cleansed. I believe it has a purpose, one involving Maria.

"I did everything in my power to clear the spirit and it... it attacked me."

On the word 'attacked,' Jade coughs again. "What the hell does that mean? How?"

240

"It was like…" Another memory flashes. One from just after high school. An evening late one night with Angie and Piper. My throat tightens. "I felt like it was forcing itself on me. Like ice-cold hands were touching me and…" I think of the basement. The black candles burning. "It was inside me."

I take a long, slow drag as the wind picks up again.

"And it knew me so well. It got in my head and made me forget what I was doing. Made me think I wanted it. It played with my emotions, making me let it in, preventing me from fighting back."

"Holy shit, Nyx…"

"Yeah," I try to laugh. "Holy shit." Another drag.

"What is that?" Jade has all but forgotten about the cigarette lightly burning between her fingers.

"I know you're with me on this but, you'll probably still laugh. Did you grow up religious at all?"

She shakes her head. "Not really. My mom was Jewish by birth, I think. But my dad never talked about religion. I think the closest I ever got to religion was that movie 'Prince of Egypt.' Why would I laugh at something like that though? I mean, what happened."

This is going to sound so fucking ridiculous. "Do you know what an incubus is?"

"That's like a… a sex demon right?"

"Yep." I nod, unable to look up from the grass. "Preys on women. Usually in their sleep. But sometimes, they're summoned."

"Nyx," she pauses. "Did this thing… were you…?"

"The point is," I say quickly. "I don't want that happening to you. Or Maria. Or anyone ever again."

"And you don't think I can handle that?" There's a trace amount of pain in her voice, but I believe even she doubts herself.

"*I* can't even handle it," I tell her. "But I have to. And I didn't want to bring you into this, but I need help. I tried an old friend, but she refused. I can't even say I blame her."

The cigarette burns out and I flick it from the cabriole, stamping it out on the ground. Jade hands me hers, only half-smoked. I take the stick and put the butt between my lips, tasting her chapstick. "Thanks."

"How am I supposed to help?" Jade asks.

"I haven't the slightest clue yet. I don't even mean to force you into this. It's only if you want to help, and even then, not for a while. Not until you're ready."

"Who says I'm not right now?"

I scoff, but not impolitely and I hope she knows that. "Do you think you are? Honestly?"

"Well... I... For you, I mean. I'd give it a try."

I wrap my arm around her and pull her in, laying my cheek on her soft hair. "Thank you, Jade."

We let the moment linger until she accepts. "I guess you're right though. I had no idea what I was doing this week. I probably wouldn't be much help anyway."

"Not yet," I agree. "But you're on your way. You're a beautiful woman with a beautiful heart. Even if you were ready now though, I'd warrant we wait. The moon isn't right anymore. The best time for spells such as the one we need just passed. It'd be another month before the time is right."

"What do you mean?"

"The waxing, just after a new moon. That's when we should do it, and I missed it. I suppose I, too, was a little distracted."

She gives me a look of confusion and I add, "Don't pretend with me, darling. It's all over your face every day. Something is still eating at you. Is Jenna a fair guess?"

"I think the Sight as you call it is my thing," she rebukes to my glee.

"Oh?"

Jade pulls herself up, out of my arms. "We chalked that night up to alcohol and moved on. Me especially."

"You don't say."

"Why are you smiling?" She laughs.

I cover my mouth. "I'm sorry, that's rude of me."

"You never liked her, did you?" Jade teases.

I shrug. "I'm a very good judge of character."

"And very modest."

"In some areas. I know I'm hot though."

Jade eyes me up and down and we both laugh at my false pride. Well, maybe not entirely false.

She then adds, "I'd go for you."

"Who could blame you?" I say sarcastically and laugh a little louder, and she laughs a little quieter.

I finish off the rest of the cigarette without further discussion between us, only the hushed breeze and the far-off screams of children on the old carousel in the park. It feels a bit strange, the revelations I have just shared with her and the book still lingering in some unknown corner of my covenstead, yet here we are on a peaceful, vibrant day as if nothing were wrong in the world. And more than that, my apprentice has become much more of a sister in this last week. Not since Nissa have I been able to sit in the park doing nothing with a friend. It's almost like high school again, escaping the building during lunch to walk down here to the stone benches under the trees. Back when my skin was unblemished by ink and the notion of witchcraft was a playful way to stand out rather than a lifestyle. Back when the ice hadn't yet left its burn. When the idea of an offering wasn't an evil thing yet.

25. Letting Logan In

He's still wearing the pointy hat while we close up the store. Jade sits on the countertop watching us, laughing at all of his silly jokes. Grabbing a wand off of one of the bottom shelves, he asks, "What's the point of doing manual labor when you've had these all along?" With a hard flick of the arm and wrist, he points to the broom and dustpan propped up behind the counter and says, "Abracadabra, clean this shit up!"

Jade covers her mouth to laugh, but I hold back my smile.

"This thing must be defective," Logan says, feigning dismay.

I drop what I'm doing, and take the wand from his hand. "It's because you're not doing it right. It's a graceful swish. You're not throwing a baseball." I gently swish the wand and the broom tumbles.

Both Logan and Jade's jaws drop in astonished surprise.

"How did you do that?" Logan asks in a way in which I can't tell if it's real amazement or not.

I don't answer verbally, just give a small shrug and a wink, and hand the wand back.

But answering the question, and ruining my moment, Willow jumps up from behind the counter, revealing herself as responsible for knocking into the broom.

"Cute," Logan teases.

"I bet she could do it for real," Jade chimes in.

"Only if you close your eyes and turn around," Logan argues, keeping his gaze on me. "She can't do it when anyone's watching."

"Logan, darling, you should know better," I say with a hint of sultriness. "It worked last time."

His face remains still, but I can see his hand grip tighter around the wand. A vein bulges from his forearm. I can already picture that strong hand on my throat.

"What do you mean?" Jade asks, breaking me from my daydream.

"Nothing," Logan and I say at the same time.

He carries on, though. "We all know she likes to show off though, right?"

I mouth the word *don't* while struggling not to blush or laugh at him.

Logan puts the wand back down where it belongs, then hops over the counter to grab the broom. As he does, he says, "By the way, you got any more appointments tonight? Deciding if I should stop by at some point. Just in case."

I bite my lip hard to prevent myself from either yelling at him or giving in to the flirting.

Jade once again reinserts herself. "I feel like I'm missing

something here. Did something happen this week I don't know about?"

I spin and try to forget Logan is there for the moment. "If one day you ever have a place like this, never let a guy like him work there."

"Where'd all the entertainment come from, then?" She asks.

"I second that," Logan adds. "It'd be real dry around here without me."

Thank God Jade doesn't pick up on the meaning. Hopefully the look on my face says "annoyance" not "attraction."

"I think that's only because there'd be no one here to mop. Care to do that after you sweep, Logan?"

He moves up from behind the counter, pushing a small dirt hill with the broom. "I will if you ask nicely. But what about your other employee? She at least getting paid to sit around?"

Before I can speak, Jade hops off the counter and jokes to me, "I thought you said he was working as an unpaid intern."

"That's not a terrible idea, darling."

Logan rolls his eyes.

"I gotta get going anyway," Jade says, her energy much lower as the words come out. "I've still got a lot of packing to do for move-in." I'd totally forgotten she'd be moving into her college dorm in the next few weeks. At least she'd still be just down the road.

I give her a kiss on the cheek. "Of course. Don't worry about coming in this weekend. Logan and I will be able to handle ourselves. But here," I retrieve a spare key from my pocket. "Monday night work with you?"

The key drops into her open hand. "Monday night," she agrees.

"Good girl."

Once she's gone, it's only Logan and I left alone in the room. He continues sweeping, but he takes his time with it as if he's not really paying attention.

I watch him while he works, the way his arms flex with each swish of the broom. When he catches my glance, he asks, "Something I can help with?"

It snaps me out of my daze. "No, just… keep working." And an idea pops into my head. "When you're done with the floor, see me in the covenstead. We'll talk about payment," I say as I slowly make my way over to the curtain.

Logan's smile tugs to the right, revealing a handsome dimple. "You really think that's a good idea, Nyx?" He stops sweeping and leans on the broom, watching me pull back the curtain. "How do I know you're not gonna do anything to me in there?"

"Have you been reading my mind?" I tease.

"Just as long as I come out in one piece."

"Maybe you won't come out at all. Guess you'll just have to find out," I say, letting the curtain fall between us.

As it does, I hear him begin sweeping again, now with a faster pace. He moves briskly through the aisles at first, then slows down until he's sweeping as lazily as when Jade left. What is he up to? I pull back the curtain the littlest bit, so I can only barely see through it. He's sweeping all right, over by the door, with a devilish grin across his face.

He's making me wait, isn't he?

Fine. He's only missing out.

If he's going to take his time, at least I have a little extra to clean up this place. I clear the tarot cards from the table, light some candles, fluff the pillows in the back, make myself look a little more presentable, adjust my breasts to pop a little more in my dress and fix my hair. Fuck, I wish there was a mirror in here.

Soon enough there's a knock on the wall next to the curtain.

"Just a moment!" I shout. I know I invited him in, but I feel caught off guard. Silently, I hop over to the pillows and lie down as Jade did earlier in the week, then pull my tits up just a bit more so my nipples are almost about to pop out.

"Come in, Logan," I say just above a whisper.

The curtain pulls back, but the fucking table is in between us.

"Nyx? Where are you?" He asks.

"Over here…"

He slowly makes his way around the table until we lock eyes again. The image of him standing over me like that, and I so ready to be taken. His arms bulge in his shirt. He could do whatever he wanted to me right now.

"Isn't it time I compensated you for your hard work?" I can't believe the sultry tone I use. I'm not sure if I ever talked like this with Damien.

Logan crosses his thick arms. "And this is how you want to pay me?"

I trace a finger up the vines inked on my leg, and pull back the hem of my dress. "Only if you think it's fair. If this is what you want."

He smirks and runs a steady hand through his hair. But all his cool is betrayed by the slowly extending, massive bulge in his pants.

"And here I thought we were gonna start having a professional relationship," Logan says.

"We can keep it professional out there… if you can resist." I begin to untie the belt around my dress.

"I don't know if I'm the one we need to worry about."

"Who's worried?" I sit up straight, and let the dress fall off my shoulders, baring it all for his hungry eyes. His cock swells up stiff, bigger than I've ever seen in my life.

"Nyx…"

I rise, and step provocatively around the table toward him, letting a finger slide along the wood. "Don't tell me now that this isn't why you wanted to be here."

There are only inches between us, my breasts practically pressed against his abdomen. When his chest rises with bated breath, it almost touches my upturned chin. I gaze up at him with wanting eyes and put my hands on his stomach, slowly lowering them down to his groin.

"You presume a lot," he says, faltering backward. There's still some of that teasing, flirtatious tone, but there's some coldness to it. He backs away toward the curtain, and in my shock at the rejection, I stumble back against the table.

"Wh- what do you mean?" I rush to collect myself and throw my dress back up onto my shoulders. "You've been flirting this whole time!"

Logan laughs, "Sorry if I took it too far, but I told you," he pulls open the curtain. "I don't go for girls that are already taken."

"I-..." I never told him. I gave Damien one last chance, and though I hated myself for it when he never showed up, I had to stick with it. But Logan never knew. I never told him.

He begins to step through the curtain and I shout, "Wait!"

He stops.

"I'm not. It's over with Damien. It's been over for a while."

Logan looks at me with disbelieving eyes. "You serious?"

I nod, biting the inside of my lip. The dress begins to slip again.

It takes a moment to process that he's already on top of me. My dress has been torn off and his hands are on my throat, pulling me into his lips. My hands grab his cheeks and our tongues collide, feeling each other, twisting around each other. His tongue caresses the back of my teeth and I bite down gently, keeping him where he belongs. At one point he almost pulls back, but I bite down harder by instinct, and we both taste a drop of blood. But he doesn't fight it. He only attacks harder, lifting me up and putting me on the table so my legs dangle.

Finally, he's able to free himself. "You're right," he says. "I have been wanting this."

And I want him. I want to sit on his cock and ride him until I can't feel my legs.

He grabs my waist and pulls in closer, and I wrap my legs around him. Even through his jeans, I can feel his rock-hard cock pressing against my groin. He rubs against me and I'm soaked. My juices leave a wet spot on his pants.

Just by grinding against me, I feel like I'm about to come.

Then he backs away, and as he's mentally controlling me, I slide off the table and fall to my knees. "I never do this," I tell him, but not to deter his intentions.

"You will for me," he says, and I'm under his spell.

My mouth opens wide.

Logan unzips his pants. His cock falls out onto my lips.

Never before have I wanted to taste it so bad, but a compulsion comes over me and I wrap my lips around him. All I want is to please him.

I spit on him, and Logan grabs me by my hair and pulls me in. His thick cock thrusts into my mouth, filling me entirely. Tears well up in my eyes but I want more, and I can only take so much. I use both hands to stroke the base, but it's still not enough. At this angle though, it's all I can do.

I push off, giving him a few more strokes, then say, "This will be better," and mount the table again, laying on my back and letting my head hang over the edge, sticking out my tongue. Logan puts his hands on my throat and thrusts in again. I can't breathe but I love satisfying him. In and out, he goes deeper than before, fucking my throat.

I want to please him. I want him to know I'm someone he'll never find again. I grab his ass and force him in deeper.

Logan moans with pleasure. He fucks my throat harder and faster.

I can barely control myself. All I feel is his cock in my mouth and throat but I want to find new ways to please him. My fingers trace down his ass and find their way around his hole. As he fucks my mouth, I slip a finger into him and hear him growl in ecstasy. I think I just found a new kink of his.

"Holy fuck, Nyx," He groans like he's about to finish.

Before I know it, he's pulled out of my mouth and turned me around on the table. My legs dangle. He spreads me open wide.

I wait with heated anticipation as he takes off his shirt. His chiseled body glistens with sweat. My legs shudder with want while my lips pulse with need.

His hands grip my waist. Logan runs his cock against my folds, teasing me.

"Please, just fucking do it," I beg.

One hand shoots up to my face. Two of his fingers enter my mouth.

"I like it when you beg," He says.

My eyes widen with pain and pleasure as his cock tears me open. With each thrust, I come a little more. My eyes roll in my head and I hear him moan in pleasure at the sight of me giving in completely to the delight he gives.

And it becomes too much. Too much in the best way possible.

"Faster," I breathe out, begging.

He grabs me by the waist and does as I ask. My legs tighten around him. It's building up with each thrust. His fingers tighten, digging into me. His cock pounds against my insides, the veins massaging me just right. Every movement is so perfect. The climax builds and builds and builds until I scream, and squirt like no man has ever made me, drenching him in my juices.

My legs go limp, and he backs away.

When I come to, I see him looking at the mess I made. He's dripping wet, with his cock hanging out over his soaked pants.

"I'm sorry," I say. "That hasn't happened in a while."

"Sorry?" He asks.

Logan gives me an evil grin and I bite my lip hard.

He closes the distance between us again and turns me around, bending me over the table. I squeal with delight.

Saliva drips down on my ass. Barely a moment later, I'm enthralled by the feeling of his thick cock in my asshole. The pain is better than anything I've felt enter me in my entire fucking life. Each thrust feels like it's going to rip me in two but I crave more. Harder, faster, deeper. I want all of him.

Logan grabs my hair and pulls me against him. His chest against my back, his hand on my breast, his teeth on my neck, I crave it all. Even when his hand moves from my breast down my stomach, I miss the touch of him playing with my nipples, but I'm impatient for him to rub my clit. I need every sensation all at once. I need to be overstimulated. I need every ounce of him. He rubs my clit like it's the only thing he's ever lived for and within seconds I'm about to squirt again. I scream as some of it gets on Logan's cock, dripping down both of our legs.

He pulls out, turns me around and I fall on the table. I look at Logan standing over me, with his perfectly defined body.

Logan forces my legs apart and goes down to pleasure me with his tongue, sucking up my cum. I grip his hair, trying to guide his movements, but he knows exactly what I need. His tongue flicks my lips just right and I come again in his face. A wave of embarrassment comes over me, but the look in his eyes tells me he loves it. He keeps going, adding his fingers into play.

We move from the table to the wall, to the pillows, swapping out who gets eaten out, and which hole he uses. When he fucks my pussy, I want to taste myself on his cock. When he's in my mouth, I want him filling pussy. Even when I'm sore, I don't want him to finish yet. I don't want this to end.

But as I ride him, grind on him while he reaches up to play with my tits, I can see it on his face that he's struggling to keep it in.

"Come for me," I ask of him.

Logan leans up and I fall onto my back. His sweat drips onto me. He thrusts harder again, then pulls out and groans as he comes. His seed shoots out across my stomach, my chest, and onto my chin.

His body goes weak (I didn't know that was possible for him), and he falls back onto the pillows.

My heart races. I can barely breathe. All I can think is, *I wonder how he tastes,* and lick the cum from my chin.

Just as good as I'd hoped.

26. Let's Keep this Professional

I watch Logan re-dress while I'm totally paralyzed, laying on the pillows. Fuck, I could really go for a cigarette right now. My entire body shivers, and even though I can't move of my own accord, I want to go again.

Logan breaks my heart putting his shirt back on.

"Headed out already?" I ask him.

"I'm sorry, Nyx," He says with a coy grin. "My boss is a real hardass, don't wanna be late for work in the morning."

"Oh yeah? What do you think she'll do to you if you're late?"

He shoots me a challenging glare. "We'll just have to see, won't we?"

I pull up a nearby blanket to cover my legs. It's not cold in the room. The heat from our bodies still lingers with the musk of passionate fucking and exchanged fluids. I just want to enjoy the comfort of the blanket, and it's a good little tease for Logan. "Being late means less of this," I warn.

"So you had more in mind?" He begins to lift his shirt back up, revealing the lower half of his abs.

"Darling, I wish I could tonight. Unless you want to run the whole place yourself tomorrow."

He drops his shirt and smirks at me victoriously.

"What happens from here then?" He asks, the smirk beginning to drop, but not entirely fade.

I sit up a bit. The question chills the room and I pull the blanket up over my shoulder. "What do you mean?"

Logan pulls up a chair that was placed by the wall, pulling it next to the table, and takes a seat. He says every word slowly and leans in. "What happens from here?"

"Nothing happens," I scoff. "We had our fun. Got it out of our system."

"Out of our system?" He eyes me hard. The hazel glow pierces through me.

"Yes. Out of our system. Nothing has to come of this if we don't make something out of it."

"So, this was just for fun?"

Yes, Logan. It was fun. It was a fun night, we had a lot of fun. What is he on about? Why is he making this such a big deal? Isn't this what guys want?

"Darling," I say, trying to speak slowly and calmly. "You just got out of a relationship and you're still living with your ex. *I* just got out of a relationship, too. I'm not looking to jump into anything new so quickly."

"So we might as well fuck around before rushing into anything serious."

Although I agree with him, I don't agree with the tone in which he says it. And all of this feels backward. I've never known a guy to be dismayed or annoyed at being the one-night stand. And this isn't even that!

"I'm not sure what you want from me, Logan."

"I'm not sure what *you* want. At all."

I reach for my robe and pull it close, putting one arm through a sleeve. "All I wanted was this. What just happened. Thanks for sticking around this long but if you keep up the attitude you can leave and I'll see you in the morning."

"Well hold on now. I'm not giving you attitude, I just want to know what the deal is. You want a quick fuck just to 'get it out of our system,' fine. Cool." He puts his hands up like he's surrendering. "You're the boss, I'm just here to do what you tell me."

A thought flickers in my mind, making it impossible for me to know where exactly I stand on my feelings for him right now. *Anything?*

He continues, "I'll admit, I'm not the biggest fan of that, but I'll take what I can get."

The words ignite something in me and I jump to my feet. The blanket falls to the floor, and the dress hangs on one arm, leaving all of me exposed. I shout at him, "You'll take what you can get?"

His eyes look me up and down once then meet mine again. "Have I mentioned yet how hot you are when you're mad at me?"

I love and hate this back-and-forth we've developed together. I hate that he can get me so worked up, and I love the way he gets me going.

Staying seated right where he is, Logan looks up at me and says, "One and done, fine. But I just want to be around you."

I roll my eyes. "Don't get all sappy now, Logan. I prefer the flirty side of you." I pull my other arm through the sleeve of my dress and tie the belt around my waist. "Even the annoying side is more fun."

His eyes follow me as I cross the room to a small cabinet in the corner. There's nothing important in there, but I feel so awkward with him pressing me like this, I just need to fiddle with something.

"I'm serious, Nyx," he insists. "I'm not asking you to profess your love or anything-"

"Thank God." I open the top door of the cabinet and see some old candle stubs. I pull the first one I see out, along with a lighter, and put it on a dish on top of the cabinet, then light it. This should help clear some of this weird energy Logan's bringing to the room.

As if I hadn't interrupted, he goes on, "I just don't want to get caught up in this friend- or, co-workers-with-benefits thing that always ends in disaster."

I spin around, trying my best to be a little playful because he's right. Friends-with-benefits never end well. "We're not co-workers though. You're my employee."

He stands, and pushes the chair in under the table with his foot, then steps toward me. "You're impossible tonight."

"You're impossible every other day of the week. It's only fair."

Logan stands tall over me. I can picture him sliding a finger down the seam of my dress and it'll just fall off again. I'd admonish him for being so bold then let him take me.

I love and hate this back-and-forth we have.

Instead of slipping off my dress, he puts a finger under my chin. "Work with me here, Nyx. For five minutes I'll act like an adult, so you better too before we end up hating each other from whatever this is."

I take a deep breath in. His presence over me tells me to take his finger in my mouth and suck on it, but he's right. This is a ridiculous conversation that we must have.

"Fine," I sigh.

"Good. Let's just both be straightforward. I like being here with you," he takes a step back. It's not a retreat, more a sign of respect for space. "And yeah, I enjoy *this* a lot. I'm okay with whatever you're comfortable with."

What do I even say? I didn't come into this night with a ten-step plan. Not even a five-step.

I take a seat on the steps up to my apartment, and Logan pulls the chair back out to sit down.

"We can keep doing this," I finally say. "I'd *like* to keep doing this. It was... quite a bit of fun."

His annoying flirty tone returns. "Best you've ever had?"

Yes.

"You can believe whatever you wish," I say. "May we get back on topic?"

He holds out his hands toward me, a gesture to say, *carry on*.

So, I carry on. "When we're working, from nine to six, it's

261

hands off. After hours, it's fair game. But some ground rules. I don't like sappy shit. Especially because this is just for fun."

"So, you can see someone else if you want to."

"Either of us can."

His glare challenges mine. Neither of us speaks.

Logan rubs his knuckles. The veins in his hands press against his skin.

As my mouth opens, he asks, "Do you *want* to see anyone else?"

I rush to say, "No."

"Me neither. So why don't we call it what it is?"

I gasp for air as my heart leaps. "Don't, D-... Logan. Don't say that."

He leans forward in his chair, hands dropping between his legs. A strand of hair falls in front of his beautiful eyes. He says in a low voice, "Why not?"

I push myself up off the step and take a step backward into the dark of the stairwell. "If we're playing this safe, don't rush this."

Logan's on his feet too now, and takes his time approaching me. "How can we rush it if we're already here?"

I throw my hand back, searching blindly for the railing. "We're not here yet." My heart races. "*There*," I correct. "We're not *there* yet."

He draws closer. "But we won't be seeing anyone else."

My hand flails. *Where's that damn railing*, I ask myself, unable to take my eyes off of him. "You know, you're much better at doing as I say when you're on the clock."

"Good thing we're off then."

"This doesn't mean-" I take a step back as I speak, but miss the step and slip, and fall back on my ass.

Logan towers over me, silhouetted by the candlelight in the covenstead. He drops down, hands on the step on either side of my head. Between my legs, I feel another craving for him, and if he doesn't take me now, I'll take him, regardless of how complicated he's made this conversation.

"Let's mean it then," Logan says, lowering his lips to mine.

I bite the inside of my lip and begin to reach back. "This is a bad idea," I whisper with only atoms between us.

Every little bit of my being tells me to go for it, except for one cold voice in the back of my mind. It's quieter than all the rest, but the only one I can hear. Just before our lips meet, I draw back.

This exchange can't go on.

"You can fuck me again right here if you want to. But another rule: no kissing. Unless you're going to tongue fuck my mouth like you did earlier, it falls under the banner of 'sappy.'"

Logan hesitates, and though I can't see it in his eyes, I know he's not happy about my decision. Regardless, he pulls back and holds out a hand.

I take it, and he helps me back to my feet. Even two steps above him, we're only meeting at eye level.

"Any other rules?" He asks plainly.

"Clear communication."

"Naturally."

"And boundaries. Do you have any?"

He crosses his arms and leans against the wall. "What do you mean?"

"Kinks."

Logan purses his lips. "Well…" he says, thinking intently. "No one's ever put their finger in my ass until you did it."

"And?" Maybe we're onto something productive here finally.

"And that's the most I'm taking. I'll say that before you get too ahead of yourself."

Well, shit. *Binds* did too much to get my hopes up. Probably would have caved completely to his sappy bullshit if he was willing to take more.

"Otherwise, I'll hear out what you've got in mind."

"Good," I say. "That's something we can talk more about later then."

"Glad we still agree on a later."

"And no other parties. I'm not calling us exclusive, but we can call it a courtesy."

"I'm fine with that."

"Anything you want to throw into this?"

He shakes his head. "Just to clarify, nine to six is off limits, right?"

"Yes. I want to keep our business relationship as professional as possible."

Logan scoffs. "All right," he says, taking a step back down into the covenstead. He pats his pockets; I hear a soft *thump* when he hits his wallet, and metallic jangling when he hits his keys. "All right," he says again. "Nine to six."

"Nine to six," I repeat.

With all of his things in order, and an agreement met, he pulls back the curtain. "Goodnight then. Nyx. I'll see you at eight-thirty."

27. On the Clock

At 8:29, I sit behind the counter with Willow in my lap. I stroke her back slowly, with a look resembling a conniving witch from an old fairy tale.

Come on in deary, see what we have to offer this fine morning. Just don't wander too far, you might just slip into my cauldron.

At every little sound, every creak, and every car that drives by, Willow perks up, jutting her gaze toward the window.

"He's coming," I console the eager cat with another stroke.

A figure walks into view along the sidewalk. We both sit up a little more, but with more than a moment to see, it's clear that it's not our well-endowed employee.

I check my phone. The numbers change from a minute until, to the half hour. Just then, something bangs against the door. I look up and see Logan yanking on the door handle. He pulls again, the sound of the metal lock ringing through the store then looks up to see me grinning wickedly at him.

Logan points down to the lock and mouths the words, *I think you forgot to unlock this.*

I bite the inside of my lip and slowly shake my head.

Willow leaps from my lap and skitters over toward the door, pawing at the glass.

Logan pulls on the door again, lifting an eyebrow at me.

"Did you want to come in?" I ask with exaggerated playful facial expressions in case he can't hear me.

He smiles back with a vicious grin. I can already tell that if I open the door now, after making him wait this long already, I'll most likely find myself pinned to the floor.

I turn and stretch, hands up high so he can see the shape of my body he won't be allowed to touch.

Logan yanks the door again. Hard. It sounds as if he's about to rip the door down. He then freezes as a cop walks by and past the storefront.

I stand and saunter toward the door, taking my time, weaving through the aisles. Willow seems just as impatient as Logan. I hear his voice faintly through the glass, "Come on, Nyx. Open up."

"I'm sorry," I pout, pushing my breasts together. "We're not open yet. But you can come back later."

He shoots a quick look up and down the street, then says, "I'd like to come *now* though."

"I bet you would," I say, inching closer to the glass so my tits press against the door. "What would you do if I let you in?"

Logan bites his lip. At any moment someone could walk by, and it'd probably be when he says the most inappropriate thing he can think of. Instead of answering, he cocks his head impatiently to the side and says, "It'd be better if I showed you, so open up."

"Hm," I say, and take a step back. "How about I show *you*." A finger lifts the hem of my dress. "You know it's crazy, I think I forgot to wear any underwear this morning."

His eyes lust after my legs, my thighs as they become revealed, centimeter by centimeter.

"You know you're only making this worse for yourself," his muffled voice warns.

"That's the idea."

Willow runs off before too much is seen. Sure, she likes having Logan around, but not as much as I do now.

I offer, "You can come in if you tell me what you want."

"Nyx…"

"Uh uh. That's the rule." I threaten to drop the fabric back down and worry spreads across his face.

"All right! Hold on! Hold on!" He does another check to see if the coast is clear, then drops his voice down real low that I can't even hear him.

I put a hand to my ear. "What's that?"

He purses his lips. One hand tightens hard around the door handle so I can see the muscles in his arm flex. He speaks a little louder, by the look on his face, but I still can't hear him.

I look up at the clock above the door. 8:45. "You're wasting time, Logan. If you wanted to have some fun before opening, now's your chance!"

Down below his penis throbs hard against his pants, pointing upward into his shirt.

Should I take this a little further?

269

I back up another step so the nearest shelf blocks me from the view of the main window. Unless someone stands right where Logan is, no one walking by will be able to see the bare breast I pull out of my bra.

"If you want this…" I say, playing with my nipple.

He mouths one more *Come on, Nyx*, then hardens his face as if he's about to burst through the door. This is it. I hear him loud and clear, "Let me in so I can bend you over the fucking counter."

I slip my breast back into the dress and approach the door.

"That's a good boy," I say through the glass, and raise my hand to the lock.

His breath leaves a circle of fog on the door.

My fingers tease the metal knob.

Logan's hazel eyes hypnotize me, force me to press harder on the knob until everything is silent in the world and we hear the fatal click of the lock.

I take a quick breath in.

The door opens.

I'm up in Logan's arms, my legs wrapped around him, tongue between his lips and his teeth. In just a few long strides he's dropped me down on the counter. His hard penis pressed against my wet and wanting lips.

"You've got ten minutes," I warn through moans as his lips move down my neck.

"I'll take how long I need."

Fuck. Me. My legs wrap tighter around him. Now *that* is the real-life smut "Binds" has gotten my hopes up for.

Between bated breaths and aroused moans, I try to say, "I'm- t- the b- buhh… fuck… the boss here."

Two of his fingers slip between my legs, circling my clit in opposite directions.

"Sure looks like it, Nyx," he teases.

Is that a challenge? Pull yourself together, Nyx. Show him who's in control here.

Composing myself as best I can, I grab his thick forearm and pull his hand up between our faces. "You have now," I pause, and lick my juices off his fingers. "Eight minutes to do what I say." I throw his hand back at him and watch as he takes a taste for himself, never breaking eye contact with me.

"Well then how can I please you, boss?"

I spin around on the counter, and push myself off, taking a seat again in my chair. He watches me as I spread my legs and pull back my dress. "This time I want *you* on your knees."

In one swift motion, he hops over the counter. Logan stands there for a moment, looking down at me, but then does as I say and drops to his knees. His hands grab my thighs, holding them apart as he draws closer. His breath alone on my wet lips makes me convulse, but his hands clench on my thighs and he keeps my legs in place.

I run my hands through his hair as the tip of his tongue graces along my fold. I take a deep breath in to contain myself. Logan licks up my juices, and caresses my clit, swirling his tongue around it before sucking me into his mouth. His teeth nibble at me, sending me into a frenzy.

"Fuck. Me. Logan."

He pulls back and says, "If that's what you'd like," and reaches for his cock.

There isn't enough time though. Regretfully, I tell him, "No, keep going like that."

He dives back in, plunging his tongue into me.

I feel an orgasm building up. He moves around inside of me, massaging my insides with his mouth, letting his lips massage my folds.

"I'm getting close," I tell him, gripping his hair more tightly, helping guide his movements.

Logan mumbles something with his face buried that I can't make out, and one invigorating movement later, my legs wrap around his neck, thighs crushing his head. I feel bad at first, not wanting to hurt him, but he does nothing to fight back. Instead, one strong arm wraps around the snake coiled around my left leg, and he only pulls tighter. The stronger my thighs squeeze around his head, the more violently he eats me out.

I try to maintain control of him with one hand, but I have to use the other to stabilize myself, gripping onto a shelf behind me.

Then, the most horrible thing happens. We should have locked the door.

Just over the top of one of the shelves, through narrowed eyes, I see the door open and the top of someone's head approach. As a moan threatens to escape me, I throw a hand over my mouth.

"Nyx? Are you open yet?" A woman's voice asks.

I tap on Logan's head to tell him to stop, but he doesn't get the message.

"Logan!" I whisper. "Logan, that's…" I can barely get out

the word *enough* as a movement of his tongue and a finger rubbing my clit brings the orgasm even closer.

"Nyx, you there? Oh! Hey!"

Spotted.

I throw my dress over Logan and sit up, hoping this customer won't notice.

But Logan doesn't seem to mind the new arrival. His tongue insists upon penetrating me.

The customer, an older woman and a regular, comes around the corner. From what I've gathered from her over the years, she's not into witchcraft for herself, but her daughter or granddaughter is, and she comes in here for gifts. That's always her reasoning: gifts. But with the regularity with which she comes in, I assume it's more of bribery from a parental figure who pushed away or made her kid feel bad about the witchcraft to begin with and is now trying desperately to show interest and win them back.

"There you are!" She says, a wide-eyed grin showing off her pearly whites. Her hair bobs like something in a conditioner commercial with each step, and her many bracelets and necklaces jangle loudly. At this point, Logan is obviously ignoring her. There's no way he can't hear, even with my thighs pressed tight against his ears.

I glance up at the clock. 8:57.

She continues striding toward me, and I lean forward as much as I can, resting my fists on Logan's covered head.

"I'm sorry, but we're not open yet," I tell her as composed as my euphoric state will allow.

The woman freezes two feet away from the counter with a

look of offense. "But, the door was open," she argues.

Logan's tongue flicks up along my folds and I jump and put a hand to my mouth.

"Are you okay, dear?" She asks.

What the fuck is her name?

"Sorry," I say. "Hiccups. Darla, yes?"

She nods, with an unreadable look on her face, somewhere between doubt and concern for me.

"Darla. Yes." I put both hands down on Logan's head and give a little nudge. "We open at 9. Not - *MMph!* - not quite ready to open yet." I stifle a moan by biting the inside of my lip.

"But that's only…" She looks at a thin silver watch on her wrist. "Three, two minutes from now. And it doesn't look like you're busy at the moment. I need a gift idea."

Something brushes against my clit. Logan's nose I guess, because his tongue is deep inside me.

"I'm…" *Think, Nyx!* "Meditating. I have to m-meditate before opening."

"Oh, lord. You girls these days with your yoga." She waves away my excuse. "Really though, are you alright? You look-"

I blurt, needing an outlet for my moans of pleasure, "I CAN'T! I need to meditate. Before opening. Please, please come back in a minute!" I throw my head back, about to come, but try to make it look like stress or even panic. Anything other than the look of a girl getting mind-blowing head but not being allowed to enjoy it.

Darla takes a step back and puts a hand to her chest. "If I had known you would be so rude today."

I slap my hands down on the counter. My hair falls sweaty

and messy in front of my face. A white lock covers my right eye, blurring out the woman in front of me. "Anything you want in the store half off, just *please* give me a *fucking* minute!"

Darla falters backward. "This is the last time I'm-"

My fingers strain on the counter. "That's fine! Please just… a minute!" I'd take a completely dead day, a dead *week* even if I meant I could have these next thirty seconds for Logan to bring me to complete bliss.

She opens her mouth again, but I point to the door. "9. I n-need to f-f-fucking m-meditataaaa! *Fuck!*" It's too late. Logan brings me to climax. I feel his head pull out from my legs as they constrict again, and I drop my head down on the counter.

"Are… are you all right, Nyx?" Darla asks. This time, the concern in her voice sounds real.

Almost weeping with pleasure, I beg her, "Just please give me a minute. I just need a minute to meditate."

"Oh- oh oh okay…" She accepts, slowly retreating.

As soon as she's gone, Logan comes up from his hiding place. "That was a close one," he says, wiping his mouth.

I reach up a weak hand to smack him, but it only lightly brushes his face.

"You can try that again later if you have more energy. I might like it, even."

I mumble back, "It's 9."

"So it is. I guess I'll get to work. Should probably start with mopping the place up."

We both look down and see a puddle of my juices.

Between heavy breaths, I say, "I don't think… anyone has ever made me… squirt like that."

"Always glad to give you a new experience." Logan pats me on the back like a chum, then walks away like he didn't almost get us caught in front of a customer.

Darla comes back a minute later, walking through the aisle gingerly. "Is now a good time?" She asks. "Are you done meditating?"

For now, I think. *But I'll definitely be doing more meditating after closing.*

28. It's Nice to Have a Friend

"Something's off about you today," Jade accuses with a confounded gaze.

Ever since she came in this morning she's been given me knowing looks, or at the very least, suspicious. But Logan is doing nothing to temper the air in here. On Saturday morning we had our adventure under the counter, and it had seemed to satiate him for the time being, aside from the "accidental" grazings we exchanged just to annoy each other. But with a day off between now and then, he came in as hot as ever. Rules are rules, though, and this day has been nothing but teasing and lustful glances.

Really, I thought that once we had sex the first time it'd be out of our systems. My system at least. Unfortunately, or fortunately depending on if it's work hours or not, things have only become more intense and harder to resist. So when Jade came in after closing, we had to be as quiet as possible cleaning up the covenstead and hiding him upstairs before she walked in on us. Logan still doesn't understand why we'd have to hide it from her, and the idea that fucking where I run a business just doesn't get through to him.

Thankfully, when Jade enters the covenstead the only thing off is my energy which she picks up on right away.

"Something happen over the weekend?" She asks as she unslings a bag from her shoulder and puts it down under the table. The contents shuffle around and thud on the carpet, like the sound of books. Spell books and guides, perhaps.

I tell her honestly, "A lot of meditating."

"You look a little stiff," she says, making herself comfy on the pillows. I wonder if she'll pick up that smell on them. Is it as strong as I think it is? I left incense burning in here all day, hoping it'd help cover up the musk.

I turn in my chair at the table to face her and let slip a knowing smile.

Jade pats one of the pillows. "Gonna sit with me?"

Everything in my body is so sore, I don't want to move. I should have stayed on the pillows when Logan ran upstairs - Fuck, I really hope he isn't doing anything stupid up there - but this looked much less conspicuous. Now I can't even move.

I jerk my head toward the table. "Let's sit here today," I offer. "I'm just feeling... really tight today."

Jade rolls her eyes and picks herself up off the ground before making her way to one of the other chairs at the table. She reaches down and picks up her bag, then pulls out (I was right) a series of books.

Without acknowledging my complaint, she picks up one of the books and separates it from the rest. "I was thinking about what you said the other day about the moon cycles and picked up some light reading."

I reach over and spin her book around to get a better look at the cover.

"Jade, darling, you know I carry this one in the store. Where'd you get it?"

She shrugs, hiding a minute sense of guilt in her almost pouting lips. "Just up the road. I feel like I'm spending all my time here." She laughs then to herself, "Didn't want you getting tired of me already."

We still have a bit to work on with her self-confidence, it seems, but that's all right. It's at least cute because of how much she's come out of her shell already and I don't feel too bad.

As I begin to say, *I could never get tired of you,* both of us are caught off guard by a bang coming from upstairs.

"What was that?" She asks.

"Willow," I tell her, although I know the honest answer is Logan. I swear, he better be staying out of my things or I'm going to strangle him in a way he won't enjoy. "You stay here, Jade. I'll be right back."

I hop over to the stairs and scurry up as fast as my sore legs can carry. Behind me, I just barely hear Jade's complaint that "It's just the cat."

I wish it was. I really wish it was.

When I open the door, Logan is sitting on the couch still only half dressed, with his feet kicked up on the coffee table. "Binds" is open in his hands.

"Well hey there. Hogwarts out of session already?" He asks, resting the book in his lap.

Are Harry Potter jokes all people can think of?

Shutting the door behind me, I demand, "What was that sound?"

"What do you mean?"

"Jade and I both heard it. Seriously, Logan, are you fucking around up here?"

He shakes his head. Then, "Oh! I mean I dropped this on accident," He says, holding up the book. "Is *this* the kinda stuff you meant the other night when you asked about boundaries? Cause holy *SHIT-*"

Before he can finish I trudge over and take the book from his hand, throwing it back down on the coffee table. "Either be quiet or you can get out from the fire escape. Your choice."

Logan looks briefly over toward the window, then back at me. "What if I don't?"

I put my hands on my hips and stare, my threshold of acceptable annoyance about to be reached. "Whatever page you just read in that book, *that's* what I'll do to you."

"Somehow I'm not surprised you'd have that kinda stuff."

"Don't test me, Logan." I point a finger at him and back away toward the door. When I open it, I whisper, "I mean it."

Back downstairs, Jade flips through the pages of her moon-spell book. She glances up as I step out of the dark of the stairwell and back into the covenstead. "Everything all good up there?"

"Yeah," I grunt. "He- *She*, Willow, just knocked something over. Stupid cat."

Jade's eyes spell doubt. "Right. Okay." She nudges the book again. Not toward me, just a little movement to remind me why we're there.

"All right, yes, the moon." I cross my hands and scoot myself into the table. "What about it?"

Jade's lips part, then close as she gathers her thoughts. "You said it was important. In the park on Friday."

"Yes?"

There is a clear strain in her voice, a tone I've never yet heard from her. "For the book. The one you took from that girl."

What is she talking about? I ask myself.

The answer then rushes to me. "Oh! Right! Yes." I throw my hands out toward her. "The summoning book. Of course, haha, how could I forget."

"Yeah," she says timidly. "Kinda seemed like a big deal the other day."

"It is. I swear it is, and it must be dealt with at the next possible opportunity."

Jade stares at me with sulking eyes, as if expecting me to say more, and disappointed that I haven't.

"What's wrong?" I ask after a moment of silence.

With a totally foreign boldness of herself, she accuses, "You."

I have to laugh. "What are you talking about?"

"You're never this... oh, what's the word? You're just off today. Like, distracted. Back the other day, that book sounded like it was the most important thing in the world."

"It is," I rush to collect myself and manage a straight face. "Really, it is. I'm sorry. We can focus on that." I push out my chair and stand. "How about some tea? Maybe I just need a cup to get my head back on right."

"Sure," she says without any conviction and slumps back in her seat.

I nod to her politely and hop back up the stairs.

Back in the apartment, Logan is still shirtless on the couch, this time reclining across it and still reading. He lowers it just below his eyes to watch me stride over the kitchen to prepare the tea. I try to pretend he's not there so I don't get distracted, but he always has to make himself known.

"I love the way your butt jiggles when you run like that."

I whisper to him, "Logan! The door is still open!"

His eyes go wide in fake alarm, then he whispers back, "I love the way your butt jiggles when you run like that."

"Sh!"

Between clicks of the gas stove trying to catch, I hear Logan swing his legs off the couch and walk up behind me. I focus on the kettle, pretending he's not there, even when his member presses against me, and his big arms trap me between himself and the counter.

"Having fun down there?" He whispers in my ear.

"Plenty. More than I would up here."

"Come on…" he spins me around and I can barely contain how much I love the force he uses. I look down and see his penis poking far out of his pants past his belly button. "Tell the truth. You were just waiting for the chance to come back up to see me." He tilts his head down and buries his face in my neck like a vampire's kiss.

One leg instinctively rises up to his waist. "Logan, you're really gonna get it if you don't stop fucking around."

"Counting on it," he breathes on my neck.

"Stop that!" I try weakly to push away, biting his ear.

He grinds against me, his bulge grazing against the thin fabric of my dress between my legs.

A low whistle whines from the pot.

My hands run through his hair.

His cup my breasts.

The whistling grows louder.

Lips are bitten.

Zippers are undone.

Logan pushes through my folds.

The kettle's cry drowns out my own, and Logan pulls out. "Sounds like the tea's ready," He laughs. "Better get back down there."

I bite my lip so hard in aggravation that I almost break the skin. "You asshole." I turn away from him and take the kettle off the stove. The whining dies down and we're back to whispers.

"Just wanna make sure you don't take too long down there with your friend." Logan winks and puts his cock in his pants. What can fit of it, anyway.

"I'll take whatever- however long I need." I just have to focus on one thing. The tea. Make the tea. Bring it down to Jade. *Teach her what she came here for!*

Logan watches me wordlessly from the other side of the small kitchen while I prepare the drinks. I can't see him, but I can feel that smug grin on his face as if our exchange had been a battle he'd won. But oh, don't worry. Once Jade's gone it'll be my turn to do the teasing.

* * *

"Moon cycles! Okay, let's do this."

Jade sips her tea patiently.

I reach across the table and slide the thin paperback back to me. I flip through the first few pages, just to see where to pick things up from, and skim the table of contents. "Have you started reading this at all?"

"Not that one yet." Color seeps its way into her face, and her eyes widen slightly from their previous subdued expression. She pulls another book out of her bag, a red and purple hard-bound spellbook with dozens of sticky notes popping out of the edges. Jade proudly announces, "This is the one I've been going through over the weekend. Just, after last week, I thought I had a lot of catching up to do. I felt kinda useless with all your clients."

"Oh, don't even think about that, darling. I mean, it's good you're doing your homework, it makes my job easier. Now, let's see…" I study the first page of the moon magic book. A few paragraphs down, I close the book with an exaggerated slap and toss it into the corner.

Jade jumps with the slap.

"If you're going to buy books on this stuff, you should really buy them here," I tell her. "My books aren't scams. Look, the moon is very simple. Life, like the moon, is cyclical. What's come before will come again. That is why we look to the moon to guide our spells. Like reading tea leaves, or the constellations, the cycle gives us knowledge.

"The new moon. Let's say, for example, you need to rejuvenate or kindle a relationship…"

Jade squirms in her seat.

"I know," I give her a silly little grin, thinking about Jenna. "We may have missed the mark on that one. *But*, as the moon cycle goes around, so do our chances to use it. The new moon is time for new beginnings. We can cast our spells whenever we need. But we must accept that we are only borrowing power from the universe. The universe *wants* to help us, those who treat nature with respect, so if we work alongside nature, nature will assist us. The new moon will help flourish spells of newness. A new job, a new opportunity… a new relationship."

There's something in her eyes. Something unreadable.

She pulls her hands from the table, retreating into the shy woman I first met weeks ago. With her movements, the candles illuminating the room seem to dim.

In the silence, a creaking is heard upstairs. My fingers clench under the table, hoping Logan's not up to anything.

"So…" Jade says, catching my attention again. When I look at her, her eyes are on her hands on the table. "So I guess… just so I can wrap my head around it… what… kind of spells have you

285

used on a new moon?" She stretches out the word 'kind,' seemingly nervous to ask.

I try to share with her a comforting smile. She should know by now she's the one person I'd share any of this stuff with. Magic stuff at least, some of the more personal stuff can stay just between Logan and myself. "Well," I begin, "last week for example, Do you remember I told you my ex and I tried something called 'Sex Magic?'"

Jade nods, blushing a little.

"Something like that is helped by harnessing the power of the moon, depending on the cycle it's in. I timed it for the new moon, a time for manifesting and new beginnings."

Jade seems to be hung up on only one aspect of this. "Sex magic?" She laughs in her restrained, almost embarrassed laugh.

"Yeah. I know it's-"

Every word brings her back to the Jade I've come to know. "No, it's… I mean, what's magic about it?"

Now I laugh. "Well, from that night, nothing. He's my ex for a reason. The goal though was to engage in both meditative and passionate sex, embracing the power of the new moon, the spark a resurgence of our love for each other. And, also, it gives you one hell of an orgasm."

We both share a boisterous laugh and another creak is heard upstairs. I cut myself off and shoot my head upward. He's up to something, I know he is.

"That damn…" I mutter.

"What? What is it?" She looks from me, to the part of the ceiling I'm looking at.

"It's, uh… it's Willow. She's doing something up there." I push out my seat but Jade jumps up with me.

"Can you forget about the cat, please? She's fine, it's just a cat."

When I step away from my seat, Jade takes me by the arm.

"Come on. We don't get any time anymore, just you and me. Not since that guy."

My gaze lingers a moment more, waiting for Logan to make another sound, but nothing comes. So, I turn back to Jade. "What are you talking about? You don't like him?"

"No, I mean, he's cool. But I kinda just figured with him working here, you'd have more time for us."

I feel suddenly defensive. "There is time for us. Right now, here, come." I pull her to the back of the room and guide her down with me to sit on the pillows. "See, it's just us."

"Sure, now. But even when he's running the store and you don't have clients, we just hang out out there. We could be hanging out, you know, just us sometimes. Not for this whole thing with the demon or whatever it is." She sniggers at the word "demon," and brings her hand higher up my arm.

"Is there something you wanted to do?"

Jade stutters for something to say, then rolls her eyes and tries to laugh it away. "Forget it."

With sincere concern, I ask, "No, what's wrong?"

She breathes out hard, like she'd been keeping all the air in the world in her chest. "Don't you… don't you want to do anything other than witchy stuff twenty-four seven? I mean, when was the last time you went to the movies, or went on a hike for the sake of a hike, not for some one-with-nature thing? Or spent time with someone just to be near them?"

I take her hand from my arms and hold it in my hands on my lap. "Jade, that all sounds like so much fun. It really does, but it's not a luxury one has when they run a business with no employees six days out of the week. I can't even remember the last time a friend asked me to just 'hang out.'"

A creak again from upstairs. I jerk my head up, but Jade's other hand guides me back to her.

"Well I'm asking you."

I smile.

"I'd like to take you out sometime, Nyx."

So this is what having friends again is like.

"I'd like that, Jade."

29. Maria's Return

I'd never seen a fall from grace so cruel as when Maria walked back into Witch's Brew. Through the overly crowded retail floor, when the door opened and the little bell rang, it rang louder than all of the voices in the room, commanding my attention. I saw her familiar hat at first, already well worn, and from the brim, straggly cords of grey-blonde hair. Maria staggered through the crowd, gradually revealing more haunting details. The other customers parted from her path, seemingly unaware of her presence, as if she were a ghost passing through. The energy was there, but there was nothing for them to see. I, though, saw all.

Purple bags hung under her hazy eyes. Small wrinkles creased around her mouth. Even the skin on her forehead hung low on her brow. She looked like she'd aged ten years since last I'd seen her. Further down, the skin of her neck and arms was pulled tight like she'd been starving herself, and her clothes hung baggy on her shoulders. The beaming energy and enthusiasm I had once known was totally foreign now.

Seeing her saunter toward me, I tossed responsibility of the register to Logan and rushed over to Maria. I nearly fled in revulsion when my hands touched her bony shoulders, but held firm, not wanting to scare her off.

"Maria, darling…" what could I say to her? It looked like I had a cancer patient walking through my store. For all I knew, that could have been the case.

I shot a concerned look back at Logan. He'd seen her recently. She was the reason he was here the night of the new moon. Is this what she looked like then?

Logan shared my expression and gave a small shrug. I'd have to catch up with him later for all of the details of that night.

Back to Maria, I ask her, "What's going on, darling? Are you feeling alright?" That should be a safe question.

A faint smile cracks her dried lips. "Fine, fine."

My eyebrows raise in disbelief. Two words? Only two words from her, not a droning million-mile-and-hour speech that goes nowhere.

"Come with me," I plead, taking her hand and leading her to the covenstead.

Maria stays grounded where she is at my first tug, but when I try again, she trudges forward, following me through the crowded store. As we move through the crowd, I sneak out my phone and text Logan, asking if she looked this bad when he ran into her. I see him steal a look at his phone just before Maria and I pass through the curtain into the covenstead. A moment later, my phone vibrates.

-She looked tired, but not that bad. Talked my ear off for an hour.

I guide Maria to one of the seats at the table and help her sit. She takes her time, staring forward past the brim of her hat, and lays her hands flat on her legs. As she moves, I spot a new tattoo on her arm, a series of pagan runes wrapped around the middle of her forearm. There are even a few on her fingers. I think back to our first appointment when she spotted mine.

"Let me get you a cup of tea," I offer. "How does that sound?"

Maria purses her lips in indecision. So, I tap her shoulder and tell her, "I'll be right back, okay? You just sit right here."

I skitter upstairs and text Logan, telling him I'll be a little while, then Jade, asking her to come over as soon as possible.

-Development with the book. We might need to act sooner. Please come by ASAP!

Her response is almost instantaneous.

-I can't rn. Busy. But I'll be over tonight.
-Need me to bring anything?

Bring anything? Why would she need to bring anything?

-Just your beautiful soul,
darling.

The kettle boils. I prepare a tea mix of my own make: Ginger, honey, chamomile, and rosemary. The ginger is the key, though, for what her situation looks like. Nausea and sleep deprivation, I'd say. *Severe* sleep deprivation.

A sound of rumbling echoes through the stairway. Teacups in hand, I rush back downstairs to see what's going on.

"Maria?" I call, slowly coming back into the light of the covenstead.

Stuff is being moved around at a rapid pace until she sees me and stops. Maria's eyes are wider now, but the rest of her face remains deadpan, totally unaffected by being caught.

"Where is it?" She demands. Cupboard doors are pulled open. Books, old candles, sage wraps, anything loose she found is thrown on the table or tossed to the side, rolling around on the floor.

When I don't say anything in response, totally at a loss for the state she's in, the chill creeps up through the floorboards, twisting around my feet and ankles like a mist.

I push down the lump in my throat and tighten my hands around the tea mugs. "I don't know," I tell her honestly. "Please sit back down, Maria."

"I need it back, Nyx." Her dry lips pull back, stretching against her teeth. At least those look normal still. She's about three steps away from looking like an old hag from a fairy tale.

Without too sudden of movements, I cross the room over to the table and slowly lower the mugs to the table. "If you sit with me, we can talk this out. Okay? Will you please sit, Maria?"

"You can't call me that anymore. My new name is-"

I cut her off with force. "I'm not calling you that. Your name is Maria."

She drops her head so the brim of her hat falls in front of her eyes, and bites her lip in embarrassment.

This is a delicate situation, Nyx, and you're not handling it very well.

"I'm sorry. I won't shout." I reach over and give the tea mug a little nudge in her direction.

She glances out, then shies away entirely. Behind the sniffling back of tears, I hear her say, "Please just give it back. I think I really fucked up."

This isn't the girl I'd met weeks ago. And although she's right, that whoever she's gotten involved with was the wrong fucking choice, whatever they're doing to her can't be made out as her fault.

"You haven't done anything wrong, darling." If she's not going to be the first, I take my own mug and raise it to my lips, hoping it eases her mind a bit seeing me so outwardly calm.

"You don't know," she argues. "We need the book back. I need him back."

"Who are you talking about? Maria, who have you been hanging out with?" *And who is this 'him'*, I ask myself. But Maria shoots back at me with violence on her tongue before I can ask her.

"You wrecked everything you selfish bitch!" Maria rips one of the cupboards from its tracks and throws it onto the ground. I jump to my feet, throwing myself back and for a moment it sounds like everything has gone quiet out on the retail floor. Dropping my eyes to the bottom of the curtain, I see a small shadow pass and stop just on the other side. Logan.

The room fills with cold air. Tingling traces up my legs. The shiver of her body and the way her eyes wander tells me she feels it too.

"It's in here," she whispers. "I know it is."

Right now, I miss her pointlessly wandering, doe-eyed speeches.

I plead with her, with as much gentleness as my shaking, terrified voice allows. "Maria, I need you to tell me who it is that gave you that book. How did you find them?"

Tears of excruciating pain stream down her face from terribly bloodshot eyes. She wraps her arms around her stomach as if there's some stabbing pain or contraction in her gut. Ignoring my question completely she says, "He won't come back anymore. He won't come. I miss him too much. I need him again."

"Who? Maria, who's this man?"

"You told me it wasn't real!" She shouts, once again silencing the rest of the building. "You didn't believe me! You made fun of me and said I needed help! And now you're taking him from me!" Maria trudges toward me, her feet stomping with strength the rest of her body doesn't show. "I can feel him now still. In this room. This is what you wanted, isn't it? You wanted to know what he felt like. You wanted him for yourself. Too lonely here? No friends, no one that really loves you, you have to take the thing I cared about from me because you couldn't stand to see someone else happy. Didn't want to be alone and miserable anymore, did you? Wanted something you could keep locked away, something that couldn't leave no matter how horrible you are to it?"

The curtain opens behind her, but I can't see anything past her bloodthirsty eyes. I try to stand but her bony fingers grip my shoulders and push me back down.

She shouts again, "Why do you have to be so selfish?"

A hand takes her by the arm and pulls her away. "Times up," Logan says casually, escorting her out of the room. "No walk-ins today. You'll have to make an appointment."

Maria kicks her legs out, flailing hopelessly in Logan's strong grip. Just one hand on her, and she isn't going anywhere except where he wants. She screams at me, "Give it back! That's my book!" and the curtain falls again between us. Maria continues to scream and shout obscenities about me all the way to the door. All I hear though is the little bell when the door opens, Maria's voice being cut off, and what sounds to be a witty remark from Logan to the customers.

The whole ordeal leaves me paralyzed in my chair. I can barely breathe, barely think. This, her behavior; it can't merely be a result of losing the book. No, this is some other influence. Manipulation from whoever gave it to her. This is a highly impressionable young woman's mind twisted by someone with malicious intent. And the name again. What was that name she said they gave her? Something with an 'H.' That could be the key to all of this delusion.

Logan pushes back through the curtain, concern washed over his face. "You okay, Nyx?"

It takes a beat or two, but I'm able to respond. "Yeah… yeah I'm fine."

"What was that about?" He tries to laugh it off - all is said and done, right? - but it comes out weak.

"I… I don't know. I don't know yet." I tell him, picking myself up out of my chair. "But I'm going to find out."

He steps forward, following me to the stairs. "What are you-"

"Stop. Please, just… work the counter. That's what you're here for. Just please give me some time."

Logan does as he's told without a word of protest. And I know it's not out of surrender by the way he nods his head in acceptance. He does what I tell him out of respect. And that little nod and faint smile makes me wish he *did* follow to help.

* * *

'H.' It was definitely an 'H' name.

Not to take away from the intensity of the moment, but I feel like I should be in some deep dark lair. Cobwebs and candles everywhere. Scrolls lining all the walls, and tiny little spiders rushing out when I grab one of them for some vital, ancient knowledge to help me on my quest. I feel like I should look like Gandalf in that one scene in "Lord of the Rings," searching for clues to the whereabouts of the One Ring. But instead, I'm sitting on the couch, with Willow on my lap, looking up witchy names that start with an 'H' on my laptop.

Hazel, no.

Hecate, no, but that sounds familiar.

Habundia, definitely not. Not that there's anything wrong with that name.

Hecuba. That's a new one, but no.

Hellawes. Nope.

Hunith.

That one. That sounds familiar. And the more I think about it, the more sure I am that is the one she said. But what does it mean? Searching "Hunith," most of what pops up is from a T.V. show, Merlin, a very reliable source. Going into the depths of the Google archives, all I find is more Merlin, and frankly, I feel ridiculous. But eventually, once all the nerdy fandom stuff is out of the way, one result proves fruitful. It's a Welsh name, meaning "Sleep." Not a very powerful name for a witch, but, sure, let's go with that for now. But why would it be buried under all this Merlin stuff?

I'm beginning to wish I studied mythology as much as I tell others they should.

All right, a search on Merlin. He was King Arthur's buddy, magician, all the obvious, yadda yadda yadda… oh! Mother's name according to some sources was a woman named Hunith. We're getting closer.

And the father…

Terror rushes through me. Even in the safety of my room, I feel the book's presence, the horrible cold.

According to the Arthurian myth, Merlin's father was an incubus.

30. Rubbed the Wrong Way

All through the evening, the demonic spirit attached to the book has cast a taunting energy over the building. Sitting on my bed, I watch people walking by on the sidewalk. Whether or not they know they were doing it, passersby cross the road or pick up their pace when approaching the store.

It knows I know its plan. And it knows my own well enough. The incubus must be exorcised tonight.

The only person who doesn't shy away from the store is Jade, who runs right up to the door and unlocks it with her key. I follow the sound of her footsteps all the way through the retail floor, the covenstead, up the stairs, and to my apartment door, throwing it open.

"Hey!" She nearly shouts through exhausted breaths. "Sorry I took so long. Busy packing. Jenna and I move in this week and my parents have been so up my ass about it."

"I thought you were excited about starting school?"

"Your text made this sound more important. What happened?"

She joins me on the bed, putting a hand on my leg, and I tell her everything, even the more ridiculous stuff. But through it all, she listens intently. I know I was right to put my trust in her for this, especially when I tell her about the name and the meaning behind it.

"Do you think she knows?" Jade asks.

"The name's meaning? Probably not. Maria isn't…" I rub my temples feeling guilty for how I feel about her. "She's not the biggest critical thinker. I knew when I met her that her perception of all of this, witchcraft and spirits, was entirely based on Hollywood. She wanted to believe in the popular thing. Wasn't a fan of reality."

At this, Jade giggles. "I'm sorry, but I don't think most people would consider everything we're talking about 'reality.'"

"No," I agree. "But you can't pick and choose nature. If there's good, there's bad. Light, dark. If there are powers of benevolence, evil. You can't accept God without acknowledging the Devil."

"And do you?"

I purse my lips. "I believe in the universe. That encompasses all. I believe in goodness, so there must be evil too."

Her hand begins to rub against my leg, just above the knee. "I feel like this is stuff you should have told me when I gave you my signature."

"I'm sorry," I tell her genuinely.

Jade scoots an inch closer and says gently, "It's okay. Not like it's gonna push me away now."

"I'd hope not. All of this stuff with Maria just shows we have to act now." I begin to pull myself out of the bed but Jade holds me firmly in place.

"Really? Now?"

"Yes, darling. I don't want this getting any worse. For anyone."

I move again, but she moves with me.

"All of this talk of waiting for the right time and you just want to rush into it? Don't you think maybe we should just…" She looks around the room, then says without looking directly at me, "Just relax or something. You know," her eyes meet mine. "Like we talked about. Someone that's just here with you."

Her fingertips graze my cheek. "And besides, spellcasting with an unclear mind?"

I appreciate her attempt, I really do. But with that book downstairs, I just can't focus on anything else. I tell her, "I know, I know, you're right, but I just-"

Jade gracefully pushes me down onto the bed. It's so sudden, but the smile on her face shows she's just trying to ease my mind.

"How about that rain check, huh?" She asks. "A back rub worked for me when I needed it."

"Jade, come on," I laugh. "Cut it out, I'm serious."

She looks around the room again. "Do you have any massage oil up here?"

I roll my eyes. She's just gonna push this, isn't she? To her credit, it is pulling my thoughts from the book. "Here," I say, reaching over to the drawer in the nightstand.

Her gaze follows, and her lips pull apart in an evil grin at an obvious reveal.

"Oh get over yourself," I tell her. "So I have a magic wand, so does everyone. So what are we gonna do? Gonna give me a back rub or get me off?"

Jade blushes. "Guess we'll just see where it goes."

She reaches for the oil and I take my top off, laying belly down on the bed. Jade straddles my thighs.

"Be careful," I warn. "It comes out fast."

Jade doesn't say anything. Instead, I feel the cold drop of the oil on my spine and drips moving lower toward my butt. Her hands press against me, working up and outward in long v's from the base of my spine up to my neck. Her fingers wrap around my neck, massaging my hairline. She then works back down around my shoulder blades, and starts over from the beginning with the v's.

"Is that all right?" She asks. "I've never really given a massage before."

I moan out, "That's wonderful, darling."

Jade works a few more rotations in, each time starting a little lower and pressing a little harder, really getting a good feel for it.

"Do you mind if I…" A finger pulls at my pants. "Don't wanna get any oil on them."

"Yeah, I don't mind."

She slides my pants down under my cheeks then readjusts, pauses to do something I can't see, and begins again.

"You're getting kind*aaaaa* close down there," I half joke when her hands trace over the top of my butt. "I told you, this stuff is *aaaaaaaa*ll about focus."

In almost a whisper, she says into my ear, "Don't worry. I'm focused on what I want." On the final word, I feel something that is definitely not her hands pressing into my back. No, no I know what that is.

I spin onto my back and there on top of me is Jade wearing nothing at all. I don't even have time to think before her lips are on mine. Her hands search for something to touch; my breasts, my face, my shoulders, my neck, anything.

When I try to push her off, my hands touch her breasts, her erect nipples poking my palms, and she holds them there, pulling me up with her.

I pull my mouth away and demand, "What are you doing?"

Jade answers with another kiss, grabbing back at my chest.

When she stops to catch a breath, I ask again, "Jade! What the fuck are you doing?"

"It's what I want." She tries to kiss my neck. "It's what we both want, isn't it?" She tries to kiss my cheek. Her hands fall between my legs and I push her away.

"Stop that!" I shout and force myself out from under her. I jump out of bed and search for my shirt which she's apparently thrown across the room.

"But I thought-"

"Oh my god, Jade." I wipe my mouth, then take a deep breath to compose myself. "What was that?"

She's no longer blushing. Her face is a deep, deep red. Tears well in her eyes. "I thought... I thought that you-"

"No!" I hate myself for how appalled I sound. But to let myself be so vulnerable with her just for her to do that to me when I wasn't expecting it. How could I expect it?

"B-but this whole time," she babbles. "Ev-everything. Y-you're alw-ways s-s-so… I thought this, I, I was what you were talking ab-bout."

I pick my shirt off from the floor and draw it over my head. "When? Talking about when Jade?"

"This whole *time!* Everything!" She spits out her words and wipes snot from her nose. "You're always s-so touchy. And th-the way you talk to me l-like… like… like what I want and all that. W-when you kissed me that night. A-a-a-and the other week. Wh-when you broke up with your ex! The way we talked, a-about the Sight or whatever it was, a-and those things you said about us craving each-ch other!"

I struggle to recall what day she's talking about. If it was after the breakup with Damien, that's probably when I was hungover. And that day… no, I do recall it. We did speak, "But I was talking about-" I stop myself.

Jade eyes me hard waiting for an answer. She still hasn't yet put her clothes back on as if she thought there were a chance to salvage a moment between us. "Who? Nyx? Who were you talking about? Because everything since we met made me feel like it was me!"

"I'm *sorry* it wasn't," I say without any conviction.

At this point, she does grab for her blouse and pants.

"You're a bitch," she mumbles.

"Excuse me?"

"You're cruel! You led me on and fed me all this witchcraft bullshit. You're fucking cruel, Nyx."

I throw up my hands. "I didn't do anything! It's not my fault you're obsessed with me." I keep my eyes on her as she trudges toward the door.

Again, she mutters, "But you loved leading me on didn't you?"

I'd kick her out if she weren't already headed for the door.

"Come back when you've got your head back on, darling."

She spins around violently from the second-to-top step. "And cut it out with the fucking 'darling' crap. You sound like a fucking tool."

I don't know where she got all of this confidence, and I do not like it one bit.

Willow jumps between us and hisses at Jade. She takes a half step up, then gets wise and flees downstairs and out of the building.

Once I know she's gone, I let myself breathe. "Thanks, Willow."

Instead of curling up between my legs, she shoots me an evil look and screeches louder at me than she did toward Jade.

"Who's side are you on, anyway?"

Either way, I decide, fine, if she was only in it because she was trying to get with me, then she wasn't someone I should have trusted with what I have to do anyway. And good. Good riddance. I can take care of the book on my own.

Except…

I can't.

And I have no one who can help me.

Once again, the room fills with a horrible coldness. All the candles in the world couldn't bring any light to this room.

31. Considerations

"Nope. No no no, out." Frank points sternly at the door. "Not dealing with any sad girl shit tonight."

I pull up a seat at the bar and glare.

"*Definitely* not doing this tonight. Go home, Nyx."

I look around the room and see we're the only ones here. Wouldn't expect much for a Tuesday night, but even this is a little disappointing.

"When was the last time you kicked a girl out of here?" I ask.

Frank plants both hands firmly on the bar. "The last time you almost made stupid choices."

"Can't expect me to learn from my mistakes if you don't let me make them." I scan the shelves for something that would properly put ease to my frustrations with Jade and the book. "You know, I don't think I've actually tried gin before."

"You can sit in the booth and have a Shirley temple if you like," he says flatly.

I throw my head into my hands. "Oh my god, Frank," I grumble. "You act like I have a drinking problem or something."

"No, I act like I own a bar and you have an attitude problem. I know how this shit goes down and I put up with enough of your crap as is."

"Me? I never give you any crap."

"You cause it. Know how many free bottles I've given away because of you and your car stealing games?"

"Oh boo-hoo. They're always creeps and they get the car back. Besides, they always offer to take me home anyway. So really, it's okay even if they're not in the car with me."

Frank runs a hand through his hair in frustration. "You're not making your case any better."

"One drink," I say. "Just one and I'll be a good girl." For good measure, I lean in and pout, "Please?"

"Won't work on me. You're like a little sister. That's weird."

"Oh come on!"

Frank pushes off the bar and reaches for something below the counter. "Here," he says, tossing me a bottle of water. "This one's on the house."

A group walks into the bar, chatting about something probably related to the horse races, and take a seat at the booth behind me.

I put the water bottle down and roll it back to Frank. "I can either make bad decisions here or bad decisions without your supervision."

Frank crosses his arms and purses his lips. We eye each

other challengingly, waiting for the other to break. But I know who's going to win this. He has to make up his mind and attend to his new patrons. Frank looks up, past me to the booth, then back down into my eyes. With a small, defeated sigh, he reaches back and takes two glasses off the shelf, placing them on the bar.

"One drink, if you tell me what's going on. *One*," he says and goes to attend the other patrons.

Sure thing. As long as it gets me a drink.

While he attends the gentlemen in the booth behind me, I take out my phone and pull up the text chain with Jade. My fingers hover over the keys. What do I even say to her right now? Do I say anything at all, yet?

-Text me when you can

is all I can think to say. Hopefully, by the time she does text back, I'll have thought of something. Some way to remind her 'Hey, we've got a book to cleanse.'

Frank comes back around the counter and pulls a few more glasses off of the shelves and pours all but two, our glasses. As he pours, he warns, "If you turn around, I'm never letting you back in here."

"You know that only makes me more curious," I tell him.

But there's no hint of play in his voice. "I'm serious. Your friend with the Corvette is back. Don't. Fuck. Around."

Well now. All that makes me think is I might have a ride home tonight.

Oh, who am I kidding? If he's not going to be a creep, I have no reason to take his car.

There's a bottle of scotch in front of me. Frank must have left it there after pouring without realizing it. With him not paying attention, I reach out to grab the bottle and pour myself a shot.

Oooooh… smooth. These guys must have hit it big at the races this week to afford the good stuff.

Before Frank comes back around, I twist the cap back on and clear the glass. But the first thing he says it, "Ya like that kind?" He takes the bottle and puts it back on the top shelf.

"It's not bad."

"Better be worth it, 'cause that's your one drink."

"Bull. Shit." I argue. It was barely even a shot. Just a sampler if anything.

"Pay up. What's eating you?"

I glance down at the black screen of my phone. "You know what? I actually have to go. Problem worked itself out."

As I rise he drops a bottle of gin on the bar.

I halt and consider. "You're not allowed to laugh," I say.

Frank untwists the cap. "We both know my sister. I'm used to it."

I sit back down and hold my glass as he pours. A tiny bit of brown from the scotch mixes with the clear gin. "How is she, anyway?"

"Batshit crazy as always. Her and that other girl Piper are still up to all their weird fuckin' shenanigans. Come on, Nyx, what's up?"

"They in town?" I raise the glass to my lips and give it a whiff. *Fuck!* I think, *Gin may not be my thing*, but I take a sip, and it's not half as bad as the smell.

"Angie comes and goes. I think she's around now but I haven't seen her. I wouldn't reconnect though, if that's what you're thinking."

"It's crossed my mind." I put the glass back down on the counter. I've only had a sip, but Frank refills it.

"If so, then you probably *do* need a drink. I don't even wanna see her. Must be something real spooky scary though if it's come to that." He fills his glass up to the brim before putting the bottle away. I guess he's expecting a slow night.

"You don't know the half of it, darling."

Finally, Frank breaks his tough guy, big brother act, and cracks a smile. "You're never gonna quit that, are ya?"

"Geez, does everyone have a problem with how I talk?"

He shrugs. "You do you, kid. Who else is giving you shit? Don't they know that's my job?"

I take a deep breath at the thought of Jade's tirade. "This…" *Friend?* "Girl… I've been working with. Somehow she got the wrong idea about us and our professional relationship."

"How so?" He sips and listens.

"We're working on this little problem together, and it would seem as though this entire time, she's just been trying to sleep with me."

Frank nods along.

"I mean, here I am, trying to get some real shit done, run a business, and work out this... situation, let's say, for a client, thinking that this girl is there to help. But no! All that's on her mind apparently is how to fuck me! I feel so stupid now, looking back. All the hints she was dropping. How could I not see it?" I take another drink. It goes down better than the first, but not as smooth as the scotch.

Frank rests his glass on the bar. "Hm. So you're mad at her because she tried getting with you?"

"No, *she's* mad at *me* because I wasn't into it. And it's totally unreasonable of her. I don't *owe* her sex. And that wouldn't even be appropriate, she's basically an employee."

Frank only nods again, then says, "And you'd never cross that line."

"Never." I agree, a twinge of guilt twisting my gut. It's not that I'm lying, it's that it's to Frank. Avoid the truth with him? Sure. There's plenty of stuff going on in my life that's not his concern. But lie? I feel gross already.

"All right then," he says. "So what's next then, other than sulking?"

"I am not 'sulking.' I'm regrouping my thoughts." I pull my cabriole with a placed cigarette from my sleeve and put it between my lips.

"Ah! Right," he says, taking the cigarette from my slot. "Because alcohol is so good at that."

"You own a bar! How do you expect to make money if people don't have bad days?"

"I make better money when people have good days and want to celebrate."

I roll my eyes. "I need to find another bar then."

"You'd hate the other bars."

He's not wrong. Caroline Street. Ew.

"All right," he says. "Regrouping your thoughts, right? What's next? Is this girl worth it? For… you know, whatever it is you need for this client."

I swirl the glass in my hand. "That's in part why I wondered about Angie." I put the cigarette back in place and light a match. Frank checks his hands, wondering when I took it back. I love pulling that trick.

"I need a witch," I say, pretending to ignore his confusion.

Frank takes the lit cigarette back and takes a puff before stomping it out. "In the back or not at all. Look, you know I don't care for at all witch stuff. But I know you do, and I know she does. So because of that, I gotta say, don't get involved with her again."

I really could have used that cigarette if we were going to get into this. Instead, I stare down at the gin. "That was all a while ago. I think we're past that."

Frank leans in and lowers his voice down to a whisper. "Nyx, you all may act like what happened was nothing, but I don't. There's a reason I like to pretend she doesn't exist. Angie should have gone to prison for what she did to you."

I *really* could have used that cigarette.

"Frank, it was years ago, and we were all idiots back then. We didn't know what we were doing."

"She did. Don't pretend she didn't."

The gin, the smell of it, the look of it, has become revolting.

313

I push the glass toward Frank.

"Look," he says. "Whatever this is, I know you're going into this with your whole heart. But if it's making you consider going back to Angie, please, it can't be worth it."

If only he knew. If only he knew and believed me. "Well, if not her, I'm screwed." I hop off the bar stool and look over at the old guys in the booth. Mr. Corvette catches my look.

"Enjoy the ride?" He asks to the amusement of his friends.

I don't have to see Frank's face to know he's mouthing, *don't*. Too bad I'm gonna.

"Wouldn't mind another sometime," I tell him, leaning on the table.

I hear Frank stomping out from behind the bar. Gotta make this quick, so while the men are ogling, I take Corvette's drink from his hand and shoot it back. The guy has good taste in cars and liquor. If I ever become a gold digger, at least I know who to go to.

Corvette pushes out of the booth, but Frank's hand is on my arm, pulling me toward the door. Corvette and I protest, but Frank argues with the old man, "It was never gonna happen."

But for good measure, in case I need more free drinks, I give him a wink and press my tongue to the inside of my cheek. It'll happen one day, in his dreams. But I haven't paid for a drink here ever before and I don't plan on ever having to.

I watch from the sidewalk Frank argues with Mr. Corvette. And while they're busy with each other, I give his keys a little jingle.

32. Pillow Talk in a Cramped Space

By the time Logan finishes, I've mostly sobered up. He's still a bit tipsy too, though he's had much more to drink than I have. We take a moment to catch our breath, and he holds me in his arms on the floor of the storage closet. His head rests on one of the pillows we stole from the covenstead, and mine rests on his chest.

"Always wanted to do it in here," I tell him, before lighting a cigarette between my lips.

He breathes heavily. "Why haven't you before?"

A puff of smoke, then, "Just never happened. No one spontaneous enough before."

Logan takes the cigarette from my lips and takes a drag. "Coulda' tried it solo."

"Yeah? Where's the fun in that?"

He hands the cigarette back. Logan's much more courteous than Frank in that way, I suppose.

"You're right. It's usually better to have someone to give a helping hand." His arm drops from around me and smacks my ass hard enough to leave a mark, giving me a little jolt of pleasure, then holds me tighter.

"*Usually* better?"

Logan shrugs. "Yeah, usually. I mean, more often than not."

I perk up a bit and rest on my forearm. "Like when?"

"Huh?"

"When for you has it been *that* bad?"

His face contorts in confusion, but he can't help but steal a glance at my chest. "Why do you want to know?"

"For my pride," I joke. "Just so I can know what makes me the best you've ever had."

"The best, huh?" He laughs.

"Oh, don't play, darling. We both know it."

Logan doesn't argue. Only purses his lips. "All right, but it's a boring story."

I pull the pillow from under his head so I have something to sit on that's not his half-erect penis or the cold floor. He gives me a mean glare, but I meet his intensity and he knows it's not a fight worth fighting if he wants a second round later. And we both know he will.

The stamina of this man.

Fuck.

"It was just one of those dates that, you know, wasn't going anywhere," he says. "We both knew it, but neither wanted to be the one to admit it, just keep things polite. The sex that night was kinda... eh."

"What, was she unattractive?" I take another drag and blow it out the doorway.

316

"Come on," he laughs in an '*Are you crazy? Look at me,*' kinda way. "No, this girl was gorgeous, but it just wasn't it. I don't think we even got all our clothes off, it was just like, 'Yeah, might as well get this over with.' Nobody finished and that was that."

I suck on the cigarette, giving his "story" a moment to breathe, then tell him dryly, "You were right. That was a boring story."

"Well if you want exciting, you shoulda been there last night."

What the fuck happened last night? I perk up but try not to show it. Instead, I ask as casually as I can, "You hooked up with someone last night?"

A coy smile starts to crease his cheeks. "No, but I appreciate that that would make you jealous."

I bite the inside of my lip. "Not jealousy," I try not to sound annoyed. "Just... that wasn't part of our agreement."

"The one that says we're not a thing with all the rules a thing would come with? Don't worry. I'm not breaking the rules." He interlocks his hands behind his head and rests on them. It's obvious that he's only doing it to flex his muscles for me. I make it painfully obvious I'm not looking.

"So, what happened?"

"Kat moved on as well."

"Did she now?"

"Yep. I got home last night after hanging out with some friends and she was moving on just fine on the couch with some new guys."

"Guys?" I almost shout, not knowing to be proud of her or sorry for Logan for seeing that.

By his laugh at my reaction, he doesn't seem all that beat up. "Yep. Guys. Plural."

"Fuck… What'd you do?"

"Went to the kitchen and got a beer. What else? What would you have done?"

I probably can't say, present company in mind.

"But… but you just broke up! And you're still living there! Isn't that weird?"

"Very. But Kat is…" he pauses, considering his words carefully. "Look, one, I'm not jealous of the guys she found. Guys that share like that are the biggest cucks. And two, I don't need a girl like that. 'Specially when I've found someone a whole hell of a lot better. Sexier too."

I roll my eyes. "Oh, quit it with the sappy shit, you know I hate that."

"That's why I added 'sexier.' You hate sap but you love praise."

It's true. I do.

"Just don't make it a habit."

Logan sits up more straight. "Why not?"

"Because I said so."

"That's not a reason." He inches closer.

"It's all the reason you need." I take a drag and blow the smoke in his face.

Logan doesn't seem bothered. "We're not on the clock.

You're not my boss. I need something better than that."

I pout to tease him and pat his cheek with my free hand. "That's too bad, darling."

His hands grab my hips and pull me close beside him in a movement so swift I almost lose my breath. "You know, you put up a hard fight but I think it's all for fun."

Stupidly, all I can think to say is, "Yeah?" And not in a playful, seductive way.

"Yeah. I just can't figure out why. I want you. You, at the very least, are unbelievably attracted to me. Why not make this more than a work relationship."

For a moment I fall into his earnest eyes. They're like a dog's, such a depth of devotion and longing to be as... needed... as it's giving to you. I could break this man's heart tonight and he'd still show up for work on Monday as punctual as ever.

"Why not, Nyx?" He whispers.

When I put the cigarette between my lips this time, it's only to stop me from biting myself. But even that doesn't work. All I end up doing is crushing the filter against my lip.

"Because I don't need it." The words come out hard, barely winning a hard-fought battle with the lump in my throat.

"Yes, you do."

"You really want to push your luck with me tonight? You already fucked me once, and it's looking like that's all you're getting." His face doesn't change, so I rush to add, "For the rest of the month."

"That's fine." He leans in closer. Logan's kissed me before. Kissed me all over my body just a few minutes ago, but his face is different now. His eyes are different. The tone of his voice when he says 'That's fine' is different.

"Cut it out, Logan." I push myself off the floor and step out of the storage closet to grab my dress off of the counter.

He's quick to follow but doesn't bother with his clothes. "Why?"

"I don't need to give you a reason. All you should need is 'no,' and leave it at that. And honestly, Logan, *honestly*, now isn't the time that I want to be dealing with this."

"Wh-"

"Please put some clothes on. It's not happening again tonight."

"Nyx, I don't care about the sex," he nearly shouts. It halts me, giving both of us a moment to think about our next move while he puts his pants back on. "Forget the sex. Fuck it, I don't care. I do not care about the sex. That's not what I'm talking about. I'm talking about us. I'm talking about *you*."

From some corner, I hear Willow's little pitter-patter. Someone wants in on the drama.

Logan continues, "Why are you so against having a real connection with someone?"

Again I roll my eyes, this time in real annoyance.

He says, "You didn't tell me what happened with Jade but I think I can take a guess. She didn't want to be some convenience for you, right? Probably wanted to be your friend."

If I could see my face, I know it'd be hellfire red. "No, I was *fine* with her being my friend. I *wanted* her to be my friend."

Logan huffs in disbelief.

"*She* got all crazy and tried to make it something we're not. Familiar situation, huh? *She* came onto me! What do you think about that?"

Logan crosses his arms. "I'm surprised you didn't go for it."

What?

The words almost can't come out, I'm so in awe that he would actually say that.

"Who the fuck do you think you are?"

"Don't pretend, Nyx. Everyone can see it, the way you are with her. Every single time you two were together, even I thought you were fucking." He points his hand at the covenstead curtain. "I just didn't say anything because I believed more that our agreement wasn't just a one-way thing. It's the way you are, Nyx. You carry yourself in this way that's so… so…"

Say it, Logan. Just say it.

"So sexual! It's like, if I didn't know you better, I'd think your 'appointments' were you just sleeping with those people. And your friend, Jade? Fuck, Nyx, if you weren't actually sleeping with her no shit things fell apart!"

I swear I could punch him so hard it'd knock his jaw off.

He doesn't even wait for my protest to add to his insults, "You take a barely legal, highly impressionable girl, who just came out of the closet, gets heartbroken by the girl of her dreams - yeah, we've talked when she's hung out around here - she puts all of her trust in you because of all these promises to help her get her life together, and the entire time you do everything you can to seduce her without actually going for it. The girl must've had blue balls like CRAZY! And you're surprised she was devastated when the girl she's into, who's been leading her on for months, rejects her and makes her feel like shit for having very reasonable emotions? Jesus, Nyx."

My nails dig into my palms. My teeth dig into my lips. Tiny droplets of blood escape my body. "Get out."

"No."

"Get *out*, Logan!" I throw my fist, but it bounces pathetically off of his chest. "Get out, get out, get out!" Hit after hit after hit bounces off him until he grabs my arms and restrains me.

"Give it a rest, Nyx."

"No!" I shout, trying to free myself from him. "If you think I'm such a shitty person just get the fuck out of my house!"

"This isn't a house, it's a store with an apartment."

I'm too angry to be crying, and his stupid no-shits attitude and shit-eating grin only make me angrier. "Get the fuck out! If you hate m-"

Of all the things to do to try to make this situation better, he does the dumbest thing possible and puts a hand over my mouth. I bite at him, achieving nothing. Then, as calm as ever, he says, "I could never hate you. Why do you think I'm telling you this?" He lets go and nudges me away, then takes a step back as well. "If I hated you we would have fucked and I'd be gone. I'm telling you this because I *don't* hate you. I'm telling you this because I care about you, Nyx. Because I know that even though you handled everything with Jade as godawful as possible, you cared about her too."

"Fine. Fine, Logan." The tears start coming. "I'm upset. I'm upset Jade bailed. I've been fucking miserable all night and things are only going to get worse. There. Happy? Do you feel better now that I've spilled my guts to you? Thrilled you get to be a hero now? A shoulder to cry on? Or are you just happy to have a win over me?"

He gives me a look like I'm the dumbest person in the world. "What are you even talking about?"

I throw my arms up in defeat. Where the fuck did I put my cigarette?

"Please leave." I don't have the strength to fight anymore.

"No."

"Please," I wipe my face. "Don't say it. Just go and make it easy."

He steps closer again. "Nyx." He puts a finger under my chin. "I'm still here. I'll go home tonight. But I'm coming back to work in the morning." Logan leans in as if to kiss my lips, but hesitates, and goes for my forehead instead, and for some reason, that makes me feel so much worse. So guilty. "I could never hate you. But you annoy the hell out of me sometimes."

My arms fall around him.

Nothing more of our emotions is said that night. I don't tell him how I feel, and he doesn't push it anymore. But he doesn't go back home. His patience with me has earned a night of quiet rest in my bed.

33. Meditations

I wake before Logan and am quick to dress in the light of the rising sun. He stirs as I slip on my dress, but thankfully doesn't wake. Or maybe he did, and is trying to pretend he didn't steal a look at my nakedness. I search through my cabinets for a notepad and pen.

Stepping out for the morning. Help yourself to anything. I trust you to run the store without breaking anything. I'll be back when I'm ready.

To be absolutely positive he gets the message, I tape it to his forehead. Logan ruffles around, but still, fast asleep. I grab my keys and am out the door as soon as possible.

I arrive at the trail for the pool before the sun is fully over the horizon. The light streams through the trees into the parking lot as a guiding light toward my destination. I am meant to be here this morning. Through my meditation, I will gain the insight I desperately need to clean up this mess with the book.

Before stepping out of the car, I remove my shoes. The gravel of the lot is uncomfortable under my bare feet, but stepping onto the dirt path I've beaten into the ground over the years is warm and soft. The morning dew on pine needles and leaves tickles the arches of my feet. Every step forward into the forest is another ounce of serenity filling my body and soul. As the forest thickens, it hides me from any unwanted eyes and passersby. I can no longer see my car, can't even hear traffic. Only the beauty of the world around me fills my senses.

About a mile in, I come up on an area blocked by downed trees and thick brush, the gate to the pool.

I recite a quiet prayer of gratitude for being allowed this place, then remove my dress and pull up the loose door of branches that block the one access point, and step through.

The pool in the forest is as beautiful as ever. Mist rolls off the surface of the water, with the last rays of the morning sun shining through them, warming the water. I step forward gently, careful not to harm any living thing; bugs, ferns, holes to homes of small animals. I am respectful of all here.

The first dip into the pool is so soothing I almost fall in and drown myself in it. I take another step in, then another, until I'm floating, drifting in the pool, and begin my meditation.

I am fasting until I find a new solution to this situation with the book, or until Jade gets her shit together and helps me again. And it had better be soon because with each day the new moon approaches, and I think the malicious energy of the book is seeping into the rest of the building.

I want to believe that the argument we had last night was spurred on by the book more than anything, and it was Logan's levelheadedness that saved us from saying or doing anything we'd regret. I want to believe it was the book, the sexual demon bound to it that pushed Jade's mind and messed with her emotions that led to her outburst. Before long, I wouldn't be surprised if the energy got to my customers. Jokes of dark magic would no longer be jokes at that point.

After too much time to count had passed, I already regret the fast. It would have been fine if Logan and I didn't have drunk sex last night, or at least if I'd had a midnight snack. But now I'm running on nothing but liquor since dinner last night. My stomach grumbles, but I have to push past this. I have to overcome my own demons, which Logan so kindly pointed out, before I can overcome the book.

I push past the pain in my stomach and ignore the dryness of my throat. I focus inward, reciting spells under my breath. The goal is self-cleansing, a spiritual detox. Ponder the flaws and insecurities in the back of my mind. Replay the night with Jade, replay our past exchanges, the moments we were alone together.

How did she act around me? What was the tone of her voice? How did her body move? What about myself? How did I really talk to her? How did she hear me? How did I move around her, and how did she read me?

The train of thought brings me to Maria. When did she turn on me? Was it that night in her apartment? I corrected her on her predispositions of the spirit.

No. No, I didn't correct her. I teased her. I made jokes about her to her face. I mocked a girl who wanted happiness and friendship, and now only feels more alone.

No, that's not true either. She found her people. What I did was let her fall down the wrong path. I could have helped her. I could have done what she asked me to do and investigated the spirit. If I had done that, she'd be safe, and none of this would have gotten between mine and Jade's friendship.

Maria wanted to be my friend, and I had no reason not to accept it except pride.

She still wants a friend. She needs one now, more than ever. A true friend. My time for that has passed, but I know someone who can help. Someone who would care about her the way she deserves.

And as for the book, I'll just have to swallow that pride and try to win Jade back. I can control myself around her. I'll be more aware of both myself and her. I won't lead her on, I'll make my intentions crystal clear. It will be a relationship of mutual, professional respect.

Everything is going to be okay.

When I open my eyes, the sun is directly above me. A cute little spider crawls up my naval toward my chest. I backstroke toward the shore, careful not to let the spider fall off and drown. When I reach the shore and lay on the ground, the spider climbs across me, along my arm to my hand, and hops off.

I lay there for a few more minutes, enjoying the summer warmth of the forest.

* * *

The phone rings and rings until it goes to voicemail. I call again. Still no answer.

What the fuck, Jade? I'm trying to be a nicer person, answer your phone!

I call a third time, and when it goes to voicemail after two rings, I throw my phone into the little pocket under the dashboard. Fuck it, if she's not going to answer the phone, I'll just have to talk to her in person.

34. A Little Bit of Help

"What the hell are you doing here?" Jade stands in her doorway before me with her arms crossed. Travel bags and bins clutter half of the room as if held back by an invisible barrier. Jenna (if they're still going to be roommates) must not have begun the move yet.

"I came to say I'm sorry," I tell her. No point beating around the bush.

"How did you even find me? Are you following me?" Jade pokes her head out of the doorway and looks up and down the hall. What she's looking for, I have no idea. But it's a question I'd prefer not to answer if I'm trying to win her back.

I push past her into the room, pull a chair out from the small desk at the end of her bed and take a seat. "I've been doing some meditating, and a little drinking, and I came to the conclusion: You were right."

Jade gives me a look of perplexity, that slowly turns into one of "no shit."

I go on, "I know I can come off a little abrasive sometimes. And…" I take a deep breath in, "Maybe I'm not always totally aware of how I carry myself. And I don't always do my best at reading others' emotions. I never meant to lead you on, and I was wrong to make you feel bad for how you read the situation."

Jade rolls her eyes. "So, it's still partially my fault, you're saying." Her hand is still on the knob of the open door.

Instinctively, I want to tell her, "Yes," but we're working on being more considerate now. "No, that's not at all what I meant."

"Then what did you mean?" The door wavers in her hand.

I rise, hoping my height advantage over her will get her to stop fidgeting with the damn door as if she's going to intimidate me out of her room before I can make amends. "I mean I didn't realize what I was doing. That's it. I'm sorry. I was oblivious."

"Kissing me and touching me like all that was just being oblivious? Jesus, Nyx. No, I don't buy it!"

"Well, buy it!" Shit, I was really hoping this would be easier. "You were right that I led you on. You were right! What else do you need to hear?"

"Nothing!" She shouts, throwing her hands in the air, and stomps over to her bed. The door swings closed. This feels like progress, at least. She's not trying to force me out anymore. "I didn't want- I didn't *need* an apology. I'm done with this. It was a waste of time from the start when you did that stupid ritual with your stupid book!"

I could bring up the fact that she *did* sign it, and that is just as binding as any other contract, so in a way, she's obligated to at least see this through. But I know that'll only push her away further.

Gotta salvage this, Nyx. Swallow that pride. Swallow it.

"You came to me for a reason," I remind her. "Maybe it wasn't the right time," I lie; of course it was the right time. Meetings like this don't happen by chance. "But there was a reason for it. There was a reason we were brought together, and there was a reason you came to me."

"I 'came to you' because you were hitting on me!"

I bite my tongue. I'll let her rant if she needs to, as long as she gets it out of her system and we can talk like forgiving adults.

"Don't you see yourself? Don't you ever consider how you're acting? You bring me in after hours, talking all sultry-like, got the candles and everything, whispering to me like that? Fuck, it was like walking into a porno. But you're good, you're so fucking good at getting people under your spell. You actually convinced me this was real, and that you cared about me. You didn't though. All you wanted me to do was help you with that damn book you stole from that girl. It was never about me, was it? It was never about being my friend. It was never about helping me deal with my problem. It was all just a game so you could get a fucking intern on your little project."

"Jade, how could you actually believe that? The problems with the book didn't come up until after we met."

She doesn't argue, only rolls her eyes.

This tactic isn't working, and I feel like I'm reduced to something I really didn't want to do. I take a deep breath, then cross the room to take her by the hand and get on my knees. But do *not* think I'm about to beg.

I say gently, "Jade. When you asked me to go out with you as a friend, did you mean it? Did you mean as a friend?"

"Yes," she says with strain, but without hesitation. "Yeah, I really just wanted to get you out of that store and spend time with you like a real person."

I nod. "Good. I really did want that too. I haven't done something like that in a really, really long time. For the last few years, if I wasn't at the store, I was with a guy I don't think I really loved. I would have loved to just take a day off with a friend. And I'd still like to. You brought so much joy to my life I haven't had since... since high school, probably. I loved having a sister again. I wish you could still be that. And I promise I won't cross any lines. I won't lead you on, I'll be aware of how I act."

Jade looks down at our hands. They tighten, but her face is still unreadable.

"I just don't trust you, Nyx."

It's a stab in the heart. Here I am, on my knees for her. I've never been this close to begging before.

"Just give me a chance to prove myself," I ask of her. "I promise. All I want is a friend."

She pulls her hands away. "Here's your chance. Tell me honestly, why did you come here today?"

Honestly? Now, that's a risk. I've been honest with her this whole time, but if we're talking about what sparked this change of heart? It probably wouldn't be appropriate to tell her about the hassling I got from Logan, the context of it at least. But, when I told her I believed she had a touch of a sixth sense, it wasn't to hype her up. There'd be no use in lying, and hopefully - *hopefully* - she will be understanding.

"I still need help with the book."

She tears her hands away and pushes further back on the bed, up against the wall.

I rush to say, "And you're the only person who can help me! But once that is done, I swear-"

"Just get the fuck out of here." She doesn't even shout. Jade says the words so flatly, so matter-of-factly. She really is done with me.

There's no use fighting it anymore.

I stand. My lips part as I think of something else to say, but there's no point to it.

The door handle feels so cold. The whole room feels cold.

I leave without another word.

* * *

It might be time to give up.

Fuck, I can't believe I'm saying this.

No, no it's not time to give up. I'll try again. I'll exorcise the damn book on my own.

Oh, who am I kidding? If I could, I would have done that a long time ago. Maybe I can get rid of it. Hide it better than somewhere in my own house. I'll secure it good and dump it in the lake with weights tied to it. That's actually not a bad idea. Maria wouldn't be desperate enough to learn how to scuba dive and find it. But her new coven might. If they're willing to summon a demon they probably wouldn't have any problem going for a swim. Even if they didn't, it's still there for someone else to wander on to. Some fisherman who fights for his life to pull up what he thinks is just a really big fish. Then this starts all over again when he pawns it off and it ends up in a store like mine for some new girl to get ahold of.

It must be cleansed. There's no other option.

Okay, Nyx, you can do this.

I pull up to Witch's Brew and... is that a fucking line?

I park the car across the road, the only spot on the street open and rush in. There is absolutely no room to move around and for a moment, I'm scared for Logan. They're going to kill him! He'll be so lost without me!

"Excuse me! I'm here! All's good! Who needs help?" I offer assistance to whoever I can but no one takes me up on the offer. Do they not know who I am?

I nudge toward one woman picking through the crystal tray, looking lost. One at a time, I can clear some of the congestion. I reach out to her, but the first voice I hear is Logan's.

"This is actually the one I was talking about. Aventurine, good for healing the heart and emotional tranquility," he says, holding up a pendant with the crystal. The girl smiles, and Logan tells her to meet her at the front to check out. I follow them both and once behind the counter, he notices me.

"Oh, hey there," Logan says with a grin and rings up the pendant. "Didn't think you were coming back. Thought I'd just assumed ownership of the place."

"You wish. Surprised you're not overwhelmed yet. How did it get like this?"

Logan shrugs and hands the customer a baggie with her new Aventurine necklace. "Fuck if I know. Was dead for a while, but- oh, hold on. Can you get the register?"

Before I can answer he's off again. Logan jumps from one customer to another, to another, pointing them in all different directions, not missing a beat with any of their questions. I'm in a frenzy to get everyone checked out as rapidly as humanly possible and, though it's a struggle, I'm trying to listen in on the shopping tips Logan gives.

Everything... and I mean absolutely everything he says is spot on. When he gives explanations of the tools we provide for witches to do their craft, he says it better than even I could. There are even little bits of information I hear that I'd never even known! Is he just making stuff up on the spot? He must be. There's no way- but it all makes sense.

The next few hours carry on like that; me stuck behind the counter, and Logan working the floor. Maybe this will be his store soon if I'm not careful. And the eyes of all the customers say he is a big reason that they're here.

Watching him work actually gives me an idea.

As soon as the last customer is out and the door is locked, I take his hand and drag him into the covenstead.

"I'm surprised you're still on your feet," he laughs, reaching for the trim of his shirt to take it off.

"Keep it on," I tell him. "That's not what you're in here for."

Disappointment creases his face and he lets go of his shirt.

"I'm giving you a promotion."

"Yeah?" He asks, still sounding disappointed. "I expect the pay is top tier, right?"

"Keep up how it was today, and we'll talk about it. But no, this is a different kind of promotion. You're my assistant now." I motion for him to take a seat at the table, and I take mine across from him. The candles in the room flare to life.

"You gotta tell me how you do that. Got a trigger or something up your sleeve?"

I ignore the question. "Do you remember that book I gave you to hide?"

"How could I forget? Every time I step in this room something interesting seems to happen."

"Focus now, darling. Look, I need your help again with it. And as my employee, I'm ordering you to help."

Logan gives me a coy smile as if this were some silly joke. "You're pretty weird." He pushes out his chair and stands. "If you want me to get rid of it I'll just throw it away." He makes his way toward the dresser and I rush up to stop him. Already though, it gives me a clue as to the book's whereabouts that I wish I didn't yet know.

"Stop! It's not that simple."

He pauses, but the mischievous look in his eyes says he wants to push my limits.

"Please, sit back down," I ask, gesturing toward the chair.

He smirks. "You know, I like it when you get bossy, but it's a lot less fun when we've both still got our clothes on." He just has to push my buttons, doesn't he? But at least he does as he's told.

"I didn't want to bring you into this," I tell him. "I really didn't think I'd ever even consider this, but…"

"Help me Obi-wan Kenobi, you're my only hope."

I shoot him a glare. "For once. For *once*, Logan, can you please take this seriously?"

"All right, all right, I'm all yours. What do you need?"

I huff out a breath before continuing. "I need you to help me cast a spell."

It's obvious on his reddening face and puffing cheeks that he's barely containing a laugh.

"Don't fucking do it," I warn.

His eyes squint. This must be the hardest thing he's ever been asked to do, control himself.

"Laugh and you're fired."

Logan covers his mouth and puts his head down to hide from my wrath. Being fired isn't a threat enough, he's too used to it.

"We're done fucking around if you laugh."

"Okay, okay!" He nearly shouts, still holding back a smile. "You got me. I can't risk that much. Okay, we're casting spells now. Cool. Always wanted to be a wizard."

"It-" I rub my temples. How the fuck did I ever get involved with this man? Worse, how did I ever let him have sex with me? Did Damien deprive me of good sex that badly?

"So, how is this gonna work?" Logan asks, arms crossed and tilting his chair back. "How 'bout I give it a quick little…" He does the sign of the cross. "Power of Christ compels you, and we call it a day."

"If it was that simple I would have done that already."

"Would you?" It's a challenge disguised as a joke.

"That's not how you deal with stuff like this."

"Works in the movies."

"This *isn't* a movie."

"Okay, all right. How do we do this then?"

I really hope that when he asked that just now, he was asking genuinely. "This won't work if you're just screwing around. This is serious to me, Logan. Even if you don't care for it, just help me out."

"I already said I would." He puts his arms on the table and leans in. His tone changes, and I know for certain he isn't joking. "I told you I'd help. I'm in, Nyx."

I don't know if it was me or him who reached out, probably him, but our hands meet. Our fingers interlock.

"I do ask one thing from you, though."

This is going to be something just to push my buttons, isn't it?

"Dinner. You and me."

I bite the inside of my lip, unsure what to say. Did last night's conversation not actually get to him? And am I going to be that disappointed if it didn't?

"We don't have to make it a date, or anything," he's quick to add. "But... just something non-work related, but still with clothes on. What do you say?"

35. Dinner (Not-a)Date

This is absolutely ridiculous. I can't believe I agreed to this. We have two days left before the new moon and have had time for nothing but work, but for some reason, we can make time for a date and not spell practice.

Not a date. It's *not* a date, I have to remind myself.

It's just dinner. It's a very well-earned dinner, I might add. If I could use any distraction instead of practicing with and educating Logan this week, it would have been other sorts of physical activity. But dinner will do.

This whole idea though that it isn't a date, but we're going somewhere nice… it just throws me off. If Logan had told me what was on his mind, I'd have less anxiety over how I should dress - for the restaurant, not for him - so, for safety's sake, I dress to the nines.

Screw it, whether or not it is a date, I can have a nice night. I'll think of it like this: I'm treating myself. I do my hair up nicely because *I* like the way it looks. I'll put a little more time into doing my makeup because *I* want to do this for myself. And I'll wear stockings without rips and a modest-but-sexy dress because I like how it makes *me* feel.

But I hope Logan likes it too.

I'm sure he's not thinking about it like that, though. He agreed that this was just as friends and I'm not ready for anything more. He'll respect that.

When I step out the front door and lock it, I expect to see him in jeans and a v-neck shirt. Maybe his hair won't be messy for once, and maybe he'll wear nicer shoes. What I didn't expect is the man standing in front of me; the man wearing fine Italian shoes, slacks, a button-up shirt, and a blazer. His stubble is freshly shaved, and the hair… still messy. But it's a mess that looks intentional and in a way, sort of professional. And there's a smell about him.

"Are you wearing cologne?" I ask.

Logan takes my hand and gently kisses my tattooed fingers. It makes me think of going to the house of a proper gentleman and meeting his family only to repulse them with this "goth-girl trash" style. I wonder what his parents are like. Would they like me? Would they be okay with a clean-cut guy like Logan dating a girl who looks like this? Or would they give me constant shit and tell me the tattoos won't look good anymore when I'm fifty?

Why do I even care? I don't. I don't, I don't, I don't, because it's not like that. This is a dinner as friends that I will not let develop into anything else.

But I do lov-

I do like the way he kisses my fingers.

"I thought it'd be better than the smell of incense I can't get off of me anymore."

He smells like mahogany teakwood. "It is much better," I say.

Logan smirks, and with his free hand, opens the passenger side door and gestures in. "Please," he says, escorting me to my seat.

I feel like I'm being led into a pumpkin coach shaped like a beat-up Chevy, headed to a platonic ball. He closes the door when I'm in and hops around to the other side and gets in.

"I thought you didn't have a car."

Logan gives me a confused grin. "What gave you that idea? Think I was walking to work every day?"

"That night at the bar when you were walking home."

Logan laughs off the comment, and I can put the pieces together.

"You said we were going somewhere nice," I say. "What did you have in mind?"

"Have you ever tried Nove?"

It's a nice place, I know, and he didn't mean anything by it. I never told him that was my last date with Damien, but it is still so hard not to roll my eyes and get out of the car. Instead, I bite my tongue. "I may have gone once or twice."

"It's a great place," Logan says, pulling away from the curb.

* * *

He pulls out my chair at the restaurant with the same grace he helped me out of the car. Every step we've taken this night so far, he holds my hand, and opens the doors. If I had a coat, I'm sure he would have taken it to hang up on the rack by the hostess. And when the waiter comes by to take our drinks, he says nothing, only gestures humbly toward me to go first. And he says nothing when I order an expensive glass of wine.

But the thing that feels the most out of place of all of this, is not once this night has Logan made any of his typical dumb jokes. Honestly, it's a little worrying.

"Are you doing all right?" I ask after the waiter brings our drinks.

No shrug or laugh, or sarcastic remark. Just a handsome smile and, "Wonderful. I'm really glad you're here with me tonight."

"I... Yeah, I'm glad too. I think I really needed this." Saying it comes with a weight off my chest from the go-go-go rigamarole I've been running with the store for so long. Even with my last date with Damien, there was a purpose behind the date: get our shit back on track. Being able to have a nice, expensive dinner for the sake of having a nice and expensive dinner is so relaxing, helped by this wonderful red wine.

"Me too," he says. "Been hoping for something like this for a while."

We all know where he's going with this. Best to nip it in the bud right away. But what can I divert to? The first thing that crosses my mind is work; the book, the store. My life outside of those two recently has been dirty books - I really do need to finish "Binds" - and working off the stress of the day with Logan. I don't know what to talk to him about that he probably doesn't already know. So, all I can come back to is the store.

"Why do you put up with me?" As soon as I ask, it sounds

like a self-pitying question, and I have to rephrase it. "I mean, look, I know how my attitude can be sometimes, and the pace around the store can get pretty intense. So, I just mean, why here when you didn't put up with anything else around town?"

His lips pull apart in a grin as if he were waiting for that question to be asked, but then he licks his lips and looks down at his gin & tonic in thought. "I guess… I don't know, Nyx, it's not that deep."

"It doesn't have to be. I'm just curious. It can't just be 'cause you have something nice to stare at all day." I catch myself flashing him a cheesy smile with the flutter of my lashes. And maybe my arms pushed my breasts together a bit. I immediately feel like an absolute fool, trying too hard to attract a high school crush. But he goes for the bait and glances at my cleavage, then meets my eyes.

"That's definitely a perk of the job." Logan takes a sip of his drink, then leans in closer. His voice drops lower like he's telling a secret just a little too loudly. "I don't know. I was working retail job after retail job. There's not much excitement in life selling cheap novelties or over-priced clothes to rich guys."

"So, why'd you keep doing it? If you want something better for yourself, there's the college right down the road."

"Sure, but what would I study? I take these jobs to pay the bills. If I knew what I wanted to do with myself I'd've moved on from retail and bars a long time ago."

"Which bar did you work at?"

"The Cellar. Was there for like…" He rolls his eyes up to the ceiling. "Maybe three months? It was weird, though. They had all these open mic nights and there was always drama."

That sounds familiar. Could he have been there that night Harry ruined Silvia and that author guy's relationship? He probably would've been the one who made my drink! What are the odds?

Logan continues, "But even though the money was good, tips were fucking great, I just didn't care about being there." He stops, then laughs. "You know, for a while I wanted to be a priest."

That's... interesting, to say the least. Although, I can kind of see it now.

"What happened to that?"

He looks me up and down again, from my chest to my eyes. "I wouldn't be very good at the whole celibacy thing. Especially if you ever came into my congregation," he laughs again. "No, I- and don't laugh - I wanted kids one day, you know? I met Kat and had to reconsider my plans. But what about you? Planning on sticking with the store for the long run?"

I don't think I ever really thought about it. The obvious answer would be yes, what else would I do with myself?

"Yeah," I answer. "Yeah, I think so."

"On your own? I can't imagine it's the easiest job in the world."

"Wait, where are *you* going? Planning on bailing on me so soon?"

Logan grins, "Not if you're gonna miss me like that. I'd hate to break your heart, darling." He takes another sip of his gin to punctuate himself.

I purse my lips and carry on as if nothing was said. "I might expand one day. I've thought about buying the property next door.

346

Or, if I ever moved out, I could convert the apartment into a second floor for the store."

"And what would you put up there?"

This isn't a conversation I've had once before in my life. I never talked about this kind of stuff with Jade, and for the life of me can't remember if I ever talked about this with Damien. "The clothing stock has been selling really well lately. Maybe the second floor could be all apparel and jewelry."

"What about a meditation room, or something like that? A place for other witches to study in good company."

It's a wonderful idea, but I'm still hung up on the fact that he asked me about the future of the store.

"I'd consider that," I say, 100% making that the goal now. "So, I guess I have to come back to my first question. Of all the places you've worked around here, why stay with me?"

That smirk again. "Is it too crazy to think that I just like being around you? You drive me crazy sometimes, your whole tough girl act, but you're a lot of fun to be around. And not just for the obvious reasons. And you put up with me too. Look, I won't make this weird. I won't say anything that ruins what we've got going on. So," he lifts his hands like a peace offering. "We'll just leave it at that. Nothing too deep. I just like you, Nyx."

* * *

"Pull off just up here," I tell Logan.

He struggles to see ahead of us in the night's fog. "What am I looking for? Parking lot?"

"No, just a little patch off the road. There."

Logan pulls the car over to the woodline. I slip my shoes off and tell him to do the same.

"My shoes? You know a friend of mine used to run around in the woods with bare feet because he thought he was a hobbit and got horrible warts all over the bottom of his feet and between his toes."

I don't even know what to say to that. "Just take them off. It's good ground on which we're walking."

Logan huffs, but does as he's told. "Got a flashlight?"

"We don't need one." I get out of the car and walk to the woodline.

He follows, and I can see him getting out his phone to use as a flashlight.

I tell him, "You don't need that. I know the way."

Logan looks up at the sky. "If you plan on leading me by the light of the moon or something like that, not gonna have a whole lotta luck."

It's true. We've almost got a new moon again and will be walking in near pitch black. I remind him, "I know the way. Come, darling." I take him by the hand and lead him into the woods.

As we walk along the beaten path, I feel him twitching from stepping on twigs or small rocks. I hear him try to muffle his grunts when a branch brushes against his face.

"How far is this place?"

"Not far."

"Be honest," he says. "You're leading me out here for some kind of sacrifice, right?"

"You know me too well, Logan. Need a blood sacrifice for all my dark magic."

"Kinky."

I roll my eyes. "Get your jokes out now. Once we're there I will tolerate no disrespect. This is a special place."

"Oh, I see." He says, and I regret telling him to get them out now. "So you're letting me into your special place? Don't worry, I won't tell anyone. I'm very discreet."

"That's comforting."

"Oh yeah, I've heard it's very comfortable. Real warm, but a bit of a tight squeeze. And really wet."

"I can always turn us around," I warn him with an empty threat. There's no going back now, though. I've taken him this far, and regardless of his annoying joke, I want him to be here with me.

When we get to the door, I fill his mind with far too much excitement.

"Take your clothes off." My dress is already off my shoulders.

He stands bewildered, even though in this light, we can barely make out each other's features. Maybe, at most, he can see the faint reflection of the moon and some stars off of my piercings.

"Are we in the spot yet?" He asks.

"Almost."

"Okay, so I can still ask if this is a sacrifice thing without you killing me early."

"I might still consider it. Now take 'em off."

This time, he doesn't hesitate. In the darkness I hear him

undo his belt, then watch the outline of his silhouette fold up his clothes and put them on a rock next to mine. I take his hand again and lead him into the pool.

Once past the barrier, the world seems to lighten. The crescent moon shines a little brighter on my place of peace. The sounds of nature are louder but ring through the area like a melody. Even Logan seems amazed by the place, for once able to stare at something other than my body.

"Come with me," I whisper, leading him closer to the water. At its edge, I let go of his hand.

His eyes fall from the beauty around us onto me. He watches as I step backward into the pool. With one finger I invite him in.

I close my eyes and float on my back. "Join me, Logan. Let your spirit wander in the void."

A moment later, I feel the ripples of the water move against my legs and along my body. He's joined me.

I feel his body next to mine, hear his breathing. It's forced, struggling.

"Don't try to stay afloat," I tell him gently. "Try to let go. You are no longer here… let your body stay behind while your mind explores the universe. Focus on your spirit. Meditate…"

"Okay… focusing," he tells himself. "Meditating."

I'm close to reaching a complete meditative state. I'm almost there, floating among the stars, but I feel Logan's eyes on me. I try to block it out, try to keep my focus, but I want to look back. Not to condemn him for failing to listen again, but to find peace elsewhere.

I open my eyes and see him looking into mine.

His arms wrap around my sides. Mine fall around his shoulder, and my legs wrap around his waist. I find a state of meditation with my lips on his. One of his hands makes its way up my spine to the nape of my neck. My head falls back into his hold, and Logan kisses my neck.

Between my legs, I feel him brush against me. I take a staggered breath at his touch.

"Logan," I breathe, but he can't respond. His face is buried in my chest.

We drift back toward the shore. Logan lies on the dirt, and I fix myself to straddle him with my hands resting on his strong chest. He slides into me and I'm filled with an ecstasy far beyond those of lustful pleasure. I fall, my lips onto his again. When we kiss it feels real. It's violent and passionate, and not at all sexual. There's a raging fire of something more than bare physical attraction between us. His hands rest on my hips, never once reaching for my butt or my breasts. I know if I could read his mind, there wouldn't be anything dirty. It's only the moment between us now.

And I just know, we aren't ever going to be able to go back to being just friends or have a "work relationship" after this. Not after we finish together in that same position by the pool. Not after three words are thought by both of us, but not said out loud.

All we do is stare up at the night sky in each other's arms, afterward. Nothing needs to be said. But I don't know when I last felt this happy next to someone.

I'm totally under his spell.

* * *

The ride back to my place is quiet, but neither of us stopped smiling the whole way there with our hands held tight. Every time I think of something to say, I hold myself back. It would only ruin the moment. Logan seems to be on the same page. No witty response from him since we did it.

I've decided to let him stay the night again. Hell, he can stay whenever he likes. He could live here for all I care. Not that it was something to worry about before, but I'll never have to worry about him being late. And tomorrow morning, maybe I'll give him a promotion from employee-with-benefits to something more traditional.

I lean my head on his arm.

When he parks the car, Logan kisses my forehead. "Ready to call it a night?"

I nod, absolutely worn out from the day. And night. I could fall asleep here in his car.

Logan escorts me back to the door and opens it for me.

I step through, and something hits me. The lights are off for one, and I don't recall turning them off. But also...

"Logan?" I ask in a daze.

"Yeah?"

"Did you unlock the door?"

"No, you never gave me a key. Did you leave it unlocked?"

"No... I remember locking it." Without another word, I rush to the covenstead and flick the lights on. Logan rushes in

352

behind me. "Where's the book?" I demand, already noticing the lack of horrible energy surrounding us.

"It's…" He begins, pulling one of the cabinets away from the wall. "Should be…" Logan reaches behind it, then looks again with the flashlight from his phone. "It's not here."

Horror fills me, twisting around my bones, and tightening my lungs. I know I screwed up, but I didn't think she'd hate me this much. I fall into one of the chairs around the table.

Logan rushes to me and drops to a knee. "What is it? Who else could have gotten in? Nyx, does anyone else have a key?"

Yes. One person does. "Jade."

36. Where's the Book

"How could I be so stupid?" I drop down onto my couch. Logan falls too, with his arm around me. "I can't believe I never got that stupid key back from her."

"Hold on now," Logan consoles. "Maybe it wasn't her. Maybe... maybe that other girl, Maria, got the key from her. Or maybe someone just picked the lock. Do you really think Jade would be that kind of person?"

"Yes," I tell him bluntly. "She wasn't before, but Logan, I really pissed her off. You should have seen her the other day. She wanted nothing to do with me."

A smile breaks on his face. It's all for show, just to cheer me up, but it's there and I'd be lying if I said I didn't appreciate it. Now's not the time for his humor either, but I'd appreciate that too if I'm being honest. "There you go," he says. "She wants nothing to do with you. That's a good thing... in this situation. A girl who wants nothing to do with you wouldn't go out of her way to rob you."

There may be some sense to that. Actually, there's a lot of

sense in that. All the sense in the world. But it's wrong. "I know it was her. I don't know why, I don't know what she has to gain from it, but I know it was her."

Logan takes his arm off of me, then leans forward in thought with his chin in one hand. His eyebrows crease. "Witches…" He says.

It's surely a comment not meant out of respect, but right now I lean back on the couch and agree, "Yeah. Witches."

He glances over his shoulder. "Probably wouldn't be dealing with all of this if y'all went to church once in a while."

I roll my eyes. "Catholic girls get possessed all the time. Haven't you seen The Exorcist?"

Logan chuckles. "Fair enough." He sighs, then says, "All right. Putting myself in your mindset, going along with all this demon shit, is it too far-fetched to think Jade might have been in league with these witches Maria's with?"

"In league?" I ask.

"Yeah, like a double agent."

I shake my head violently. "No, there's no way. I can say for certain, she knew nothing of any of this before I enlightened her."

"Okay, well if you're so sure she did this, she's gotta have a reason." Logan rises from the couch and grabs his blazer.

"Where are you going?" I ask, picking myself up off the couch.

"Let's go ask her. She'll ignore your texts but she can't avoid us when we're at her door. You know where she's at, right?"

* * *

We're a day away from the new moon and things have to make a turn for the worst now. Wonderful. Logan leads the way to the dormitories as if he belongs there. The main door to Jade's building is locked, so he turns to me after yanking on the door and asks, "You know any spells that can get us in? What's that one from Harry Potter?"

I cross my arms and glare up at him.

"All right, all right, don't get pissy. Only trying to help."

"Any other ideas?" I ask.

"What floor does she live on?" Logan glances around the corner, and spies rooms with their lights still on.

"Third. Why?"

He purses his lips. "Damn. If she was on the first we could just bang on her window. Second, we could throw rocks at it."

"What's wrong with the third floor, then?"

His lips crack into a grin. "I was never good enough for the baseball team. Also don't want to wake up the whole neighborhood shouting up at her." He yanks on the door again.

"You're going to anyway if you keep doing that."

"Should we have waited until morning?"

If we did, we'd be losing too much time. If I'm right, that is. And I'm pretty sure I am.

"No," I tell him. "We have to see her tonight."

Logan nods. "Got it. I'll be right back." He struts past me and disappears into the night before I can stop him.

"Logan!" I whisper into the darkness to no response.

With him gone, I pull on the door one more time. Yep, still locked. Maybe I'll get lucky and Jade will walk by, or even better she'll walk up the path to the door from the parking lot and I can catch her like that.

A minute later though, a different familiar face struts into view from the dorm hallway, catches my disbelieving eyes, and politely opens the door.

"Lose your key?" Logan asks, blocking the open doorway.

"How did you get in?"

"You tell me your tricks and I'll tell you mine. But if you don't have an up-to-date school ID, I'm afraid I can't let you in."

"Oh my lord, move over, Logan." I try to push my way in, but he stands firm.

"Sorry," he laughs. "I'm starting to think you don't actually go here. Do I have to call campus security?"

"We don't have time for this. Do you want to stay at my place tonight or not?"

He considers, just to waste time.

Fuck this.

I flash a tit and walk past him as he gawks and loses all resilience. "Cheap move," he laughs.

"That's the best you're getting tonight," I tell him, speed walking toward the elevator. "And I'll be sleeping in a parka just to make sure you don't get any ideas."

The elevator bell rings and we step in together. We take a quick ride up and close in on Jade's dorm.

Logan comments, "Pretty quiet for a Friday night. You'd think there would be more parties."

Is now really the time for small talk?

"Maybe we could crash one sometime. I've never been to a college party."

"Party crashing? What are you, twelve?" His answer doesn't matter anyway, as we've arrived at Jade's room.

I raise my hand to knock, but Logan grabs my wrist. "Let me." He lets go and bangs hard - and I mean, HARD - on her door. "Campus police! Open up!"

I grab his hand and whisper, "What the fuck are you doing?"

Logan whispers back, "Really think she'll answer again if it's you?" He bangs again with his free hand, "Hurry up or we're breaking the lock!"

A door a few yards down the hall opens up and a young man with dirty blond hair pokes his head out. We're definitely getting arrested tonight. I nudge Logan to tell him about the witness. Logan spins, and without missing a beat, points at the kid. "Back inside, punk, or I'll call your mom."

The kid does as he's told, for some reason, and Jade's door opens. But it's Jenna who answers. She has an "oh shit" look on her face as if we are worse than campus security.

I step forward, putting myself in the doorway so she can't shut it on us.

"Where's Jade?" I demand.

"Who?" The confusion in her voice is genuine. I don't remember if Jade told me whether or not she ever went by her real name around Jenna.

Logan speaks up and flashes his driver's license in his wallet like it's a badge. "Campus police, Ma'am. Where's the girl?"

I throw my hand back to smack his chest. "Quit it, Logan." Then to Jenna, "Zoe. Where's Zoe?"

"Don't try to protect her," Logan adds. "We've already got a dozen witnesses testifying against her. She's got a one-way ticket to the slammer."

"Jesus! Logan! Stop!" I take a deep breath. "Jenna, I'm sorry for bothering you like this. But it's very important. No one's in trouble. Just please tell me where Zoe is."

It's not Jenna who answers next though. Jade steps out of the dorm's bathroom in a towel, fresh from the shower.

Logan steps away from the doorway and hides behind the wall. "Don't worry, I'm not lookin'." I glance at him and see he's looking in every direction down the hall to avoid looking in the room. I'm glad he got me in here tonight, but as always, he is running out his welcome.

"What do you want?" Jade asks defeatedly.

No use beating around the bush. "Did you go to my store tonight? The door was unlocked and the book-"

"Yes." She says flatly.

My eyes go wide, and even Logan peaks in. Jenna stands in the back, completely lost.

"W- why?"

As if this were just another thing, Jade says, "Someone asked me to."

Almost like she is totally justified, Logan adds, "Maria.

Makes sense. She asked me too. Probably shoulda seen that coming."

Jade glances up at him with a look of annoyance, like she never liked him, then says, "No, not Maria. Someone else."

"Who?" I ask, almost lunging at her.

"Some friend of hers. I don't remember, started with a 'P.'"

"You broke into my store because someone you never met asked you to?"

"It's not yours anyway. Who cares what she does with it? It's just a stupid book. It's not worth all… this." She places her hand on the door and starts to swing it closer. I put my hand out to hold it in place. Logan too steps a little closer in case the extra strength is needed.

"You don't get it, do you, Jade?" I ask, trying my best not to unleash my rage upon her.

Totally unaffected, she tells me back, "I don't care."

The words weaken me. Jade tosses me her spare key from the top of a little toiletry trolly just inside the bathroom, then closes the door with no resistance. Even Logan seems to not know what to do.

We stand there in the empty hallway like idiots.

"Do you want me to knock again?" Logan asks.

He slowly raises his hand in a fist, but I take it into my own, staring blankly ahead.

"No," I say, almost in a whisper. I hate that I know exactly who Jade was talking about. And if she has it now, there's almost nothing left to do. Almost. The clock is running. Tomorrow night we'll have a new moon. Whoever is planning a big ritual is gonna have a hell of a night. Gears turn in my head. Plans fall together. If I play my cards right, if I'm right in my assumption of who is manipulating Maria, I might still have a very good new moon. It's a thin chance, but I have to go for it.

I look up into Logan's eyes and think, *with a little help.*

37. Potions Class

Did you think this could be a story about witchcraft, called "Witch's Brew" without at least one potion actually brewed?

Logan joins me in the covenstead first thing in the morning and watches diligently as I dress the room properly, say my prayers for a successful brew, and prepare my ingredients. When I put my cauldron on the table - just a little one, nothing crazy - Logan huffs a not-so-subtle laugh and shakes his head.

"You can walk away at any time," I tell him without looking up from my checklist of ingredients. If Maria and her coven already have the book back, there's no use in cleansing it anymore, and trying to steal it back would be a waste of precious time if we don't know where exactly it is. Chances are, it's not being let out of sight of any of these witches ever again. For the most part of this plan, Logan will have to take a backseat. Hopefully, at the very least, though, he can learn something.

The water in the cauldron comes to a boil, and I begin mixing in the first few ingredients as instructed in my potions book.

With each one dropped, Logan shares another thought best kept in his head.

"Eye of newt." *Plop*. "Tail of newt." *Plop*. "Hand of…" I hold the rosemary leaf above the boiling water, waiting for him to finish. "Mouse." *TSSSsss*, the leaf drops.

"I thought you read all those books we sell here." I sprinkle in some cinnamon.

Logan leans over the table and looks into the cauldron. "I did. This is honestly kinda disappointing. Thought you'd be using a lot more weird pickled stuff you had hidden in jars in the basement. Not even a drop of 'blood of a virgin?'"

"Not in this kind of potion," I say and conjure an athame. "Just blood of an obnoxious idiot. Hand." I hold out mine for him.

Logan pulls back and laughs awkwardly as if he doesn't know if I'm joking or not. "Ahhh, wish I could help. But I don't think I count in that area. Obnoxious average IQ person maybe. Slightly above average but just poor social awareness. Your spell books get that specific?"

I put the knife away and return to my task. "I'll be sure to update it for next time with 'Penis of a man named Logan.'"

The laugh this time is slightly more confident. "You'll need a bigger cauldron for that one."

I look up at him with a grin. "I'm not too sure about that."

The aroma of the brewing potion carried by the steam now fills the room. I take a deep breath in, and Logan imitates.

"Ah, yes," he says. "Quite potiony, isn't it."

"Not yet." I turn from the cauldron and rummage through

one of the cabinets. In the very bottom drawer is a lock box with some very, let's say, alternative, ingredients.

"Hold on, now. Nyx, what the fuck are we doing? That's not a potion, you're just giving them drugs! Where did you even get those?"

"They're not *drugs*," I correct, but I have nothing to back myself up with. When his intense accusatory glare persists, I give up and say, "All right. Fine. But trust me, it'll be fine. They're called 'magic' mushrooms anyway."

Logan falls back a step. "No, no way. That's not what I thought we were doing."

"What *did* you think this was?" I ask, already putting a few of the dried mushrooms in a small strainer to let boil. Then, thinking out loud, "Probably should have done this part upstairs by the window."

Disregarding my last comment, Logan complains, "I thought this was going to be some, like…"

"Don't say 'Harry Potter shit' again."

"That. Yeah, exactly."

With the mushrooms in the mix, I tell him, "This isn't what you think. They won't be tripping out or anything."

Logan only purses his lips and crosses his arms in disbelief.

I continue, "When I first went to Maria's house, I felt many strong spirits lingering. That house is a major focal point for supernatural energies, and from what I felt, overwhelmingly positive. If their minds are opened to them… if they're distracted, we can disrupt their ritual and end this."

His face doesn't change. "So, you're going to make them trip and then steal the book."

The chemicals from the mushroom have begun to seep into the potion. "Not gonna get very far if they're all totally there." I point to my brain. "Are you having second thoughts about me now?"

That smile. "Nyx, I've been having second thoughts since I met you," he laughs. "This, though, this is something else." Logan takes a deep breath. "Against my better judgment, I'll still tag along. You take this seriously, so I'll take it seriously. But if anything gets out of whack, if it's just a bunch of goth girls chanting gibberish around a pentagram and you drugged them because you think demons are gonna possess someone, I'm calling the cops."

It's a pretty shitty threat, all things considered. Here I am, trying sincerely to help a girl in need, and this guy I thought I might be developing something with threatens to get me arrested. What a crazy world this is.

There's so much he doesn't understand yet, though. Stepping into his shoes, sure, all of this still might sound pretty crazy.

After a long, drawn-out breath, I tell him, "Wait here," and take the cauldron upstairs so the steam can escape out the window. Logan does as he's told and pulls out a chair at the table. He pulls out his phone just as I step up the stairs. He's not calling the cops *now*, is he? If that asshole is dropping an anonymous tip, then I swear…

Willow passes me on the stairs, navigating between my legs. She pays no mind to me or the cauldron I'm carrying, only makes her way past and leaps for Logan, who takes her with open arms.

When I return to the covenstead, Logan is on the floor

playing with Willow. The cat nuzzles up against his chest and lets him scratch the back of her neck.

"Do you want to know why I'm willing to do this?" I ask him.

Logan's eyes dart up toward me, but his attention is still primarily on the cat.

"I know these girls Maria has fallen in with. Two of them, girls *I* used to call my sisters, Angela and Piper."

Logan fixes himself, sitting up straight against the back of one of the chairs. Willow curls up in his legs and nudges his stomach expecting more scratches.

"They got me into all of this when we were in high school, along with one other girl, Abby, or Nissa, as she goes by now. It was just stupid fun at first, like a glorified book club. We hung out all the time, drank wine, lit candles, and read books about witchcraft. Then we started getting really into it and tried practicing all of this stuff. We even tried basing how we acted off of stories from the Salem witch trial era, like signing our names in the black book to each other. Nissa was the first one who got cold feet. She thought we were taking it a little too far and got out. But Angie and Piper were my only friends at the time. Even when things started to get weird, I kept up with them.

"At first it was moonlit rituals in the woods for bright futures after high school, success in college, and all that stuff. Then drunken nights led to darker stuff; ouija boards, seances, and eventually, drawing pentagrams and summoning. I thought it was just for shits when we started. Just drawing lines on the floor and lighting candles then singing some chants. Nothing was coming out of it, and we got a little thrill out of 'messing with powers from beyond.' But Angie didn't want to play around, it seemed.

"She made the first blood sacrifice. It caught Piper and me off guard. Myself more so, I later found out. Piper'd apparently been the one to bring up the idea. I still don't know why they were doing it. But whatever ritual Angie was performing, or, whatever goal she was reaching for, she didn't achieve. So, her attempts became more aggressive. I mean, she actually sacrificed a poor animal, a precious little cat, trying to summon some spirit. I knew then I was getting in too deep with these girls, but I was too scared to abandon them. That, and a part of me hoped it was just a phase. They'd see how stupid they were being and move on. We'd go back to meditating in the woods or crafting brews that helped heal our spirits. Piper, the one with all the ideas, actually inspired me to open this store. At the very least, she didn't give Angie her worst idea; why I'm so terrified for Maria.

"When all the other sacrifices didn't work, Angie turned to me. She said we needed a willing vessel for the spirit she claimed to be communicating with. She didn't tell me what she meant, although, I think deep down I knew. I just didn't know how to say no to her. Everything about my life revolved around these women. They were my sisters. Nothing they did would be to hurt me.

"We waited for the next new moon. Angie had this notebook full of stuff she'd collected, spells she'd created, and apparently, instructions she was given. They drew the pentagram and lit the candles, and told me to lay in the center. That's when I first felt this… this demon. It was cold. It was an icy, invisible mist crawling all over me. I wasn't bound, but I felt it pinning me to the ground. I couldn't escape from it.

"Once it was there, I tried to get free. I screamed for them to help me, but Piper held my wrists to the ground. And Angie… A- Angie… she tried to… she pu-…"

Logan wraps his arms around me and wipes away a tear with his thumb. "You don't have to say it," he whispers. Another tear falls for him to catch with his thumb. This man would wipe them away until the world ended.

I let my head sink into his shoulder. Not even Nissa knew all of this. Not even Frank knew the extent. No one did.

"I need to," I tell him. "Someone has to know."

His gentle lips press against my head. "Okay."

Deep breath, Nyx. "It wasn't the spirit that took advantage of me. But it was there. Maybe it just wanted to watch Angie do the work. Piper never even considered stopping her. When it was over, no one gained any powers, or insight into the future or world beyond. All they felt was defeat, and all I felt was shame. At first, it was for thinking I'd failed them. Then, with time, I felt like I should be ashamed for letting it go that far. I saw the signs but didn't do anything to stop them."

Logan sucks in and I hear a sentence form on his lips. It's bound to be something I've told myself a million times, some form of genuine sympathy that I've been dying for ever since this all happened, but it doesn't feel right. Not yet. Not until it's all over. Then I'll let him say whatever he feels necessary. Even if it's a condemnation of me ever getting involved in this, to begin with.

I press on, "That's why I care so much about Maria. I know what they're going to do to her because I was already in her place. And when I held that book, when I felt that spirit attached to it... I just wish I had put everything together sooner."

Logan squeezes me a little tighter but is careful not to overwhelm me. Willow hops up again. This time on my lap, not his. She pushes her head under my arm, a clear sign she wants to be scratched. It's her way of saying she's heard me.

The three of us sit together for a while, not saying anything. I suppose Logan is just taking it in, considering again if the magic mushrooms are worth it yet.

Eventually, I produce a cigarette and light up. I feel Logan's eyes on it, so I take out another and hold it up for him. He takes it, and I give him a light.

"Still surprised you smoke in here," he says. "*Especially* in here," Logan emphasizes, referring to the covenstead.

"It's my place. I can do what I want," I say with a puff.

We smoke until the embers burn to our fingers. Mine burns a little bit faster, and Logan smokes like he's trying to keep pace.

Logan doesn't even finish his cigarette. When mine's through, he extinguishes his. I take them both and dispose of them in a little ashtray on the cabinet. He watches me move, and then asks, "So, we're really doing this, huh?"

I nod over my shoulder. "If you're still willing to help."

Logan rises with a grunt, wipes the cat hair from his pants, then says, "All right. Well, we can try your way. But there's something I want to do just in case."

* * *

"I cannot believe you dragged me to this," I whisper under the chanting of Saturday evening churchgoers.

Logan shushes me with his head down and eyes closed. He mutters a prayer under his breath.

"I thought you just wanted to get some holy water or something. I can already feel my soul burning." I stick out my tongue like I'm gagging.

"Sh." Logan silences me again. "You're fine."

I protest, "I'm not taking the communion."

"There's wine too, you know."

An old couple in the pew in front of us turns around and gives me a disapproving glare. The tattoos and piercings definitely don't help their perception of me.

They return to their hymnal singing and I whisper to Logan. "At least I could have worn something appropriate if I'd known you'd take me hostage here."

Without opening his eyes, he says, "What you're wearing is lovely. You look nice in brighter colors like this."

I look down at the dress I didn't realize I was wearing, a much lighter purple than I usually do. I didn't even know I had a dress like this. Must not have been paying attention when I got dressed today.

Logan makes me sit through the whole service. When it's time for communion, I walk up with him just so I'm not in everyone's way as they pass through the pew. Once in front of the altar though,

I accept the bread and wine out of not wanting to stand out. I don't know if that's allowed or not if I'm not Catholic, but the priest handed them both over pretty willingly, and when we sit down, Logan has a little grin.

"That didn't kill ya, did it?" He teases.

I roll my eyes. "Just get your holy water on the way out. Don't want to be late for Maria."

38. The New Moon

The sun sets behind the trees surrounding Maria's home. Rays of light shine around the edges of the roof. As the light dissipates, a cold breeze blows through the summer heat and ruffles my hair, and I know it's not autumn beginning early.

We parked a few blocks away from the house and kept close to hedges and trees on our approach. We weren't trying to hide, but weren't too keen on being seen either. Although we had no reason for neighbors to think us suspicious, it'd be preferable not to have some jumpy old person thinking two punks were up to no good. I don't think the cops would care too much for some of the not-so-legal potion ingredients I have on me.

From the looks of it, no one's home yet. I don't see Maria's car, nor any other. And it will be hard to keep an eye out for Angela's or Piper's if they've gotten new ones in the years since we parted.

"What if they fly in on brooms?" Logan jokes.

I purse my lips. "I wouldn't be surprised if they did. Just look out for hooked noses and warts."

"Either of them have green skin?"

I nudge Logan in the side and stifle a laugh. It's time to get serious. I feel around in the inside breast pocket of my dress, just to make sure for the hundredth time that the vial with the potion is still there. At the same time, I see out of the corner of my eye that Logan is gripping a cross necklace he donned after we left the church.

"This would probably work better for protection if you want to wear it." I hold my necklace with a Teiwaz rune pendant of protection an inch off my chest.

Logan smirks. "I'm good with this one," he says and gives it a kiss before putting it back under his shirt.

"Suit yourself. Let's go."

With no one around, we walk up to the front door as if we were awaited guests. Part of me feels like we are.

Once at the door, Logan lifts a fist. "Think we should knock?"

I reach out and twist the door knob. Locked. Glancing back toward the street in search of our expected company, I tell him, "No. If they didn't leave the place unlocked, maybe we should look for a way in around back. Maybe a window was left open." I wipe a bead of sweat from the center of my chest.

"Before adding breaking and entering to our rap sheet, you so sure they're going to be here tonight?"

I begin to lead him around the wraparound porch, looking for an open window. "Do you feel the energy around this place?" I try a window, but it's locked shut.

"No," Logan says flatly. "Not at all. All I feel is hot." He fans his shirt to cool himself.

"Well, if you pay attention, you will. They're all around us. This house is oversaturated with supernatural energy." I try another window on the side of the house. From here, we're well concealed by bushes. "Angie and Piper would want to take advantage of a place like this, drawing on the natural energies to empower their ritual."

"If you say so," Logan says, then looks around. "Up there," he points. "Someone left their window open a crack."

He's right. I look up and see one of the windows on the second floor open just a bit. To prove it so, a bug flies up to the window and disappears underneath it.

Logan pulls me close and crouches down. "Come on, I'll lift you up." He cups his hands for me to step into.

"You sure you can get me that high?"

Logan doesn't even have to answer. I look again at his bulging arms and take a step into his hands. The man nearly tosses me into the air. Then, the thought of that puts a dirty idea in my head that I have to put away until this mess is over.

I grab onto the ledge of the window, supported on my toes by Logan. I call down to him, "Can you give me another inch?"

"I can give you eight but I don't think that'll help right now. Actually…"

"Logan, if you're looking up my dress right now I'll fucking kill you."

"Calm down," he laughs, and I picture different places I can hide his body. "Here ya go." He pushes me up another few inches so I can get the window more open. But from here it's all Nyx and her poor upper body strength. Maybe I should start going to the gym with him if we get out of this one alive.

Pulling myself up and through the window is one of the most physically challenging things I've done since who knows when. And with the summer dusk heat, I'm burning up. Sweat careens down my back. Below me, Logan is hyping me up. "You got this, Nyx. Come on, babe, you're almost there."

With his motivational boost, I'm able to pull myself through the window and tumble into what looks like a storage room. It's dusty as hell, filled with totes and banker boxes, many of them unmarked. But in a clear tote, I see some Christmas tinsel and an ornament with a picture of a young blond girl with the perkiest smile sitting on Santa's lap.

Logan's voice carries through the window. "I'll meet you at the front door!"

I pick myself up and turn to stick my head out of the window, seeing him waiting patiently down below. "No, go to the back. I'll let you in there."

"Got it," he says and starts to jog over to the back, but I stop him again.

"Is this how you got into the dorms? Just looked for an open window?"

Logan cracks a grin. "I knocked on some girl's window and told her I lost my key. Not as exciting as this." He picks up his feet, but once again, I have to stop him.

"Wait!" I call.

He gazes back up at me.

"Did you just call me 'babe' a second ago?"

Logan shrugs. "Maybe like, thirty seconds ago, but yeah. Why? Still not there yet?"

I bite the inside of my lip. I feel like a high-school girl calling down to my crush from my bedroom window. "No, I... just... don't get carried away with it, darling."

Logan winks and I *melt*, then he's off to the back door.

All right, pull yourself together, Nyx. He's just a boy, and you've got a job to do. There's no time to waste.

Very carefully, I make my way out of the room and down the hall to the grand staircase of this nearly ancient mansion. Just because there are no cars around, doesn't mean no one's home. It's probably something I should have considered before breaking in and shouting back and forth with Logan. We may have only gotten lucky, no one paying attention and running to the storage room, and I'd rather not risk anything now.

One step on the staircase sends a loud creak throughout the house. I freeze, hoping no one pops a head out and catches me. After a moment's hesitation, I assume I'm still in the clear and step gingerly down the steps, making sure to keep close to the railing.

From somewhere down the hall on the first floor, I hear faint tapping on glass. I peek my head around the banister and see the shadow of a hand behind the curtain of the back door window. Logan knocks again, and I tip-toe-hop down the hall to the door, flick the lock, and let him in.

"Why would you knock like that? I could have been anybody."

"Or you could have been the girl I helped sneak into the window. No one's home, we're fine." The sun is nearly gone behind him. Just barely visible behind the trees in the backyard, the last bits of orange and pink light the sky. It's barely enough to light up the inside of the house.

"Or it could be a trap."

Logan rolls his eyes. "I don't think girls trying to summon demons would be that smart."

"We're almost done. Just don't blow it now, please?"

Logan puts his hands on my hips and turns me around, then gives me a little pat on the butt. "Lead the way, babe."

I hiss at him, "You're overdoing it," then lead us up the stairs to the third floor, Maria's apartment.

"Can't see shit in here," Logan complains, reaching for his phone.

"Stop, no flashlights. I know my way around." It's like walking through the woods just before the dawn. Hard to see, but not impossible, and I've been here enough to know where I'm going in the low light.

Drawing closer fills me with a sense of dread. The book is up there somewhere, and it feels like we're walking closer to a giant ice box. I breathe out and swear I can see my own breath as if it were the middle of winter.

Logan whispers from behind me, "You all good?"

"Fine," I tell him.

By the top of the stairs, the light has completely diminished. "You can use your phone now," I tell him, taking out my own. "But not the flashlight, that's too bright. Just the screen."

I hear the *click* of both of our phones unlocking and hold my phone out to see down the hallway to Maria's apartment.

"You feel that yet?" I ask Logan.

"Feels like someone left the AC running a little high."

Good. This close to the book I don't think even the hardest skeptic could ignore it.

Maria's door is, thankfully, unlocked. I turn the handle, but something inside me refuses to push it open. Logan senses the hesitation and pushes forward, being the first to enter.

"Keep an eye out for the book," I tell Logan, who gives one of his silly salutes.

When I first came here with Maria, we were blessed with the light of a full moon. The night was so warm and cozy. I had a chance to make a new friend that night, maybe even gain a sister. Now there's no moonlight shining in through her glass balcony door. If I could see anything in the pitch black, it'd be safe to assume I was wandering through a snowy waste.

Logan snaps his fingers in front of my face. "Hey! Still with me?"

It brings me out of my daze. "Yeah, I'm here."

On the word "here," another loud *click* is heard from down on the first floor. My eyes shoot open and I rush back down the hall to the stairs. The front door opens, and a moment later, the lights turn on. Maria walks in first, looking like a corpse. She's followed by Angela and Piper, who look happier than ever, a stark contrast from their newest companion.

As quietly as possible, I rush back into the apartment. "They're here!"

"Bail?" Logan asks.

No, of course we're not going to bail! "See if we can climb down from the balcony. Quick!" Logan jumps over to the balcony door while I look around the kitchen for a kettle. There's an empty one still on the gas stove, and into the kettle, the potion goes.

Logan rushes back into the room. "If we aim for the bushes we should be okay."

The third-floor hallway light turns on. "No time," I whisper. "Into the closet!" I shove him into the nearest one just in time for the three women to come in and turn the lights on.

"Hunni…" Angela's voice. "Why don't you make some tea for us, dear?"

Maria moans back, "I don't think I'm really in the mood right now."

Piper scoffs, but Angela is still the one to speak. "Don't be silly. You've been groggy all day. It'll make you feel better. Have you been drinking that mix I gave you?"

Through the slits of the closet door, I see Maria nod.

"Good," Angela says. "You make some of that, and I'll get everything prepped."

Piper chimes in, "Do you need anything from me, Angie?"

Angela doesn't reply but disappears from view into either the living room or Maria's bedroom.

My head is firm against Logan's chest and I can feel him breathing. He whispers, "This is getting exciting, isn't it?"

I watch as Maria brings the kettle to the sink. She swishes it around and for a moment I'm terrified she's dumping it out. But relief washes over me when she fills the kettle, with the potion still in it.

I whisper to Logan, "Now all we need to do is wait."

Maria puts the kettle on the stove and ignites the flames. Then, Piper walks into the kitchen with a contorted face. "Did you put the mix in the kettle?" Piper asks.

Groggily, Maria asks, "What?"

"It smells weird."

Fuck!

"It's probably just the spring water from the tap."

Piper takes another sniff. "When was the last time you cleaned this?"

Maria sighs, exhausted. "I don't know, Piper."

Piper puts her hand on the kettle handle and everything seems doomed. I'd prefer to get out of here without any evidence, but if worse comes to worst, maybe Logan wouldn't mind fighting them off to get the book back.

Just then, Angela calls Piper to join her wherever she is. Piper puts the kettle back down and lets it boil.

Thank God.

Even Logan's heart is beating fast.

I crack the door open the littlest bit, careful not to make a sound. Maria doesn't notice, as her attention is on the kitchen wall, staring blankly. I look around back toward the living room. The light is on in the bedroom, and there are bundles of something on the bed. Candles litter the entire room.

It's time.

The kettle whistles but it takes Piper's shouting at Maria for her to notice and take it off the stove. Being yelled at seems to really kick her awake, and she rushes to prep the tea cups for the three of them. She pulls a jar from one of the cabinets with little homemade tea bags and puts them in the cups with the hot water. If my potion was crafted properly - and it is, it's mine - the scent should be canceled out by whatever mixture is added to it. But, one can only pray.

Angela and Piper return to the kitchen, grinning like devils. "Ready for your big night?" Angela asks, taking a teacup from the counter and sipping without a second thought.

Logan whispers, "Let's goooo."

I shush him, watching the others drink. Now we just hope it kicks in before they can get into the ritual.

"Come now," Angela says, nodding toward the bedroom. "Let's do some matchmaking."

Piper puts her cup down, not having drank in full, and takes Maria's wrist, leading her in with Angela.

"Are we good to leave now?" Logan asks.

The bedroom door closes.

"Not yet, we have to make sure it works, or we go to plan B."

"What's plan B? You never mentioned a plan B."

"I just thought of it."

Muffled noises are heard from the bedroom. A thump, a scratch.

I push the closet door open, feeling safe from being caught. If they're starting, they won't leave the room until the ritual is over.

"You run in fast and grab the book back, then…"

"Yeah?" He presses.

Then what? Go to the police and say they were trying to rape a girl? If we stopped it, there's no evidence that they were if she's doing this willingly, then *we're* the ones being questioned on why we're there. If we don't report it and just run away with the book, they'll try again another way. No, plan A has to work. Scare the shit out of them so they see the folly of their actions.

"Forget plan B. Plan A will work."

Logan reluctantly accepts my indecision. "When will we know it's working?"

From the bedroom, we hear an indistinguishable voice say, "I don't... I don't feel right." Please tell me it's the mushrooms.

We tip-toe up to the door and I press my head up against it to get a better listen. Then, clearly, I hear Angela. "You'll be fine, dear. You're doing great, just lay still."

Then Piper's voice. She's saying something incomprehensible, definitely not English.

"What the fuck is that?" Logan whispers.

"She's reading from the book."

It becomes clear that the first voice was Maria. If she's the only one who gets affected by the potion, I'll forever hate myself for making things worse.

Maria pleads, "I really don't feel good. I'm so cold. I... I don't think this was a good idea."

Angela consoles her again, but slightly harsher this time. "You'll be fine."

"The... this is too tight."

Logan and I look at each other. *What's too tight?*

383

I put my ear back against the door but am immediately pushed off and throw my hand over my mouth so I don't scream.

Logan grabs me and gives me eyes that ask what's wrong.

I mouth the word 'frozen.' The door is as cold as a block of ice. It's in there.

The room shakes. The mushrooms haven't kicked in in time. Plan B has now become "make it up as we go along and hope for the best."

From the other side of the door, Maria cries, no, whimpers, "Please. Please, I don't want to do this anymore! P-please untie me! I don't want to do this!"

Logan senses my thoughts and moves me out of the way. He twists the knob but it doesn't budge. I reach for it, but Logan keeps me back.

Maria screams louder for help, but Piper only reads louder, overpowering her screams.

Logan's face hardens. He turns to the side and then throws the full force of his body into the door. When he bounces off, there is a huge crack in the wood.

Then Angela's angry voice. "Who's that? Did you tell anyone about this?"

Maria screams, "No! I promise! I didn't, just please untie me!"

Logan throws himself against the door again. The crack widens.

That's when the most horrifying cry I've heard in my life erupts in the house. "No!" Maria screams. "Leave me alone! No!

Please! Please, oh God, please! Help me!"

Piper's incantation fades away and is replaced by a mimic of Maria. "I don't feel so good either, Angie."

Angela rebukes her, but the intensity in her voice softens. "Quit it, Piper. Just... just keep reading."

All throughout their brief exchange, Maria continues screaming.

One more good throw and we're in. But he holds himself back.

I shout at him, "Logan! Do it again!" But he's frozen, staring through the crack in the door.

"What the fuck is that?" He asks, just above a whisper.

I step in his way and look through the door. There, hovering above Maria laying naked on the bed with her legs pulled apart, the beast appears.

I grab the doorknob, turning it as hard as I can while throwing myself into the gash in the door Logan's made but it does nothing to get us in. "Logan, help!"

He returns to his senses and pushes me out of the way again, then with one final thrust, breaks the door in two. We both fall into the room and a horrible wind sweeps through. Between Maria's screams for help, the wind, and the shrill icy screech the demon emanates, nothing can be heard.

"Do something!" Logan shouts at me.

I don't know what to do! I don't know any spells for this! I don't know if spells would even work at this point! The book. There should be something in the book.

Angela and Piper don't notice us. They don't notice anything apparently. Their eyes are glazed over, and they sway back and forth.

Piper asks dreamily, "What is that?"

In their daze, I rush over to her and attempt to pry the book from her hands. Logan pushes past Angela and falls to the side of Maria's bed to undo the ropes holding her wrists down. But once he does, the room shakes violently again. I'm pulled from what I'm doing and see Logan pushed into the corner, blocking the sight of the demon coming down on him. Logan yells at it to go away, to leave us alone. It descends slowly on him.

I have to do this. I try again to pull the book from Piper's hands. Her grip tightens and she asks, "Who are these people?" Tears well in her eyes. "Angie…" Her voice rises in fear. "Who are all these people? Angie!"

Fuck it. I ball my hand into a fist and land one on her cheek. It hurts like hell, but Piper drops the book and falls into the corner of the room.

When I turn around, Angie is already balled up on the floor. She screams, "Leave me alone! Leave me alone! Go away!" But it's not directed at the demon.

"Nyx!" Logan shouts. "Do something!"

The demon turns, facing me with eyes as dark as the void and burning hotter than Hades itself.

My frozen fingers flip through the pages, but none of these words are legible. How the hell did Piper learn this?

Maria screams through tightened lungs. A pathetic whimper only barely escapes her lips, as if a hand is squeezing her throat. I glance over at her, and bruises in the shape of claw marks imprint themselves on her neck.

The demon floats toward me, like a hurricane tearing up the room. A voice says in the back of my mind, *I wondered when I'd meet you again.*

I shout, "You have no right being here! You have no domain over me! You have no domain over Maria!" I fall back up against the wall as it approaches, unfazed by my words. Behind it, Logan is back on his knees, untying Maria from her bonds. I shout again, "I command you to leave this home!" If only I knew the name of this demon!

The voice laughs, *I have domain over whatever I please, Samantha.*

I hold up my necklace, mouthing a prayer of protection. Icicles form in my nose. The air in my lungs is sucked from me. I can't breathe. I can't see. I can't even move. Claws grip my ankles and pull my legs apart. I fall to the floor on top of Piper's unconscious body. The Cold trails up my legs, between my thighs, and I scream when my loins are assaulted.

Through my tears then, just beyond the horror surrounding me, Logan rises with his hand held out. His voice is louder than anything in the world. For once in my life, I'm happy to hear this phrase. "The power of Christ compels you!"

Icy fingers pull away from my legs. The demon turns its attention back toward Logan. The room shakes. The bed rumbles off the ground. Books and pictures fall from their shelves. Angela holds her head as if it's about to explode.

Logan shouts again, "The power of Christ compels you,"

like he's reenacting The Exorcist.

The demon screams, but Logan is louder, standing tall and firm. He looks like nothing in the world could knock him down like he's strengthened by otherworldly powers.

"The power of Christ!" he shouts. "The power of Christ!"

I see in his hand the small crucifix necklace is glowing. This small wooden carving, glowing, as if it were made of gold. Not only that, it looks like it's made of pure light.

"The power of Christ compels you!"

With the demon distracted and unable to stop me, I turn back to the book. I recite my incantations to cleanse the book without resistance.

From the other side of the room, Angela moans, "Leave me alone, leave me alone!"

Logan continues to shout it away, and the demon falls, shrinking away by the base of the bed.

I say my incantation, and Logan shouts one more "Power of Christ."

A final burst of cold air blows through the room, a bright light emanates from the center, and just like that, it's gone. Just like that, we're midsummer again. The room is overpoweringly hot.

Logan's grabbing a blanket from Maria's closet and throws it over her.

"Are you okay?" He asks.

Maria can't say anything, but she nods hurriedly.

Logan then turns his attention to me and hops over the bed and meets me on the floor. "You okay?" He brushes a lock of hair behind my ear.

"Yeah. Yeah, I'm okay."

His worried eyes shift to joy. "Good," he laughs. "Told ya it would work."

39. Relationships

The three of us; Maria, Logan, and I, sit on the balcony under the stars. She sips at a glass of water. She already looks more full of life.

"What happened to them?" Maria asks.

"Yeah," Logan says. "Who were they talking about?"

I take a drag of a cigarette. "Maria… this is a wonderful home. You're very lucky to live here."

Her eyes drop to her glass. She may not believe me after such a traumatic experience, but it's true.

I tell her, "Many wonderful, happy spirits live here. Spirits like that don't wish for harm or negative emotions to be in their presence. I put something in their tea that opened their minds to these spirits. When they could see them, they were overcome with guilt for what they were doing, summoning something so evil, because they could finally see the good." I take a drag. "I hope it was enough to turn them from all of this for good."

Maria shrugs.

The energy between us tells me that even after this, she doesn't want me around.

"I'm sorry, Maria."

Her eyes meet mine. There's obvious distrust in them.

"I'm sorry I treated you so poorly. I should have been a better person. I should have been your friend."

Logan puts his hand on my leg and winks. *You're doing great*, his face tells me. Let's just hope Maria thinks the same.

"I know I fucked up, and I don't expect you to let me make things right again. I... I just want you to find happiness."

"I tried to," Maria says softly. "Everyone just..."

"Maria, if you trust me one more time, just once, there's someone I'd like you to meet. She's the nicest woman I've ever known, and I think she can really help you through this. Just trust me on this one thing."

Maria forces herself to look away from me, and up at the stars. "What are you going to do about them?" She nods her head back to the bedroom.

"We call the police. Tell them they were on drugs and tried to..." I'm not sure what the right word is to make this easier on her mental health.

"They tried to rape me." Maria says. "They took drugs, drugged me, and tried to rape me."

What am I even supposed to say to that? It's basically what happened, but to have it out there, to acknowledge it so bluntly.

After a few moments of silence, Maria asks, "Who's this person you want me to meet?"

I sigh in relief. Everything might be okay. "Her name's Nissa. She's a good witch."

* * *

Logan drops me back off at Witch's Brew. I step out of the car, but he doesn't follow.

"You coming in?" I ask.

He never turned off the engine. He only looks forward, with a hand on the gear shift.

"Logan?"

"That was pretty crazy back there," he says.

"Yeah. It was." I want to laugh about it all; demons, spells, Exorcist moments, but Logan isn't laughing.

He looks at me then, his face totally unreadable. "I didn't take this job to be getting into all this."

Don't do this to me now, Logan. Not when everything's starting to look up.

"Is that it, then?"

"Nyx... this isn't the kind of stuff... this wasn't in the job description. And if we're just... whatever this is..."

"This is too serious for a not-so-serious relationship. Is that it?"

Logan nods.

"What if I got serious, then? No more tip-toeing around what we're both thinking."

"Think that's gonna get me to reconsider?"

I bite the inside of my lip. It's a new moon tonight. There's still a chance something good can come out of it. I look up the street and see a sign outside one of the stores that reads "Bookends Reopening Soon!"

Logan turns the car off. "'Cause that's what I've been waiting forever for you to say."

Epilogue

I use garden shears to cut the pumpkin stems, but Nissa is more practiced, and can get a clean cut with one slice of a sharp knife. She lifts the pumpkin that's almost as big as her stomach and carries it to her truck, dismissing my offer to carry it for her.

"I'll tell you when I get tired," Nissa sighs. She stacks the pumpkin against the small pile in the trunk, then stretches with her hands pressing on her lower back.

"Looks like you're getting tired already," I tell her and try to lift an oversized pumpkin that's about to tear a muscle. Nissa watches with a grin then steps in and picks it up like it's no big deal.

"I'm pregnant, I'm always tired. But not too tired to do my job. Besides, it's good for the baby."

I wipe sweat from my brow and watch her load another pumpkin into the truck. Other than her constant stretching, Nissa looks like she hasn't done more than move a few pillows. The only other clue that we've been working all day in her garden is the dirt patches on our knees. Nissa better be making a fortune off these at the farmer's market for the amount of work I've put in.

"That should be enough," she says and turns back to me. "Drink?"

"Please. But I don't think you're allowed at the moment."

Nissa giggles and helps me up. It feels very backwards and I am *not* looking forward to the day I'm in her place, even if she makes it look so easy. "Cider," she says. "Not the hard kind. The homemade kind."

I don't recall seeing any apple trees around, but her property is so dense with vegetation that they'd be easy to miss.

When we step inside Nissa's cottage, her husband Brian is sitting quietly in the living room with an equally quiet Logan. They both jump up as we enter and look elated that there's something finally to break up the awkward air. Nissa crosses over to the kitchen to fetch the cider and I push Logan back down onto the couch to sit on his lap, throwing my arm around him. Brian sits down too and his eyes search for his wife.

Logan pulls back a strand of my recently dyed bleach blond hair and whispers, "Thank God you came in. This guy is *so* dull."

I stifle a laugh and whisper back, "You poor thing."

Nissa doesn't take long to join us with drinks. She places two down on the coffee table for Logan and I, then gives one to Brian and takes a seat in her reading chair with a deep groan. The day's work has finally caught up with her.

"How's everything been with Maria?" I ask Nissa. "She does go by that, right?"

Nissa gives me an odd-but-polite look. "Of course. What else would she go by?"

I ignore the question and Logan and I take a sip of the cider.

"She's been good. Coming around a little more, I think. She's usually pretty quiet, but I can tell she enjoys the company." She then looks over at her husband. "Brian likes her because she doesn't make any noise when she comes over."

He chimes in, "Lot of conference calls."

Fun, I think to myself.

"Think she's ready to talk to me again?"

Nissa purses her lips, then looks down at her drink. "Not yet. I don't think."

I didn't expect any major revelations. Only hoped that after all this time there'd be some small progress.

"But," Nissa adds in, "I see it happening very soon."

"Yeah? What makes you say that?"

"Next Wednesday is the new moon."

Acknowledgements

This book really came out of nowhere for me and I couldn't be happier with how it came together. But I by no means can take all the credit, and a lot of the time writing this, it felt like I could only claim a small percentage of credit with how much support I received, like it should be someone else's name on the cover.

Thank you to the **readers of "Bookends."** That book was a leap of faith for me, putting out my heart and soul to the public and it was received with such open arms. Every review I read filled me with such joy and motivated me to keep going on my writing journey.

Thank you to my **ARC readers**! This book, like "Bookends," was originally published for free on Inkitt as a first draft. Thank you for the feedback and the wonderful reviews!

Thank you to my fellow **indie authors**. We haven't exactly met face-to-face, but I watch your journeys as well, and I feel like we constantly support each other, validate each other at every book signing and festival we do, and every post we make sharing each other's work.

Thank you **Jade Nioma**, author of "Fate's Tether." Your story, both as a human being, and your book, has been an inspiration to me. You showed incredible support to "Bookends" when it came out and I hope I can repay that debt to you.

Thank you to the creative team at Valenza Publishing. **Dr. Stephen Hull**, my editor, and **J.T. McGee**, author of "Thrall," you have been invaluable as creative voices, always there for me to bounce ideas off of and pushing me to better myself as a writer. Dr.

Hull, every time I saw your excited comments in the draft of this, freaking out about a plot development you were hoping for, I was laughing. J.T., if we could make our stories overlap that would make me so happy. Maybe one day we can collaborate on a project.

Thank you to my **friends and family**. I try to be humble, but every time of of you showed interest in or asked me about my work, I'm sure you saw how I exploded with joy and were quickly annoyed with how I didn't stop talking about it. Thanks for suffering through my rants!

Thank you to my **mom**. I know you said you would read this even though I warned you about the adult content, and again, I'm sorry about that. But I will argue that it was integral to the themes of the story and character, and again, I did warn you. Anyway, you have been a rock for faith in our family, even when we got a little rebellious and pushed it away. You were always there to be a voice of reason and listen to us, and educate us when you could or point us in the right direction. I'm sorry I didn't always listen.

Thank you to my **wife**. I'm sure, especially within the last year while I was working on this, you would have appreciated a few more nights together. But you always did encourage my writing nights, and those moments when you said, "you haven't done much writing lately," as a push to get me back into it didn't go unnoticed. I love you THIIIIIIIIIIIIIIS much. Nem Nem.

And most importantly, **I thank God**. It's funny I write this acknowledgement on Easter Weekend. The power of God is infinite and will always claim victory over any evil, sometimes through means you never see coming. Everything I write, whether for enjoyment, to spark discussion, or to share a piece of myself that needs to be voiced for the world, all comes because a friend introduced me to God in college. It is because of that love that I can recognize the gifts he has given me and use them, hopefully, to share his truth. Not the dirty stuff in this book, the real good stuff.

I hope you loved this book as much as I loved writing it!

About the Author

Ella Madeline Hayes lives a peaceful, quiet life in Saratoga Springs with her wife. She's an avid reader of all things romance, fantasy, and science fiction.

Please leave a review on Amazon or Goodreads!

Follow us on social media!

Ella M. Hayes
@Ella.hayes.books - Instagram

Valenza Publishing
www.valenzapublishing.com
@valenzapublishing - Instagram/Facebook/Threads

And support indie authors by checking out these
incredible books!

"Fate's Tether" by Jade Nioma

"The Chosen" by J.M. Gokey

"The Maiden's Husband" by Morgan Christensen

"Witness to the Revolution" by Kiersten Marcil

www.ingramcontent.com/pod-product-compliance
Lightning Source LLC
Chambersburg PA
CBHW020013120726
47903CB00004B/1267